THE PSYCHOLOGIST'S JUST BEEN…

First Published in Great Britain 2015 by Mirador Publishing

First edition: 2015

A copy of this work is available through the British Library.

ISBN: 978-1-911044-42-0

Mirador Publishing
Mirador
Wearne Lane
Langport
Somerset
TA10 9HB

To Tim.

Best wishes

T Lindsay

The Psychologist's Just Been…

Tom Lindsay

This book would not have happened were it not for the persistence of our sons to “write down those stories, Dad.” Throughout the drawn-out process of putting thoughts and ideas into various electronic devices, my wife has been there for me, typing, proof-reading, commenting and supporting, all with a great degree of patience and affection. The book is therefore dedicated first and foremost to my family but I’d also like to acknowledge those friends who gave of their time to improve the manuscript in a myriad of ways. Any errors of fact are mine alone.

CHAPTER 1

IN THE BEGINNING…

"You're a complete idiot when it comes to examinations."

"Yes, Mike."

"What on Earth possessed you to witter on about killer sharks and giant squid in the Palaeontology Final?"

"Don't know, Mike."

"Mmmh!"

These, and similar remarks, formed the substance of the review of my Final Examinations' results for the degree of Bachelor of Science in Geology. Notwithstanding my long-suffering tutor's acerbic comments, I was the recipient of an Honours degree, despite the fact that I have always loathed examinations. This isn't because I don't know the answers to the questions. They and I have always had a fighting chance of being in the same dimension at the same time, but examinations cause me intense sciatic pain, which seems to divert my thought processes. At least, that's how I recall the matter and I find no reason to disagree with this plausible explanation for one or two below-par performances over the years.

Another reason why I was not feeling much remorse or regret at Mike's remarks was that I had a job already, almost. All I needed to do to remove the adverb was to present my would-be employers with incontrovertible evidence of my academic prowess, and I would then be magically transformed from layabout student into overpaid professional. Hindsight would add the phrase 'ha, bloody ha' to this utopian vision.

Some three months later, towards the end of the glorious summer of 1975, I was uncomfortably ensconced in Seat 47H on South African Airways flight 201, outward bound from London Heathrow to Johannesburg, via Ilha Do Sal in the Canary Islands. SAA was not allowed to overfly most of Africa so had to go round 'the bulge'.

I was on my way to South Africa to begin my chosen career, working for a large mining house as a geologist in a gold mine, whose precise whereabouts had not been divulged, but which, I had been reliably informed, was somewhere in this large country. My luggage comprised the clothes I wore, plus an overnight case in the hold, legacy of one grandparent, containing the remainder of my meagre wardrobe. Underneath the seat in front of me lay my briefcase containing a South African residence permit, my letter of appointment to the mining house and a bar of Cadbury's chocolate. My American relatives had convinced me that it wasn't possible to obtain decent chocolate outside the United Kingdom, so I was taking no chances. In my wallet resided thirty South African Rands and ten crisp Royal Bank of Scotland travellers' cheques, each valued at the princely sum of ten pounds. I hadn't, however, managed to find anything to fight off 'they lions and the like' which Great Auntie Meg had assured me roamed the streets of Johannesburg, but I thought I might just take my chances.

The bravado of ignorance deserted me and the thrill of flying seemed to be losing its glamour as the 747 headed south. For all my jaunty outward appearance in the previous few weeks, a somewhat apprehensive twenty-one-year-old was emerging. I knew the geography of the country and a little of the geology, but there had been a lot of talk at university of apartheid, which was the underlying reason the flight had to take the long way round West Africa. I was politically naïve and not well-equipped to judge the veracity or leanings of newspaper articles, magazines and statements about what comprised the South Africa of the 1970's.

The book 'Gold Mine', by Wilbur Smith, had just been made into a film starring Roger Moore and Susannah York and their lifestyle, albeit cinematic, looked pretty fair from my perspective. The job market being fairly dismal at the time, with the choice being between freezing bits of my anatomy off on a drilling platform in the North Sea or getting a tan whilst raking in the loot, I thought I would go south and see for myself. But what if I didn't like it? How was I going to get back?

My contract stated that I had to repay the cost of the initial airfare if I resigned within three years, so I would have to find that money and the cost of the return in any case. The night passed, my mind in occasional overdrive, but I must have dozed for a while because when I woke up, the sun was coming in over the left-hand fuselage. Standing in the queue for ablutions, when I looked down from the window in the emergency exit door, all I could see was a vast expanse of brown. I asked someone where we were and was told that we were just coming in over South West Africa. "Looks a bit boring," I thought. Prophetic words indeed.

The Jumbo landed amid much cheering and whistling, not, as I first thought, in appreciation of the pilot managing to stay awake and get us down in one piece, but because at least half the plane's human cargo was returning to the land of 'braaivleis, sonskyn, boerewors and Chevrolet', as a popular radio advertisement would later tell me, *ad nauseam.*

Immigration formalities were surprisingly simple. I showed the sun-tanned, stern and moustachioed officer my residence permit, he duly stamped it and my passport and welcomed me to 'Seff Effrica.'

Luggage retrieved, I went off through the Green Channel, and exited in the Arrivals Hall. Here, from what my letter of appointment had said, I was expecting that I'd be met and looked after. This was a little wide of the mark. There wasn't, as far as I could see, anyone rushing forward to greet me and whisk me off to wherever it was that I was to be whisked off to. Instead, after walking round the concourse, I found a black man dressed in a yellow coat with 'Hertz' prominently labelled on the back, carrying a placard with two names on it, one of which was mine. Well, my surname at least.

I asked him if he was from the Saint Kilda Corporation but he said he didn't know about that, only that he had to meet the two misters on his board and take them to a hotel in the city. On the basis that I would at least have a hotel room, I pronounced that I was indeed one of his passengers-to-be.

Having found the owner of the second name on the driver's board, we embarked for the Victoria Hotel. The first view of Johannesburg in those days was a curiously mixed sight. A metropolis of towers and high-rise buildings in the distance, surrounded by bright yellow, steep-sided, flat-topped but man-made mounds of powdered rock, set amidst the mainly rusting headgears of the gold mines on which Johannesburg was founded. At the hotel, my erstwhile travelling companion, a geologist of some years' standing with my new employers, checked in, said, "See you later", then disappeared in the lift and left me at the reception desk. Somewhat despairingly, I asked if there was any correspondence for me, and was duly given a couple of envelopes.

In my dark wood-panelled room, complete with double bed and comfortable sofa, but no television (I would have to wait another year before South African Television aired for the first time), I opened the envelopes to find a confirmation of the room reservation and very little else.

"Well, sod it," I thought, "I've travelled half-way around the world to a place where I know not a single soul, I don't even know exactly where I'm going to work, I've got precious little cash and the best the company has done is get me this room." I phoned my putative employers.

"Good morning, Saint Kilda Corporation, how can I help you?"

"Good morning, my name's Lindsay, I arrived this morning from the UK to begin work with you, except that I don't know where."

"Ah, you'll need to speak to Personnel, please hold."

"Good morning, Personnel Department, how may I help you?"

"Good morning, my name's Lindsay, I arrived this morning from the UK to begin work with you, except that I don't know where."

"What are you employed as, Mr. Lindsay?"

"I'm a geologist."

Silence at the end of the line, then, "Do you know which Division you are meant to join?"

"The Gold Division, but I haven't yet been given the name of the mine."

"Please hold the line Mr. Lindsay, I'll try to find your file."

Several minutes passed, without muzak, as it hadn't colonised the world at that point, then, "I'm terribly sorry, are you sure you work for us?"

"I've a letter of appointment here, stating salary and so on, so I'm pretty sure that I do have a job and anyway, someone's booked a room in my name at the Victoria Hotel."

"Oh dear (how often was I to hear those two small words spoken over the ensuing years, especially by or about the Personnel Department), I'm not certain what to do?"

"That's OK" I said. "I'll be around at 2 pm, and I expect that someone will find my file by then."

"I'm not sure..." came the response.

I said, "Oh, but I am, and I'll be there at 2 pm sharp, goodbye!" With that, I put the phone down.

I settled down for a refreshing snooze - it had been a very long flight - set my travelling alarm clock, and drifted off, recharging my mental batteries for the next part of the adventure. Personnel Department, hah!

CHAPTER 2

KERNOW

When I was still a student I obtained a temporary job on a tin mine in Cornwall. It was a Summer School, whereby not only were we undergraduates given training and work in the department of our chosen profession, we were also given the opportunity to visit others such as metallurgy, surveying and mining. The bonus was that we were paid!

The mine that eight of us lucky lads were working on had recently been rejuvenated from some fairly old workings. Mining on this spot had taken place over a number of periods in history, including when the Phoenicians had bought tin and copper from the inhabitants of this part of Britain, and we would occasionally encounter ancient excavations filled with a reddish-yellow mud which had settled over the centuries. In the vernacular of the Cornish miners, this was 'treacle'.

The whole Summer School was a delightful experience in many ways, one of which was that from some of the shallower working stopes we were able to climb up to the surface, sit on sunny flower-covered banks at lunchtime and eat our cheese sandwiches, or Cornish Pasties, or whatever our landlady had chosen for us for that day. Lunch over, we'd descend into the depths again, revitalised and ready to seek answers from the rocks.

Cornwall was and possibly still is a strange place to those who are not Celtic. Cornish people have their own society, the Sons of Kernow, and are pretty friendly on the whole. They can occasionally be a little xenophobic, depending if aspersions are being cast about their roots, or the way English is spoken, or perhaps the way some things are done.

I shared my work experience with an English geology student who had the misfortune to have a rather plummy Home Counties accent which didn't go down too well with some of the Cornish miners. When we two students were allowed to go underground on our own, which was after only a couple of weeks of training, some of the less tolerant miners frequently and purposely misdirected him.

He would ask, "I say, would you mind directing me to Stope 13A?" or something similar, and some grizzled miner would reply, "Aarr, go down 'ere about a hunnert yards, take the left drive, when you see the squizzly box 'ole, turn right," and so on.

My colleague would occasionally spend much of his day wandering round different levels, never actually knowing where he was. It didn't seem to bother him overly much.

My near-impenetrable Scottish burr didn't prove nearly so much of an issue to these would-be 'Cousin Jacks' and fortunately they gave me much less of a difficult time, but on one occasion I was sitting on the station at the five-hundred-foot level, having finished my shift, waiting to go to the surface. I was talking to an old Cornish mine captain. A mine captain is basically equal to a NCO in the army - but mine captains are not always mining engineers with a degree, and many have worked their way up to this position from starting as a learner miner.

In general, they are very knowledgeable, but can be a little tyrannical. They are the 'keepers of the mine' and make sure things happen in an ordered fashion. Fred Symons, a veteran of over fifty years, man and boy, was asking me what I thought of what I was doing, where I was planning in going in my career, and what did I think of Cornwall?

"Ah, Mr. Symons, Cornwall. It really is a pleasure being here. This is my first time out of Scotland and it's great to be in this part of England."

At this point he leapt up and bellowed. "You're not in bloody England here, you're in bloody Kernow and don't you bloody forget it!"

I mollified him by admitting ignorance, but this dislike of being lumped in with England, or the English, was a trait I would encounter, in many guises and peoples, over the coming years. Not least in South Africa, the country in which my professional career was about to begin.

CHAPTER 3

WELCOME

At the appointed hour, I walked into the imposing granite building which was (and is) one of the bastions of the Saint Kilda Corporation empire. It's not as impressive as the building across the street where the company gods lived, as I subsequently found out, but it is of sufficient grandeur to induce second thoughts about showing outward annoyance in those less bloody-minded than I was at that moment.

I reported to Reception, whereupon I was directed to Personnel. Profuse apologies were offered for the underwhelming welcome I had received. It transpired the officer who was assigned to meet me and sort out what I was doing had actually gone on leave and had, ha-ha, absent-mindedly forgotten to tell anyone I was coming. What a silly chap! What a let-down! However, I was given one hundred Rands, roughly half the value of my travellers' cheques, to cover incidental expenses, then guided upwards, by a Personnel Officer, to the office of the Deputy Consulting Geologist of the Gold Division.

"This is it", I thought. "Now I'll find out where I'm going and perhaps even what I'm supposed to do."

The Personnel Officer murmured a few words in the ear of the Great Man, who was sitting at his desk, then this august personage unfolded to a lofty height, shook my hand and proceeded to converse somewhere above the top of my head.

"Ah, so sorry, yes, well, glad to see you've joined us. Yes, yes, very good. Well, um, you've been appointed to this ah, position in Welkom, in the Free State, at one of our mines. Gold mine. Eastern Lands. Jog along to Rand Airport, Germiston, on Wednesday morning at six o'clock, get the flight and the, ah, um, Resident Geologist will meet you. Any questions?"

"How much time have you got?" I thought. What I actually replied was, "Fine, sir, how do I arrange this?"

"No, don't worry, we'll arrange a car to pick you up. Do enjoy your career with us, I'm sure you'll find out you made a good choice. Goodbye."

With a firm handshake, I was ushered out of the office, Personnel Officer in tow, taken downwards in the lift and then shown towards the front door.

"Don't worry," said the man from Personnel. "We'll organise everything and send you a note at the hotel. Enjoy looking around Jo'burg until then."

"Like you arranged my welcome," I thought, rebelliously.

I wasn't hugely more informed than I had been earlier in the day, but I was now much wealthier and it seemed as if I really was employed. I spent the next day or so wandering around the centre of Johannesburg, finding out what made the City of Gold tick, which was, surprisingly enough, gold (and platinum and diamonds and coal and steel and so on) and at the appointed hour on Wednesday morning, arrived at Germiston airport.

I'd seen one in films, but it wasn't clear before that point that a Douglas DC3 - the 'Dakota' - requires some agility to enter, as unlike modern aircraft, it rests on its tail wheel so you have to climb up the aisle to find your seat. I managed this feat without falling on anybody. Just.

The flight took place in early September, which is the tail-end of winter in South Africa. The brown landscape, which I'd seen in South West Africa seemed to be here too, so I asked the man in the next seat how far it extended. He thought for a moment and then said, "Pretty well all the way to Cape Town."

Explaining that I was new to the country, I then asked how far Cape Town was and he replied, "Another four hours or so." Great!

After about an hour and a half of uneventful flying over the sepia-tinted land, we circled and landed at Welkom airport in the Orange Free State. As the old saw had it; yes, there are plenty of oranges, but nothing's free and it's in quite a state. As I stood there, my suitcase in one hand and briefcase in another, a flustered, agitated-looking, floppy-haired Welshman appeared and enquired if I was Tom Lindsay. Upon receiving an affirmative he grabbed for the hand clutching the briefcase, and said, "Jeff Warden, Resident Geologist, Eastern Lands, welcome to Welkom."

He grimaced only slightly then continued with, "Let's go and sort you out."

We climbed into his battered, ancient VW Beetle and headed towards my new home.

Jeff spoke. "Have you, um, actually been down a mine before? See, I don't know much about you, I only got told two days ago you were coming, as a matter of fact, but we're desperate for a geologist so it's good luck that you're here."

I replied cautiously, "I was a student on a tin mine in Cornwall last year, so I know about stopes and raises and suchlike."

Jeff's brow cleared. "Duw," he said. "They've sent us a live one at long last!"

He hurried on to explain that many graduates who arrived after the weeding-out process in London were First-Class Honours 'chaps', as the weeders-out felt that the Corporation deserved the best. Unfortunately, many of these academically desirable lads - women were then not allowed to work underground - were not eminently practical and could only handle a few months of the cramped, smelly, dusty and noisy three-dimensional maze that constitutes a mine, before returning to the sanity and well-ordered existence of the academic fold.

We chatted about the usual inconsequential things which a new subordinate and a new boss do, then arrived at the Single Quarters. Those last two words should be highlighted in dayglo neon, because the subject will recur, probably more than once. At that time, on most mines in South Africa, nearly all single men, irrespective of their status within the company hierarchy, were accommodated in single quarters. If you were black, you were housed by tribal affinity and very definitely not in the same place as the white members of the single population. Single women were a rarity and if they existed at all, were usually billeted in the Nurses' Quarters.

The testosterone-painted barracks contained rooms of around eight feet by twelve feet with a parquet floor, a wash-hand basin in one corner, a bed, a chair, a chest of drawers and a built-in cupboard. Toilet and shower facilities were shared with between twelve and sixteen other men. Not all were house-trained, it needs to be said. The quarters were equipped with a central dining room and a single pay telephone. They were not unlike Halls of Residence at university, except that someone else could be paid to do the laundry. The Quarters' manageress busied about with forms and keys and addressed me in Afrikaans, then switched to English when she noticed a slight lack of reaction.

"Meneer Lindsay, you are in Room 4. Here are your keys, please sign this. Will you be eating all your meals here, please sign this. Please fill in this laundry sheet twice a week."

And so on. A well-meaning lady, who hadn't worked out that it was the other person who was supposed to answer and required only a scribble of assent from her charges for her to be contented.

Formalities over, accommodation secured, Jeff and I went off to the office. Not, as I'd fondly imagined, my office, as Jeff had the only enclosed space with a door; the rest of us perched on stools around various drawing tables in a large room next to the Survey Department.

"Andy, meet Tom."

"Tom, this is Peter."

"Oi, Baz, you scruffy Australian wombat, this is Tom."

The niceties of civilized introduction having been observed, Jeff took me aside.

He said, "Look, there's not much for you to do for the rest of the morning, so do you want to do things like open a bank account, or let your folks know you've arrived or get unpacked or what?"

"Unpack two shirts and three pairs of socks?" I thought.

"Thanks, Jeff, I think opening a bank account would be a good move," I replied. He didn't bother with checking whether I could drive, but just gave me some rudimentary directions and the keys to the Beetle.

It felt strange to be driving in a new country, even if the road signs were quite similar to those in the UK and South Africans drove on the proper side of the road. Four-way stops were a bit of an interesting novelty, as were signs telling me of a robot approaching. "A robot!" I thought. "What on Earth do they want with a robot?" I passed several of these signs before working out that 'robots' were, disappointingly, traffic lights. There were also some directions painted on the surface of the road, between direction arrows, telling me that the lane was for Slegs Only. I didn't know what a Sleg was, so I kept a sharp lookout.

The CBD of Welkom proved to be one block of buildings and a horseshoe-shaped boulevard. 'Barclays Bank', declaimed a sign outside one of the more stern-looking edifices, so in I went and up to the counter which said 'Enquiries/Inligting'.

I seriously doubt even now whether the teller had ever heard of Scotland, let alone its Royal Bank and their travellers' cheques.

I suppose an enquiry along the lines of "HelloI'mnewinthecountry, wanttoopenanaccount - here'ssomemoney," all delivered in a contemporary Scottish accent might have been a bit much. That, and the teller being an Afrikaans speaker, ensured that formalities took a touch longer than expected.

I emerged triumphant, however, with a temporary cheque book and navigated my return to the mine. I kept an eye out for any Slegs.

Later that afternoon, Andy dropped me off at Single Quarters, advised me to “take it easy, I’ll pick you up in the morning” and left me to my own devices. At the evening meal, the usual formalities associated with the entry of a new male into the herd surfaced. Nods were given.

“Hello, you new?”

“How long have you been here?”

“One day.”

“Praat jy Afrikaans? Nee, dit maak nie saak nie!”

“Fancy a beer?”

I awoke next morning bright and early, ready to begin my career, show my mettle and similar worthy sentiments. The choice of clothing wasn’t a problem, but as I pulled on my left shoe, it became clear that I’d forgotten Rule Number One, according to the Boys’ Own African Explorer’s Handbook, 1905. I had neglected to shake out my footwear and in the toe of my shoe was something with more legs than me.

My immediate thought was ‘scorpion’ so I gingerly removed the shoe, turned it upside down and a very large cockroach scuttled out and disappeared into the cupboard. Relief washed over me; I wasn’t going to die on my first day, or, at least not before breakfast.

CHAPTER 4

KICK-OFF

In Afrikaans, geologist is pronounced as 'hee-o-loogh', which, with a bit of vocal strain, becomes 'heel-ooch' which is spelled geel-oog and which is, literally translated, yellow-eye. Hence I was now a member of the Yellow-Eyes department.

Only ten days after arriving in Welkom and I was back in the Transvaal, sixty kilometres west of Johannesburg and ten thousand feet underground on 100 Level. The country was more-or-less metricated but mines always labelled their vertical measurements in feet, for some inexplicable reason. It was a little confusing having to work in a metric system, but to have to refer to the working levels by a numerical contraction of their imperial designation.

No, I hadn't been fired, but had been transferred to West Witwatersrand Deep, then and now one of the deepest mines in the world. The reason for the transfer? It was a simple matter of there being a married geologist (him) at West Wits Deep, but with no spare housing, and a single geologist (me) at Eastern Lands, but which could provide married accommodation. As we were both brand new to our respective mines, the powers-that-be decided a swap was in order and the decree went forth. Planning is a wonderful invention. Personnel Department take note!

After to-ing and fro-ing which involved the mighty Dakota once again, I arrived at a very similar Single Quarters, set on the side of a hill, or kopje, within the mine property. The outlook was definitely preferable to the unending flat landscape of the Free State, but I had to go through the signing in, new-kid-on-the-block routine again.

On my travels, someone had explained that my new boss was a red-haired Scotsman with quite a reputation, who had only recently taken over at the mine. I had visions of this kilted Hielander, striding about the place, muttering fearful Gaelic imprecations. Instead, I met a slight, sandy haired Englishman with a strongly Scottish name, a man of immense charm and wit who immediately put me at my ease.

Fergus Cameron, who was and is one of the best bosses that anyone could wish for, explained how the Geology Department fitted in to the mine hierarchy - it didn't - what services we were expected to provide, and how the work was divided up.

There were two main shafts on the mine, each with two sets of vertical sub-shafts, going down to around thirteen thousand feet below surface. The gold was mined from two 'reefs - layers of quartz pebbles separated vertically from each other by about three thousand feet of rock - both heading downwards at an angle of twenty-one degrees from the horizontal. These reefs were not overly thick, only a matter of centimetres most of the time, and were mined by blasting slots (panels) into them in a pattern which looks on a plan, and from some distance away, like a stylized Christmas tree. The official designation is longwall mining - a mining method more common in coal mines. The panels, more often called stopes, were about thirty metres long and barely a metre high; blasted material was removed by scraping the ore down the slope with a cable-driven metal scraper blade, into a horizontally excavated walkway - a strike gully. From here, it exited into the main haulage below via a boxhole. Much of my job would be to find out why, from time to time, the reef would go missing and then to propose a solution to finding it again.

Here was born Lindsay's Principle of Gold Mine Geology.

If you (the geologist) don't know where the reef is, pronounce loudly, with conviction, "Down a couple of metres, I believe, I'll be back next week to check."

The reasoning behind this principle is that in the unlikely event (heaven forbid) that you've stuffed up in your geological interpretation of the problem, it is much easier for the miners to fill in a hole in the floor than it is to make good a large (and probably getting larger by the day) excavation above their heads. Especially when there's over six thousand feet, at a minimum, of rock above said heads!

So, what was I doing underground? Strangely enough, not getting lost, just attempting to follow a suggestion from the second-in-command, a somewhat volatile individual of the Latin persuasion, Sergio Rotollo.

The previous day, I had gone underground with him on a visit to one of the development ends. These are the working faces which extend the tunnels along which underground locomotives haul ore, waste and personnel, following behind the advances of the mining faces above. After checking out that I was physically fit, I had been kitted out in the uniform of hard-hat, boiler suit, boots and a lamp. We arrived at the requisite level via vertical descent in a succession of cages; these are like lifts, without the amenities of carpets, music or opacity (the cages are made of metal mesh). We met up with our team of underground assistants - the team of men who would carry all the paraphernalia we required - and after a walk of a few kilometres in hot, humid and odoriferous tunnels, arrived at the place of work. Sergio pointed out all the salient geology and the important fact that we were working not on a scale of metres but of a very few centimetres.

This was a bit of a new concept for me, as was trying to keep my spectacles unfogged long enough to see what he was trying to impart. The work completed, we returned to the office by mid-day, via the changehouse and a shower. Sergio suggested that the next day I should, if I felt confident enough, go back underground by myself and repeat the exercise just undertaken. "Fair enough," I said and we left it at that.

The next morning, shoes checked for scorpions, having previously worked out the shaft was about two kilometres from the Single Quarters, and also having arranged to meet my assistants underground, I set off early, on foot, for the changehouse. Resplendent in my shiny new gear, I went underground, found the team, did the work and re-emerged triumphant. One of the shaft's mine captains gave me a lift back to Single Quarters and I returned, post-lunch, to the office, to find a scene of panic.

Sergio asked me, "Where in da-hell you been? What-a you been doing?"

I replied, quite reasonably I thought, that I had been underground just as he had suggested I should. I said I'd done the mapping and if he cared to look in my notebook, he'd see my results. This answer seemed to generate much relief, mixed with astonishment.

Apparently it was understood, although not by me, that I was to have been picked up by one of the other geologists, taken to the shaft and then brought back from the shaft when I'd finished my stint underground. When I had not come to the office in the morning, and could not be found, everyone thought I had decamped. My nonchalant return restored the office equilibrium for the day, although I did manage, in the following three months, to add more excitement to the previously boring existence of the Yellow Eyes.

To be fair, only one incident was truly of my making, but I initially managed to sustain an injury by a steel scraper cable, when the driver started the winch without warning. The one-inch diameter rope snapped across and up, catching Terry, my colleague and mentor, in the vasectomy area, and striking me across the forehead, causing blood to pour from the wound and smashing my spectacles. Shortly after that, again with Terry in charge, I managed to fall down a twelve-metre vertical boxhole. I was following instructions, but as I grabbed a hosepipe used to supply water to the rockdrills, it parted rather suddenly on a join and I suffered an 'uncontrolled descent'.

Terry fell victim to 'mentoritis' at that point, so Chris took over for the next month. In true Monty Python fashion, nothing happened!

Incident number three occurred after Fergus had suggested, now that I knew the geography of the mine quite well, that I map an area which I hadn't yet visited, on my own! Mapping consists of asking one of your assistants to sit at the top end of the panel and hold one end of a measuring tape, whilst the other assistant goes to the bottom of the stope, reeling out the tape as he goes. You then slide down on your backside, in a controlled fashion, and make written notes about what you see, and where, noting distances and measuring all sorts of geological oddities.

Michael and Spaceman, my assistants, and I duly navigated to the correct panels, but found that the access to the top of one particular stope was blocked off by an open boxhole in the gully, over which we couldn't pass. There was nothing for it but to descend to the next level, climb back up the face itself and begin mapping from the top down. Halfway down I began to feel rather unwell.

Two-thirds of the way down I thought, "I'm getting out of here, something's not right with me."

As I reached the bottom of the stope, and the access walkway, I started to vomit copiously. This is not a good sign in general, but particularly not underground. I attempted to walk back and out to the miner's box - the entrance to the working face where a miner keeps his tally books and suchlike. At this point I fell over. I was still vomiting, trying to drink cold water to settle matters, but it was all coming back up in a fairly steady stream. Spaceman went off and found the miner who came down and between them dragged me to the miner's box.

The miner, Salvatore, hosed me down with cold water, saying I probably had heat exhaustion. He also opened an air hose (used to power the jackhammer drills) and forced air all over me to cool me down. I sat there for an hour or so, with Salvatore, but each time I felt better, so I'd be sick again.

He eventually decided that I would have to be taken to surface. As I couldn't walk, I was placed aboard a stretcher and, somewhat ignominiously, carted along the haulages, between various levels and thence upwards to the changehouse where I was met by an anxious Fergus.

No doubt I looked (and felt) awful, but Fergus didn't look much better.

"After all," I thought raggedly, "it's not every day that one-sixth of your workforce manages to bring the entire schedule of a shaft to a complete halt!"

However, that issue didn't worry Fergus in the slightest because his concern then, as always, was for the welfare of his staff, however inconsiderate they may have been. Getting out of the boilersuit and into the shower was an effort, with much diverting sideways to the toilet to vomit again (where does it all come from?), but with Fergus' help I eventually made it, clothed and semi-lucid, to a doctor's surgery in town.

One injection, two spoonsful of liquid glucose, some orange juice and eighteen hours sleep later, I knew again I would live. As I walked to the office, every bone felt as though it was made of shattered glass - but - I was vertical and not vomiting!

It transpired that I had contracted a fairly severe stomach bug which, when subject to the effects of the heat and humidity underground, multiplied and hastened the normal effects several times over. Lesson learned – if there was any sign of incipient ill-health I would never again venture underground.

CHAPTER 5

FANAKALO

West Wits Deep - the "Dumps" as it was affectionately known - employed a workforce of around 24,000 people, of whom most were migrant workers from all over southern Africa. All of the different nations, and the tribes within the nations, spoke not only their own official language, but also many others, not necessarily including English or Afrikaans. This enviable faculty was largely denied those not of African origin. Nonetheless, as part of the management, one had to be able to communicate with all and sundry. Prior to going underground, part of my training required me to learn a *lingua franca*, for want of a better term, called Fanakalo (Fana ka lo), which loosely translated means 'like this'. A hybrid mixture of Zulu, Xhosa, probably traces of various Indian languages (it originated in the Natal cane fields), English and others, it allowed basic communication between all the language groups.

On one of my first solo trips underground I had two assistants who I hadn't worked with before and perhaps through ignorance, or perhaps through arrogance, I addressed them straightaway in my halting Fanakalo. They responded likewise, although more fluently, so off we went to the work area.

Working underground requires quite a detailed knowledge of the layout of the mine, let alone the geology. The long and the short of it was, I became lost. I knew where I was supposed to be going to but didn't quite make it. Having wandered round for about an hour not quite in ever-decreasing circles but finding dead-ends here, there and yonder, I decided now was the time to call for assistance. In my best Fanakalo, I asked Robert, my chief assistant, to go and find the shift boss for the level and get directions for finding the stope. He duly took off, then returned with the requisite knowledge and steered me to the work area. We finished the job and I managed to get the cage back to the surface at the right time, leaving rock samples to come up with my team who would ascend a little later.

That afternoon, my assistants duly arrived at the office with my kit and samples. Fergus greeted them in his usual courteous manner and asked how things had gone that day.

Robert replied, "Fine, Mr. Fergus. Mr. Tom got a little lost underground but we managed to find where he wanted to go - see you tomorrow."

All this delivered in perfect English. I felt minuscule.

Nevertheless, I persevered and became quite fluent in Fanakalo, as much as its limited etymology allows, and was only reprimanded on my use of this language on one occasion in Pinetown, in Natal Province, when refuelling my car. The pump attendant, a Zulu, suggested I either speak English or Zulu to him, "Not that kitchen rubbish!"

Many years later, in Scotland, the phone rang - an out-of-area number - and our younger son, eager to be of help, answered but could make no sense of what the caller wanted, apart from my name. He passed the telephone to Sue, who had no more luck, so she passed the handset to me.

"Tom Lindsay here, can I help?" I said.

"It's Philemon Makango, - we met four months ago in Botswana and you gave me your card. You said you'd call me if there was any work at the mine site. I hear you are hiring - why haven't you given me a call?"

I replied. "Philemon, I haven't forgotten, but we're only hiring drilling assistants just now and you're a driver. We don't need drivers for the time being and there's nothing more going to happen until we get the results from drilling. That won't be until early next year. If the results are good, I'll give you a call when the next work programme begins."

"But, Mr. Tom, I need work now," he said.

"Philemon," I said. "Sorry, but I can't just make a job. You said you wanted to be a driver, and all I have available right now is fairly low-skilled work; there's no way I can pay you anything like what you've been getting and anyway, I did say it might be a year before anything really happened."

"I know, Mr. Tom," he said. "But I want to work near my home, not far away in South Africa with those *boerkie*, so I did not want you to forget me!"

We chatted for a little longer but really, there was no more I could add and we ended the call.

I turned around to see my son's very wide eyes.

"Daddy, why are you speaking so funny?" he asked.

I looked at Sue. "Don't ask me," she said. "You were doing your gobbledygook thing again - whatever you were speaking, it wasn't a language I recognise!"

Fanakalo is truly my second language - I don't have to translate anything, it is simply *there* - and Philemon didn't speak English and I don't speak Setswana, so he'd just resorted to the language we both knew. I looked at my son. "Don't worry, sometimes Dad just has to talk to people who don't speak English - perhaps one day you'll learn another language, like you started to do in Botswana - remember?"

"OK Dad," he said, now quite unfazed. "It'll be like that snake language in Harry Potter, eh?"

CHAPTER 6

THE PSYCHOLOGIST

At the end of each calendar month in a gold mine there is a frenzy of activity called measuring. During the month, surveyors go underground on a daily basis and measure the progress of whatever mining is taking place. From time to time, they survey in marker points which are stamped copper tags affixed to the roof (it's called the hangingwall). Once back on surface, the position of each tag is calculated from the survey measurements and then plotted on a master plan onto which the outlines of the stopes and the positions of the gulleys are regularly updated.

Miners were, in those days, paid by the number of centares (square metres) broken in a stope, or how many metres advance had been made in a drive. Their income therefore derived from the figures recorded by the surveyors on Measuring Day.

The miners, meanwhile, tried all sorts of tricks to increase those numbers. Accidentally on purpose replacing a 'fallen' tag a few metres back, so that the distance from the tag to the face was a few metres more than it should have been, was not exactly uncommon. They'd be found out, eventually, when a check survey took place, but the attitude tended to be, 'Who cares?'

When a surveyor was likely to be frantically busy and not able to get to a particular area on Measuring Day, he might ask me to measure up for him. On one occasion my friend, Roy Clark, asked for my help because there was a lot going on in one particular section on Two Shaft, owing to a blocked gully between two areas on 97 Level. I arrived at the appointed panels and had my usual chat to the miner, Sarel Odendaal. This was not just simple courtesy, as after all he was legally appointed to be in charge, but made sure that my and my crew's presence had been noted in case of accidents. I said that I'd be mapping his three panels, but also that I'd be doing the measuring for Roy.

"Ja, that's fine, Tom," he said. "Maar maak seker dat ek nie kort aan meter is nie" (make sure I'm not short on metres).

The miners were the first people to whom I reported any problems with going 'off-reef'. I wasn't supposed to, as my reports were to be given to the Section Manager, who would then harangue the Mine Captain, who would take out his displeasure on the Shift Boss, who would then vent his spleen on the miner. I found that it made life easier, and won me more cooperation, if, after finishing my work and had found any issues, that I just quietly told the miner, who would have a solution to the problem underway before the arrival of the Shift Boss a day or so in the future. As this wasn't the way the mining hierarchy worked, because it was largely based on bullying, and I was nominally a 'Senior Official', the same level as a Mine Captain, I was a little difficult for the miners to pigeonhole. However, on that particular day, there were no issues with Sarel's panels, so I completed my work and headed back to the station and the exit cage.

Back on surface, I met Roy in the Survey Office later that afternoon. He said that he'd actually managed to get to the area and just as a precaution, thought he would measure up so we could compare notes. Sarel wasn't one of the usual suspects when it came to funny business, but it did no harm to have the occasional check.

The measurements tallied, so, as expected, there was no issue. However, Roy looked at me quizzically and said, "Don't get me wrong, but I'm not sure what you're up to these days."

I looked up, puzzled. "Why, what're you talking about?"

He continued. "I know you like to chat to the miners, but they've obviously got the wrong idea of what you do. I was just starting to measure up Sarel's panels, when he appeared in the northside and said to me, 'Don't bother, Roy, the psychologist's just been!'"

CHAPTER 7

SHAFT SINKING

Shaft sinking is, I have long since decided, an activity to be undertaken by others. It is fundamental to the creation of a deep underground mine, but it does require skills and attributes I don't really possess and an attitude to personal danger I will never acquire. The most suitably qualified individuals, quite possibly on day release from the asylum, undertake all the various tasks.

When you think of a shaft thirty or sixty feet deep, or perhaps even a couple of hundred feet, it sounds like a fairly innocuous undertaking. However, in the supermine I was working on, we already had two shaft systems; one down to 6,600 feet from surface, with the next one starting where the first stopped and going on down to 10,000 feet. The whole secondary shaft operation of winders, headgear and ancillary equipment was housed in a huge underground excavation. The new third shaft, the one I was involved with, went from the 10,000-foot level down to 13,200 feet. You might ask why the need to put three shafts in, when one longer shaft would do the job?

There was the small problem of the wire ropes. In the 1970s, to have a rope longer than about 7,500 feet was limited by the technology of rope-making at the time and because a rope any longer was liable to snap under its own weight. Additionally, the available winders and their technology could not accommodate any longer rope. Often, access to deeper levels was achieved by the use of inclined shafts from within the underground workings, but they tended to be slow, cumbersome and didn't do the job nearly as efficiently as vertical shafts. With the reefs on this mine reaching depths of over 15,000 feet at the southern boundary of the property, it had been decided to sink a Tertiary Shaft below each main shaft system and to develop the lowest levels from this excavation.

My introduction to shaft sinking came about during my training period when Terry introduced me to its delights. The only means of getting down or up a shaft under construction involves the use of a thing called a kibble. A kibble is basically a large, cylindrical bucket which, in general, has three welded anchor points along the top circumference, from which three chains are then hitched on to a hook at the end of the hoisting rope. This glorified bucket is then lowered or hoisted down the shaft in the same way as a cage, except there is no shaft infrastructure such as guide rails. The circular nature of the top of the kibble also causes issues when trying to exit this contraption at the station bank. This is the edge of a station - the Level - nearest the shaft, cut horizontally into the side of the shaft. From the bank, tunnels are developed to allow new parts of the reef to be accessed. Most kibbles have two guide ropes running down the side so that the bucket doesn't stray off course and bang into the side of the shaft.

My first meeting with a kibble was at 100 Level - 10,000 feet down - where I was told to get in it. It was constructed of fairly thick mild steel and on the outside there were toe holds into which you could stick your boots in order to climb into the thing. This I duly did, accompanied by my fellow geologist and our assistants. The onsetter - he who is in charge of the kibble - rang the bell system to communicate with the hoist driver to have the kibble lifted up a few feet; two trap doors opened below us and then we dropped into complete and utter darkness. Apart from the kibble and its guide ropes, there were some ventilation, water and compressed air pipes in the void, taking those necessities down to the bottom of the shaft, and a number of cables spaced along the circumference - shafts are nearly always round - on which a device called the 'stage' was suspended. The stage is basically a platform which sits just above the working face at the bottom of the shaft and from which a mechanism called a cactus grab, which looks like a child's version of an excavator, picks up the broken rock and places it in the kibble. The stage is lowered or hoisted up on the ropes when blasting of the face - the floor - takes place so it is not blown to smithereens...which did happen occasionally when those responsible forgot to raise it before blasting.

We dropped, in darkness apart from our cap-lamps, for some two and a half thousand feet until we reached the stage, where the kibble stopped and we climbed out. The kibble was then lowered to the bottom of the shaft and we clambered down the outside of the stage on a rope ladder, to the same spot, avoiding the arms of the cactus grab. The noise was quite horrendous with air-powered jackhammers going, the grab working and people all yelling at one another; normal conversation was not possible.

We checked the geology, looking for faults in the rock and for water-bearing fissures, measured and logged everything in our notebooks and then came the time to exit this subterranean bedlam. The kibble had, by this time, been filled up with broken rock and had been hoisted back up onto the stage, ready to go up and be emptied. We climbed back onto the stage with some difficulty and I stood waiting patiently for an empty kibble to come and retrieve us.

Terry motioned me across and said "What're you standing about for, get onto it!"

"But," I said. "It's full of rock."

"Well," he replied. "It's either get on it now or wait for a few hours. Just put your boots on the edge, lean inwards, grasp one of those chains and hang on for dear life."

Something I haven't yet pointed out is that I suffer from vertigo. Very bad vertigo. Standing on top of broken rock on the edge of a cylinder, clinging on for dear life as this thing rose through open space was not my idea of fun, then or now. However, there seemed to be no option, so along with a few other lunatics, I duly climbed aboard, saying to myself, "My boots will not slip, my boots are perfect. They have one hundred per cent grip. My arms will never unlock from this chain. I will not fall off and smash myself to smithereens on the stage."

The kibble lurched, then rose majestically up the shaft in complete silence. Looking down, which is not a very clever thing to do when one suffers from vertigo, I could see the few lights on the stage, blinking and disappearing into the black distance. I stopped that activity quickly and looked up at my watch. I looked at my fellow travellers on top of this mound of rock inside a bucket. Anywhere but down. Things were going better until the kibble stopped. Not at 100 Level, but somewhere in between. It stopped for what seemed about three hundred years - probably about five minutes - but long enough. Then we started up again, through the trap doors at the top, and the moment the doors clanged shut I leapt off like a person possessed, vowing loudly that I'd never undertake such a perilous nonsense again. That was a youthful mistake to make and, as things turned out, more of an optimistic wish, destined to remain ungranted.

Not long after this episode, my charming and erudite boss suggested that we needed to have the 113 Level mapped.

"No problem," responded the eager young geologist. "I'll do that."

“Well,” said Fergus, “there is, ah, a small technical problem. You have to go down the sinking shaft to get to it, because it’s being developed from the vertical shaft southwards, to meet the old inclined shaft.”

Oops.

So, not long after New Year, in fact altogether too close to New Year and the after-effects of its celebration on the nervous system, I went back down to 100 Level, climbed aboard the kibble with my assistants and off we went to 113 Level. The kibble was filled with jackhammer drill steels, wire mesh, rock bolts, sundry other accoutrements and apart from us, one other man, the onsetter. It seemed to me, at that point, that all the stuff in the kibble was facing in the direction I would have to get out when we reached the station level.

The same procedure took place as before, the kibble lifted, the trap doors opened and I asked the onsetter. “How am I supposed to get off at 113? Do we go to the bottom, chuck all this stuff out and come back up?”

He said “No, no, no. You’re getting out as we go down. It’s quite simple.” He explained as if to someone of limited understanding. “When we get to the station, we’ll stop at the bank, the banksman will run a walkway out and out you get.”

I said, “Yes, but I can’t climb safely over all this stuff you’ve got in here.”

“Oh, no problem,” he said. “What we do is we swing the kibble on its guide cables and when it reaches its apex, I’ll try to hold it until you get onto the bank.”

The kibble swung, I balanced on the edge, trying to land on the walkway, which was probably one and a half metres long at the most, and then I attempted to leap onto this bit of board which had some chain handrails. At this point, my spectacles steamed up because the air coming down the shaft was colder than the air coming out of the level. I think I may have achieved the longest jump on record from a kibble; I don’t recall that I actually touched the walkway but I certainly landed on the bank and stood there wobbling quietly. My nonchalant helpers climbed out onto the little walkway, put our gear together and waited for me to go mapping. I expect my writing may have been somewhat shakier than normal that day, owing to a majorly sustained burst of adrenaline.

We then had to return to the station and to get into the kibble by the reverse of method we’d got out. Fortunately, at this point, a couple of hours later, the kibble was actually empty so no swinging on the cables was required by the onsetter. Success. However, this was not the end of my shaft sinking career, although I should have learned my lesson and the limits of how frightened I could be.

On the neighbouring mine, or rather a would-be mine belonging to a sister company, the main shaft was being sunk in precisely the same way that's been described. However, with the development of rope technology, the main shaft was going to be considerably deeper than on our mine. No geologist had been appointed to the mine at this juncture, so all work fell under our remit.

Sometime in 1977, Sergio and I went to check the progress being made. I was feeling reasonably happy because the kibble in this case was about three metres high and once inside, of course I couldn't see out, or see anything at all apart from the smooth metal wall. It seemed quite a nice way to travel. Coming back up, the kibble was empty. Everything went very well, we began ascending at quite a rate, until about half way up the shaft, when the kibble started to develop a bit of a speed wobble. You can imagine what it felt like, standing in the bottom of a bucket, bouncing about quietly with nothing to hold on to. Perhaps not so quietly. There was the shaking externally and the quaking internally. We felt also that if it wobbled much more, the kibble might hit the side wall, in which case we would be tipped out rather ignominiously towards a rather sticky end 7,000 feet down. The fact you're hearing the story indicates we survived.

I have been shaft sinking since in much smaller shafts, in much less apparent danger, but it's only a matter of perception. It is still a highly nerve-wracking business and best left to either those who don't suffer from vertigo or those who possess an inordinately well-developed sense of balance. Or a death wish.

CHAPTER 8

THE BUSH

Towards the end of 1978, I was becoming quite frustrated with life. I was still living in Single Quarters because mine management simply would not countenance the concept of three single men occupying a house. My married colleagues could get on with normal lives, having friends around for dinner or drinks or buying furniture, paintings and the like, but my choice of being single condemned me to living in a small room to which little could be added and also to which no more than one person could be invited. Additionally, I discovered that despite a promotion, my salary was barely half that of similarly qualified engineers or metallurgists. I really enjoyed working for Fergus, but it seemed to me that I was constantly becoming irritable for the smallest of reasons and that really, I needed a change of environment.

I discussed this with Fergus, because the route out of the gold mines into exploration or to other metals and minerals seemed to be closed, owing to a lack of geologists choosing to work on the very deep South African gold mines for precisely the reasons I now wished to leave.

The company's executive management tried to keep the staff they had by dint of neither money nor promotions, but by a steadfast refusal to acknowledge that a crisis situation existed. The effect of this deliberate belittling of employees' concerns was to further annoy many perfectly able geologists and to cause mass resignations. We had explored my possible resignation when he suggested that he contact an old boss of his, for whom he had worked in the company's Diamond Division in West Africa and Australia.

"Don't know it it'll do any good, Tom," he said. "But I'm in Johannesburg next week and I'll see if Campbell might have a solution for you."

Fergus was as good as his word and Campbell both listened and acted. He secured a transfer for me to the Diamond Division, so, after a break in the UK, I packed my car and set off from West Wits Deep to Windhoek in April 1979.

Located almost in its geographic centre, this was the capital city of South West Africa, the country not having yet become Namibia. There is an ethereal beauty about the very stark southern part of the country but there is also a sense that if you break down or get lost here you're going to die. It's probably not quite as bleak as that in actual fact, but that was my first impression on the long second day's drive from Upington, in the Northern Cape Province. This time, my car contained a little more luggage than I had owned on my first arrival in Africa, some three and a half years earlier, and I duly found the motel I had been advised to stay in for a couple of nights. I sampled the very fine Windhoek lager. It was just what suited me then and it suits me equally well now.

My next two and a half years in this marvellous country were overshadowed, perhaps 'shaded' might be a better term, by the fact that there was a war taking place. The war for the liberation of the people of South West Africa from Pretoria's control. Of course, I had been aware of this before leaving my comfortable, if dangerous, gold mine, but it's all a bit different when the action gets a bit close for comfort, as I was to find out. Nevertheless, Namibia, as it is now, is still, without doubt, my favourite country in Africa; it ranks pretty highly in my Rest of the World stakes as well.

The following morning, washed, brushed and polished, I turned up at the appointed hour, at the appointed place, to meet my new boss and colleagues. Frederick Louis van der Staal - 'Frik' - was in charge. He had spent time as a young geologist in the mine I had just left so there was common ground on that subject, at least. Avuncular, burly, occasionally temperamental and, as I later discovered, possessed of a snore that could demolish houses at one hundred metres, this was the man who would guide the next stage of my career. Frik informed me that I had arrived at just the wrong time to meet anyone else, because the geologists had all come in for the monthly get-together the previous weekend and were now back out in the bush. I'd unfortunately been delayed in leaving the gold mine by six weeks, owing to an acute lack of eager, or indeed any, replacements for my position, but had finally managed to escape.

After establishing that I had no idea about the practicalities of diamond exploration, which he brushed off with an "Ag, you'll learn quick," Frik explained that the region I was being assigned to was called Kavangoland, whose northern boundary was, and is, the south-eastern Angolan border, demarcated by the Okavango River. To the south there was no real border but the area graded into what was known as Bushmanland, where the true Kalahari Bushmen still lived their nomadic lives. Frik handed me over to his temporary second-in-command, the real one being on leave, for further instruction.

This imposing personage was well over six feet tall, had a chin Desperate Dan would envy, sun-bleached blond hair and, to my surprise, because I was sure I had just met a textbook Aryan, an almost Sandhurst accent. Ralph Fitzroy-Walker, graduate of Exeter University, reincarnated as a geologist from a previous existence as a swashbuckler, but now with substantial diamond exploration experience gained in Angola, explained what my duties would be, once I had actually made my way to the bush.

"Tom, you'll be it, the man-in-charge; chief geologist, lawyer, doctor, accountant, personnel manager, marriage counsellor and mechanic. And anything else that needs doing."

He went on, "You'll have overall charge of thirty or so geologists, field assistants and labourers and your job is to find kimberlites. That's the rock in which diamonds are found, in case you've forgotten your igneous petrology."

"Of course," he said, "there's a few tricks involved so get your notebook out and let's go through some."

What Ralph didn't over-emphasise was that I would have almost no regular communication with base and that some of my field assistants, and other colleagues, would have only a passing acquaintance with sanity, but more of that later.

I was duly introduced around the office, including the laboratories and workshops, then taken off to a company flat to get myself sorted out.

"What a well-placed flat," was my first impression. "Situated next to a cinema and a brewery."

I would have three companions in this abode but two had yet to be recruited, so I had a choice of bedroom and bed. Not quite my own place, certainly, but immeasurably better than what I had been used to.

Windhoek was then, and is now, run with an efficiency which has to be experienced to be believed. Clean streets, supermarkets with great continental delicatessen sections, good cafes and restaurants, and a slight air of 'I might be in Africa, but my standards are best German'. Just driving through the city was a tonic.

Back at base, I was introduced to the two most important pieces of the puzzle that was my new life as an exploration geologist. My cook and my Land Rover. Both had worked for others before me; one had a good record and one a somewhat murky history. My Land Rover never let me down in all the time I had it. Solstice Muhanga provided me with many lessons in human ingenuity and the concept of communal property. If it wasn't nailed down, it was his.

After a couple of days of getting organised, I filled up the trusty Land Rover with the supplies requested from my camp-to-be, all my new exploration clothing and equipment, much of my food for the next month in a technologically advanced Frik-designed coolbox, and Solstice. With all his goods and chattels, of which there were many; Solstice was an avid entrepreneur.

I was warned to expect roadblocks from South African Defence Force troops and their in-training Namibian counterparts on our 800 kilometre journey north. These mainly conscripted soldiers would search for supplies, arms and ammunition destined for the freedom fighters (or terrorists, all depending on your viewpoint). As expected, we met a roadblock somewhere north of the town of Otjiwarongo. The barrier consisted of a stripey wooden pole and a policeman waving cars down. Also, an armoured car with its barrel pointing fairly and squarely at the driver of any vehicle stopped for inspection. That was me. I pulled up.

Four armed soldiers came over and positioned themselves at each wheel, automatic rifles pointed at the tyres, then the sergeant in charge came to my window and asked what my business was, where was I going and all the usual roadblock pleasantries. It was a little tricky as he spoke in German; I didn't and still don't. We managed.

I unloaded the Rover and his squaddies all had a good look whilst I tried to explain the contents. You try explaining the purpose of a whole lot of equipment and chemicals of which you have little idea to someone who truly has no idea! However, all seemed satisfactory, so I proceeded to reload the vehicle, up to the point that the sergeant pulled out his pistol and told me to put my hands on the side of the vehicle.

He commanded me to lift up each foot, then he inspected the sole of each boot. He asked me where I acquired my footwear and I told him 'somewhere in Jo'burg'.

He said that I would have to be careful. The tread pattern of my beautiful new boots was near-identical to the tread of the boots worn by the baddies. Apparently, if the Defence Forces came across those particular tracks in the bush, they were liable to shoot first and ask questions later.

After this cheerful nugget of information was duly digested, I took off north yet again with the aid of a hand-drawn map - courtesy of Frik - and many dusty hours later found my way off the main road, such as it was, into the hinterland. It was an area of scattered big trees and wide, but mainly dry rivers in deep valleys; altogether a quite spectacular place with abundant game, or so it seemed. Little duiker antelope darted about and we surprised a couple of gemsbok going about their lawful business.

About twenty kilometres short of camp, the vehicle suffered a puncture, so Solstice and I quickly unloaded the Land Rover again to get to the special 'bumper' jack - the usual sorts of jack don't work well on an off-road vehicle. At that point, a Land Rover pick-up arrived in a cloud of dust in front of us. This proved to contain Johan de Beer, my Field Officer, out looking out for his new geologist. After a brief handshake, we completed the repairs and headed for camp.

We followed him, or at least we tried to, but as he went off in a cloud of dust I couldn't see where he was going, so we followed the dust cloud. Some twenty minutes or so later, I stopped the mighty Land Rover (Series III for the afficionados out there) in front of what I could see was a very large tent. I was informed this was the mess tent which had been liberated from the Defence Forces, and, as darkness was impending, if I would step this way, I would be shown my house, which was just that.

When I say a house - shades of a Monty Python sketch here - it was actually a concrete slab for the floor, into which were inset some tarpoles with cement-washed hessian stretched round them, a door and a corrugated iron roof. The hessian went half way up the tarpoles, with the upper half being filled in with wraparound fly screen which kept out the bigger insects and the larger varieties of mosquito. There was an attached kitchen and an office made of the same materials, all centred on a large wild fig tree which delivered shade during the day, and, as I would find out, the occasional snake.

Having offloaded my goods and chattels, and Solstice having found his quarters and some old friends, I was taken back to the mess tent where I was properly introduced by Johan to the remaining members of the supervisory staff - the Field Officers and Assistants.

Fernando was from Angola and of Portuguese origin. Mikki was of Danish stock, but brought up in Namibia, and Serge was Swiss but had spent his last few years in South Africa. Pieter was the only true South West African citizen, having been born and brought up in the far north-west homeland of Ovamboland, although his tribal affinities were never made clear, owing to the tense war of freedom situation.

Fernando asked if the "Senor Engineer would like a *cerveza*?" Guessing, correctly for once, that this was me, the Senor Engineer responded with an enthusiastic "Yes, please" and proceeded to demolish a bottle of very cold Windhoek lager. Fernando's only remaining beer, as it turned out, which he had been keeping especially for the new boss. After more cold beers had been located by other individuals and consumed, with supper, I eventually went to bed.

In daylight, I could see that the camp was laid out east-west, in a roughly figure-of-eight pattern of cleared bush, with the two circles occupied by living quarters. The point where the circles met was where the workshop and stores were located. A sandy track - a firebreak - ran around the perimeter, with exits to the north, south and east. The landscape here was flat; scrubby thorn bushes were interspersed with occasional large, tall, maroela and 'false' mahogany trees and smaller, numerous, common wild fig trees, the latter of which had densely-packed dark green leaves and small red berries. There was no view as such, just cleared bush, caravans and small accommodation structures like my house. Water was provided by a borehole which pumped directly into a large plastic tank, set high above the camp on a platform and from which, buried plastic pipes supplied the various parts of the camp.

In the morning, before breakfast, Johan and I went to my vehicle, hooked up the High Frequency (HF) radio to the battery and joined in the morning radio call. Radios back then in the 1970's were not very high technology, or at least those we had most certainly weren't, and much depended on the aerial's height and orientation, not forgetting the atmospherics of the day. Getting through to base in Windhoek was convoluted, as it involved a landline connection from the radio hub at Walvis Bay to Windhoek, owing to some strange law preventing anyone within three kilometres of a telephone line from being allowed to possess or use a radio. This connection was heavily used by those ordering weekly shopping, delivering sermons or ordering spare parts for roadmaking machinery, so speaking to base was only undertaken in an emergency, or at a minimum, once every ten days or so.

On a daily basis, it was expected that each camp would communicate with its nearest one or two neighbouring camps, simply to be sure that there were no untoward incidents or accidents which needed attention. My nearest neighbour was in Tsumkwe, the major settlement - one police station, one store and a few huts - in Bushmanland, some 200 kilometres to the south. Moreover, he was also Scottish! After Johan had introduced us, Willie McGhee and I then chatted for a while, much to the amusement of the not-really-listening field staff who didn't understand a word that we were saying. It wasn't quite the "Hoots Mon, it's a braw bricht moonlicht nicht the nicht," levels of faux Scottish, beloved of many comedians, but in truth, it probably was not too far removed, at least to those not-really-listening untrained ears.

Johan then confided that he was going on month-end break the following day but would be back in a few days' time. Which was fine, as this had been cleared by Head Office, except that I hadn't a clue about who did what and what the master plan was for the month. However, Johan despatched the workforce to their allotted tasks and took me on a crash-course in camp management and exploration work, followed by the preparation of maps for the draughting office. The next morning found me, after radio call, facing my exploration crew, standing in a semi-circle around the Land Rover.

Apart from the United Nations contingent of supervisors, the remainder of the crew were Africans; some from Angola, some from Hereroland, some from Ovamboland, a few from Kavangoland and a couple of Basters. These latter two gentlemen hailed from Rehoboth, south of Windhoek. The Basters are a people descended from European settlers and the Khoikhoi (the indigenous Southern-African population).

I took the bull by the horns and said in English who I was, what I had done ... and asked who spoke English. A few hands went up - a good start. I then asked who spoke Afrikaans and again a few more hands went up. When I asked who spoke Fanakalo, a whole host of hands went up. Someone asked me, in Fanakalo, if I spoke Portuguese, but I had to answer truthfully and say "No, except for *cerveza*." Communication having been established, the crews set off on their day's work, leaving me to go through the office and sort out what my predecessor had left me.

The reason that there was no geologist in charge was that a very urgent new project had come up further south in the country in Damaraland; my delay in leaving the gold mine meant that the camp had to be looked after by Johan until I could get to site.

Thus began my life as an exploration geologist. With just over three years under my belt in one of the toughest mines in South Africa, I certainly wasn't lacking in self-confidence, but I hadn't had a huge number of people working for me and me alone. Working with peers and professionals in other disciplines was not a problem, but having to be the man on whose livelihoods, and lives, depended was going to take some getting used to. I looked forward to the opportunity very keenly.

CHAPTER 9

GUNS

Although I was quite familiar with shotguns, .22 rifles and airguns, courtesy of growing up in rural, (often very rural) Scotland, I had never considered a personal sidearm as necessary or even desirable. However, the South West Africa of the late 1970's was a potentially dangerous place, owing to the war of liberation then ongoing. Those opposing the South African controlled government didn't distinguish between mere employees of a company - me - and those with a family or historical link to the country, often in the form of a farm.

With my camp being home to many Land Rovers, trucks, earthmoving equipment, fuel and supplies of food, its bush location, some 90 kilometres distant from the nearest centre of habitation, meant that it was a 'soft' target for those intent on attacking farmers further south. Those of my colleagues working in the farmlands in the centre of the country were deemed to be even more at risk.

Frik had decreed that all geologists should be armed but there was a hitch. The company could only buy and supply arms to anyone who was a temporary resident - which meant most of the geologists except me and two others. We were fully fledged residents, owing to us having migrated to South Africa from our home countries, so we were obliged to buy our own weaponry. In my case that initially took the form of a Brazilian-made 'Taurus' .38 calibre revolver.

Automatic pistols are all very well, but sand and dust are the natural enemies of almost everything but an AK-47, so a virtually foolproof six-shooter seemed like a better choice. It was never used in anger, apart from a couple of incidents with snakes, but I never quite got over walking into the bank to pick up the camp wages, wearing a gun in a shoulder holster, with nobody paying the slightest attention.

Guns were commonplace in those times, perhaps even more so now, and policemen always sported sidearms. The local traffic policeman - local as being in the nearest town because there were no roads in the bush, only tracks - was a very large person of Afrikaans extraction and a big fan of the 'Dirty Harry' movies then on release. In these films, much was made, by the eponymous Harry Callahan, of the .44 Magnum, 'the most powerful handgun in the world!' Our intrepid keeper of the vehicular peace decided that this was an item of hardware that he just had to have and he ordered a Ruger Blackhawk from the local arms emporium. On taking delivery, he also picked up a few boxes of hollow-point bullets and proceeded, in an orderly fashion, to the town firing range.

Having loaded the gun, he then stood in the approved Dirty Harry stance and took aim, one-handed, at the target. The weapon went off with a deafening 'boom', closely followed by a less noisy 'thud', as our guardian of motoring law hit the ground, having been knocked out by the barrel, the gun having recoiled sharply owing to the power of the cartridge. There is a good reason for a two-handed grip on a handgun, apart from the aim, and he had just found out why.

In the face of a potential attack by automatic weapons, my .38 Special was, in truth, of doubtful use. Although a number of the Field Assistants were Defence Force Reservists, and thus obliged to keep their rifles with them - Heckler and Koch G3's, for those that are interested - we mere residents were not allowed to purchase automatic weapons. I decided, as the conflict began to escalate, that I might be better off with a shotgun, but not just any old twelve-bore. What I eventually purchased was a very fine piece of Italian craftsmanship, a Luigi Franchi semi-automatic twelve-bore shotgun which, with a magazine extension, held eight shots. This weapon required only one 'cocking' pull of the loading bolt and then the gas produced by each exploding cartridge reloaded the gun automatically.

I duly bought some cartridges, including some fearsome 'Rottweils'. These shells do not contain a number of lead pellets but instead, have a single, self-rifling lead slug which closely resembles the top of a soft-serve ice cream cone. The theory is that this missile emerges from the gun barrel turning very quickly - it is 'rifled' - and so is more accurate and devastating when hitting a target than is the spread of shot from a normal shotgun cartridge.

On my return to camp, one of my Field Officers, Fernando, immediately went into raptures when he caught sight of the new arsenal. Fernando had been in the Angolan equivalent of the British Commandos as a younger man; tales of his ferocity in dealing with insurgents were legendary from those who knew him in those days. We never heard a word from him on his exploits because he was simply not that type of person, but his admiration for the Rottweils was evident.

"Tom," he said. "These are-a fantástico balas. You shoot (the bad guys) in the middle and they go 'poof' and explode!" "Wait", he continued. "I show you, *com a sua permissão*."

With that, he found an old 44-gallon oil drum and filled it with water, then asked if he could demonstrate. One shot into the drum showed a neat entry hole and a gaping, jagged exit. Into a human, there could be no way that such a hit would not result in instant death from the shockwave, if not from the slug.

At this distance in time, it all sounds rather gung-ho and macho, but we were in a war zone and there were virtually no prisoners taken in this very dirty bush war. Neutrality was not accepted by either side and I was not going to be shot at without having the means of some retaliation. Nor was I planning on leaving a job I thoroughly enjoyed, so I had no qualms about defending my right to life.

A few months later, spending a few days over Christmas with some colleagues in the Tsumkwe camp, we were given a most unusual Christmas present by the local policeman, who, along with his family, we had invited for a traditional dinner at camp. Pine (Willem Pienaar) arrived in the police Ford F250, suitably laden with beers and other festive fare, and then proceeded to offload a large ammunition chest full of captured 7.62mm rounds. Although these were suited to AK 47's, they also fitted the G3's and the L1A1 FN rifles issued to Defence Force personnel. There were a few lads with both these types of weapon in the camp.

Not for us a Boxing Day eating turkey leftovers or overdosing on chocolate. There's nothing quite like the noise, smell and adrenaline of a major target practice to clear out the cobwebs!

CHAPTER 10

SNAKES

Johan, my Field Officer, was a very good and keen wildlife photographer, with a particular interest in insects and reptiles. He discovered that by putting a snake, suitably wrapped up in a woven cotton sample bag, into a deep freeze for a short time, it would calm down sufficiently to the point where he could arrange it nicely on a suitable backdrop and take a photograph with no harm to the snake (or to himself). After the photographic session, he would allow the reptile to warm up in the sun and slither away.

Shortly after my arrival in camp, he had captured a greenish, non-poisonous sand snake. During the shoot, he explained to the mad Mikki, a creature devoid of a gram of commonsense, that some snakes could change their skin colour to suit the general background and that in more desert areas, this variety could be browner in hue.

Denmark's answer to Allan Quatermain went out sampling the next day and came back very excitedly with a sample bag in which there was something wriggling. He announced to all and sundry that he had found a sand snake which was, in fact, brown, just what Johan had explained. He was told to empty the bag well away from where everyone was standing, which he duly did. What emerged was a rather angry boomslang.

This highly venomous back-fanged snake is usually quite docile and prone to disappearing quickly in the face of danger, but for whose bite anti-venom has to be obtained on demand, in addition to massive blood transfusions. As the bag emptied, Johan was noted to be a hundred metres away in the opposite direction and accelerating.

The games with snakes continued, when Mikki appeared one afternoon a few months later, with another full sample bag saying, very proudly, "I've just found this python!" Using his well-known common sense, he then upended the bag. A metre-long python duly emerged, looking a bit dazzled from its sojourn in the bag, and promptly slithered up the tent pole in the middle of the mess tent. In reasonably fluent Anglo Saxon, I told him to recapture the creature and put it back in the bush.

He insisted he wanted to keep it as a pet but I said, paraphrasing, "No chance, get it out of here and get it back where it belongs." Mikki was a bit put out but off he went, taking his snake with him. The next day at lunchtime, we supervisors were sitting down in the mess tent and a strangely similar python appeared - sliding down the tent pole this time. Mikki went to grab it and it bit him three times.

"Juss," he yelled, "it's got the hell-in."

Understatement of the day. Pythons are not poisonous but have large fangs and can carry tetanus - an inoculation for which we did not carry in the camp. I sent Mikki to the nearest hospital, around ninety kilometres away, to get tetanus shots and the snake was shown the wide open spaces. The daft Dane returned, chastened, but with no added sense injected from the snake bites. I could only hope that the snake did not suffer unduly from its experience.

Snakes were reasonably common but fortunately, incidents were rare. One of the more vivid occurred on a Sunday. Sunday in camp was my day off and woe betide anyone who woke me before a reasonable hour or bothered me for reasons that were not of earth-shattering importance. I was woken by a very agitated labourer banging on the door of my bedroom. He insisted that I must bring my gun and 'come shoot a huge snake which is eating all the chickens'. Well, although not quite cataclysmic to the human race, it was sufficient reason to get me to pick up my trusty .38 Special, my shotgun still being some time away in the future, and with a box of shells in my pocket, I headed off to the encampment where the labourers lived.

I was fully expecting to see, at the very least, quite a large python which I had no intention of shooting, but hopefully of scaring off. I enquired as to where the snake might be now and one of a group of lads said it had gone up a tree. Which was not unusual, as some pythons are arboreal, but it was quite a small, skinny, if leafy, tree they showed me and I couldn't see a huge python up this particular specimen. In fact, I couldn't see anything but leaves. Then, at about eleven o'clock on the tree, a small brown head appeared, about the size of a grown man's thumb nail. I was urged to shoot this snake.

I could see the snake was a boomslang, not one of the best varieties to have around the camp. Africans are, in general, inordinately fearful of snakes and would not, I knew, calm down unless the snake was demonstrably gone for good. With a short-barreled .38 Special and at a distance of about five metres this was, despite what all the Westerns show, not easy. Twenty-four shells later, a few bits of a somewhat tattered boomslang dropped to the ground and the chicken thief was no more. As was my stock of cartridges. Apparently, the chickens were fine, as the snake hadn't actually eaten one, but it 'might have done'.

Not long after that we were out sampling, the underlying reason for being out in this part of the world. Kimberlites, the rocks which bring very rare diamonds up to the surface from about one hundred and fifty kilometres deep in the Earth, also contain many 'pathfinder' minerals which, through time, are eroded out of the kimberlites and distributed into streams and soils. There is a much better chance of finding these minerals than there is of finding even one diamond in a few kilograms of earth, so soil samples are frequently collected on a grid pattern, taking a sample of a pre-determined area or volume at a pre-determined interval. Our samples were shoveled into strong canvas bags and taken back to camp, where the process of extracting these pathfinder minerals began.

The countryside in Kavangoland can best be described as flat-lying semi-desert in the south, with thorn scrub giving way to semi-tropical woodlands of scattered large trees and bushes in the north, all of which are cut by omurambas - dry river beds. To facilitate sampling, it was common practice in many parts of Africa to use 'cut-lines'. Tracks, the width of a truck, were established by a grader, following a man blazing a trail whose direction was determined by using a compass on North-South or East-West bearings. The lines would be five or ten kilometres apart and could be as much as twenty kilometres long. Even in those days, care was taken not to damage or remove big trees and to create as little disturbance to the surface as possible.

Sampling teams of up to six people, supervised by a Field Assistant or a Field Officer, would be dropped off by truck at a pre-determined point on a cut-line and would then walk through the bush to the next cut-line, collecting samples at a regular spacing. There, they would leave the accumulated samples to be picked up by the truck, move along the cut-line for a few hundred metres, then return to the first cut-line, again collecting samples as they went.

After dropping off the last team, the truck-driver would then proceed to retrieve all the samples left on the various cut-lines and would be in place to pick up the returning teams. This gave him plenty of time to collect firewood for the camp, or have a sleep. Multi-tasking was but a few short months away!

On one such return journey at the end of the working day, we were a few minutes away from camp with the driver, a field assistant and me in the cab of Mercedes 4x4 truck, and the bulk of the team members in the back. At one point, the cut-line was in the order of three to four metres wide as it skirted around a large tree, when we noticed what looked like a grey-green ribbon, draped over the entire width and sides of the track. When we were almost upon this ribbon, one end reared up to the height of the cab, somewhere around one and a half metres in height, and hit the windscreen. This rearing creature was a Black Mamba or, in any case, a goodly portion of annoyed black mamba.

The driver let go of the wheel, I went under the dashboard and those in the back flattened themselves on the floor.

Mambas are notoriously nervous and wary snakes and anything between them and their home or where they want to go, they will simply attack. If bitten, one has a very short time before serious symptoms set in, not least of which is death within an hour, if the bite is not treated.

Owing to the depth of the cut-line, the truck continued onwards until the driver regained the wheel, but none of us could see behind to see if the mamba had been crushed. We were also all hoping that the mamba hadn't wrapped itself round the axles or the differential, because it was not unknown for this to happen, or so the received wisdom went.

Back at camp, we drove around looking to find anyone who could tell us if anything was dangling from the truck, but no-one could see any mamba coils.

"Boss," said the driver. "You're the only one with a gun," implying that I should get off first in case mambacide was called for.

"Yes," I replied, "but it's in the safe in my office!"

I instructed the driver to park the truck well way from any of the accommodation in camp, then I undertook a standing-start long-jump from the passenger side mudguard. Beating any Olympic record by several metres, I turned around and scanned the underside of the truck for any suspicious-looking potential passengers but saw nothing.

Unsurprisingly, no-one else would get off the truck until I had fetched my trusty revolver and returned to despatch any mamba-like hitchhikers. I would probably have been better off shooting myself had I been bitten, as the chances of me nailing a mamba were slight to none! However, the snake had obviously gone on its way and we were able to get everyone off the truck with no mishaps.

Perhaps surprisingly, given later adventures in different countries where there are often quite large numbers of poisonous snakes, spiders, scorpions and centipedes, I have not, to date, been the recipient of physically injected venom. Much of this is down to my being less than silent as I blunder about the boondocks, allowing the animals to get well away, but I believe I've been lucky in this respect. Long may that run of luck continue!

CHAPTER 11

COOKS I

The exploration for minerals generally takes place in remote parts of the world, some of which eventually acquire the trappings of civilisation if the geologists have been good at their jobs, or lucky, or both, and found a mineable deposit. Kalgoorlie, Kimberley, Johannesburg, Welkom, Sudbury, Broken Hill… the list goes on, but without the discovery of minerals, it is unlikely any of these iconic cities would have come into being.

Geologists working from the 1930's to perhaps the early parts of the 1980's, before fly-in fly-out became an established way of working, often spent months in the field, living in semi-permanent or, quite often, highly temporary camps. In the earlier periods, one was expected to live off the land but as the packaging of foodstuffs became more sophisticated, it became possible to stock up for a few weeks on store-bought goods and this practice largely died out.

A common thread throughout exploration is the camp cook, and more particularly in the African context, one's own personal cook. This being was not only responsible for making sure the geologist was fed reasonably regularly, but also that laundry was done, that accommodation was kept clean and tidy, that the 'donkey' was full of hot water at the end of the day and that food stocks were monitored and any replenishments required were brought to the geologist's notice before they ran out. As many geologists will testify, this latter requirement is one which can take some time to implement. I can't think of how many times I've returned to camp from a gruelling drive to and from the nearest town only to be told "We've just run out of…"

My first cook, Solstice Muhanga, taught me many things, some of which still make me shiver. Such as how to open a beer bottle using only one's teeth - it can be done, but definitely not with my particular dental set. A tall and slender man, he was given to wearing cook's whites when on duty, and when off-duty, a peacock assembly of finery. Always, but always, topped off with dark glasses.

On my first morning in charge of a camp in the bush, in northern South West Africa, Solstice was nonplussed. He'd asked me, in Afrikaans, because he didn't speak English and I didn't speak Ovambo, how I liked my coffee.

"Ek drink nie koffie nie (I don't drink coffee)," I said.

"Tee?" he queried.

"Ek drink ook nie tee nie (I also don't drink tea). Net a bietjie koue water asseblief (I'll just have some cold water, please)."

Moving onto safer ground, he queried, "Vir ontbyt? (for breakfast?)"

"Ek verkies 'n omelet, asseblief (I'd like an omelette, please)."

His face lit up - something familiar to be done for this odd stranger who was his new boss and very definitely unlike anyone he'd worked for before. Imagine not drinking tea or coffee! He took himself off to the kitchen and from my office next door, where I was busy unpacking maps and the like, I could hear the gas being lit and the sounds of breakfast being prepared.

Ten minutes or so later, he appeared, cook's hat and apron duly affixed, and announced that my breakfast was on the table in the kitchen. I took my place; there was a rather large perfectly cooked omelette awaiting destruction. I nodded my appreciation and tucked in.

"Aargh!" I spluttered. "Wie op aarde eet jam omelette? (who on Earth eats jam omelettes?)"

Solstice looked at me strangely. "Ek doen so (I do)."

I think I just confirmed in his mind that I was slightly mad but I didn't make a big issue of the matter, because I hadn't explicitly said *not* to put jam in and still, we were just beginning to get to know each other.

One of life's little pleasures, at least in my mind, is macaroni cheese, and I had bought plentiful supplies of both ingredients for my first sojourn in the bush. Solstice, however, wasn't altogether sure of what I asked him to make when I requested this for supper sometime during our first month together. To prevent any catastrophes possibly involving marmalade, honey or Marmite, I said I would show him what to do.

I made the roux and blended in the cheese as the macaroni cooked quietly in its pot of boiling water.

"Ah," said Solstice. "Nou weet ek wat om te doen (now I know what to do). Loss dit, ek sal klaar maak (leave it, I'll finish it off)."

I left him to it, thinking that it wouldn't be long until he'd married the two essentials together and finished it off in the oven. An hour later, I was still waiting but I couldn't find Solstice. The kitchen was clean, the oven was off and the pots and pans washed and dried. Eventually I located him at his quarters, cooking his own supper.

"Solstice," I asked in Afrikaans. "Where's my supper gone to?"

"Dit word net koel (it's just getting cool)," he replied. Sure enough, in the paraffin-powered deep freeze, there was my congealing supper. He couldn't explain, or perhaps more likely I couldn't understand, why this cheese-heavy dish, ordinarily served bubbling hot, was to be presented to me as a frozen offering. It didn't happen again.

We eventually parted company when I was unable to return to camp for several weeks following my Dad's early death while I was in Windhoek one month-end, and my subsequent unplanned trip back to the UK. When I did eventually arrive back at my dwelling in the bush, it was to find it not only Solstice-free but also bereft of my liquor supply, two pairs of boots, most of my bush clothes and a number of personal items. Apparently he had returned from his month-end and been brought back to camp by my hastily-organised deputy but had then departed shortly afterwards on a passing vehicle with a rather heavier suitcase than the one with which he had arrived.

Enter Fulai Antonio, a slight, Portuguese-speaking individual, originally from southern Angola but displaced into Kavangoland by the events of 1975. What a cook! He had obviously been taught very well and his food was always tasty, but, more often than not, much better than this simple description. Fulai and I got on very well, despite the language differences, so much so, that when I was asked to deputise for the Deputy Field Manager in Windhoek for three months in 1981, I asked him if he'd like to accompany me and live in the big city for a while. He was very pleased and we set up our quarters in a company house.

In my temporarily lofty position, I was called upon to entertain from time to time and Fulai's excellent cooking was often remarked upon. One or two of the more senior company personnel hinted that Fulai should think about moving to their employ but neither he nor I were keen on this and all attempts were stonewalled. The only real problem Fulai encountered was the washing machine. This was something we didn't have in the bush and it took quite a while until he'd mastered the controls and the laundry wasn't perpetually covered in suds.

During my travels, I had acquired a made-to-measure lightweight three-piece wool suit, cut from a particularly good British cloth, which I had to wear from time to time in my Windhoek sojourn, where formal meetings with those in the upper echelons of the company's executive management were not uncommon. After a couple of these meetings, I laid the suit out on a spare bed, intending to take it to the dry cleaners to be freshened up, but I forgot to pick it up in the morning as I left for the office. I arrived back that afternoon to find a very worried-looking Fulai hopping from foot to foot. He was clutching something behind his back and was babbling away incoherently.

"Stop, stop," I said. "What's wrong?"

"*A máquina de lavar roupa tem comido suas calças* (the washing machine has eaten your trousers)" he said, producing my grey wool suit trousers, considerably reduced in size but markedly increased in density.

They may have fitted a five-year-old, but they definitely weren't going to fit me again! Most of my clothes were made of pre-shrunk cotton and Fulai hadn't been aware of the effect that prolonged immersion in hot water has on wool, owing to the fact that in the bush, most laundry is done in cool or cold water. It wasn't his fault, and it certainly wasn't done with any intent other than for me to have clean clothes, but I did point out the Woolmark to him and cautioned him against ever using any washing machine for clothes with this mark on their label.

The incident did, unfortunately, preclude me wearing that particular suit again, but as fashions were changing and slightly flared trousers were going 'out', it probably prevented me from looking more than usually behind the times. Not, as my friends and family will assert, that this issue has ever figured largely, or at all, in my life.

CHAPTER 12

BB PILLS

Most of the workforce in my camp in Kavangoland, South West Africa were either from local villages or from the nearest town, Rundu. Each Field Officer or Field Assistant - the supervisors - had his own team of samplers, compass-men and the like and when, once a month, these supervisors had a long weekend in Windhoek, so their team also had a long weekend at home.

My month-end visits to the capital coincided with those of most of the other company geologists scattered around central and north South West Africa, which allowed us to have meetings about staff movements, to discuss results, to take part in good bitching sessions and to drink too much beer. As the leader of my camp, I did not have a team, as such, so those personnel who did not fit into a team - the camp mechanic, the carpenter, Solstice, my cook, and a few other worthies - all came with me and were dropped off where required.

Rundu, back then, was not exactly possessed of too many shopping facilities so each month-end I agreed to purchase a few items for my 'lads' which were only available in Windhoek. This was undertaken on a cash-only basis, with no mark-up and with the agreement that I would do my best, but if something or other was not available, there would either be a suitable replacement or if not, no purchase would be made.

'Oris' watches were a favourite, as were cigarette rolling machines (and papers), good knives and for some reason, a never-ending request for 'BB' pills. These items were available at the OK Supermarket, a branch of a well-known but low-end South African supermarket chain and no prescription was required, nor was there any limit on the numbers which could be bought. I asked one of the lads what was special about them and was told that, "They're really good, give you lots of energy..." and other cruder but heartfelt approbations. I never bothered to look at their composition until I was distracted one weekend and checked what was written on the side of a packet.

As far as I could ascertain, the bulk of each pill comprised chalk and the outer covering was sugar, with a blue food dye added. Out of curiosity, I tried one with my evening beer. There was no discernible increase in my energy level but I did notice that I now had bright green pee! The effect wore off quickly and I saw no need to repeat the experiment.

As my camp was the furthest distant from Windhoek - over 800 kilometres - it was quite a trek to Windhoek with Frik's rigidly-enforced ninety kilometres per hour speed limit, which he checked up on by installing a tachograph in each of the road-going vehicles. Although I was usually last into town, I would begin my journey by leaving camp on a Thursday at around 4 am. A couple of hours later, I would change vehicles and assorted baggage in Rundu, from the Land Rover to a bright orange Peugeot 404 pick-up which we kept at the Police Station and which was used solely for the trips to and from Windhoek. With fuel and food stops stretching the journey time, I usually staggered into my shared flat late in the afternoon and would head straight for the beer fridge which, with luck, might have one or two frosty offerings not yet demolished by my colleagues.

On one rare occasion, I happened to be first into the flat on a month-end Thursday and was enjoying a glass of amber nectar when a windswept apparition burst through the door and headed, wordlessly, for the fridge of salvation. "Hello Trev," I said. "And good afternoon to you too!"

"Hello yourself, you Scots git," replied my erstwhile colleague and sometime guitar player. "I'm bleeding knackered."

Having established that Mr. Callaghan had endured an exhausting five-hour journey, poor fellow, I sympathised with him over this toll on his well-being and then said, completely without foundation, "And you look terrible, by the way! Those bags under your eyes are bigger than my briefcase. You not sleeping well or what?"

Trev, a hypochondriac of noted proportions, looked worried, "Does it show, then?"

"I've seen you looking better," I said.

"It's been like this for a couple of weeks," he said. "Caught a bit of a bug and I can't seem to shake it off."

I said to him that he need worry no longer because I had a solution to his health issues.

"What's that?" he asked.

Putting an earnest tone into my voice, I replied, "BB pills!"

Trev hadn't heard of these but I assured him they were just fast-acting vitamin tablets and that I would get him some in the morning, when I was planning to pick up an order I had placed at a nearby chemist's for a top-up to the camp's first-aid supplies.

The following evening, after all of us five or six geologists had quenched our respective thirsts, I handed over a couple of the bright blue pills to Trev and said they worked best if taken with breakfast. This he duly did and as was our custom, a few hours later, we headed to the rooftop garden of the swanky Kalahari Sands Hotel in the centre of town for a leisurely Saturday mid-day barbeque. This particular weekly event was something of an institution because the barbeque contents were heavily German-influenced and rarely have there ever been, in my experience at least, such fantastic wursts of various descriptions, marinated meats, beautifully prepared salads and the like. This feast was accompanied by quantities of the excellent Windhoek lager, which, after a time, began to make its presence felt.

"Look after my seat, would you?" asked Trevor. "I've just got to nip off to the bog."

I awaited his return with some interest. He reappeared, looking mildly flustered.

"You bastard," he said. "You complete bastard!"

"What's the problem?" I asked with a palpably false air of concern, struggling not to laugh.

"There I was", he said. "Pissing sodding emeralds and thinking 'bloody Lindsay and his bloody BB pills', when the guy next to me started looking at me like there was something horribly wrong."

"So," he carried on. "I turned to him and said, 'Ah, pardon me for remarking, but as a consultant urologist, I suggest you make an appointment with your specialist as soon as you can. A couple of pills will cure the problem.' Then I hopped it. He'll be ages trying to work out what's going on."

"Anyway," Trev continued. "How long does this green colour last? I could cause some mischief with the boss…"

I dissuaded him from trying to engage in any discussion about medical issues with Frik as they were at a currently frosty phase in their relationship.

We all knew that the first two hours on a Monday, for reasons never disclosed, were a period when one did not speak to Frik. Around ten o'clock, the normal Frik reappeared and conversation, as we knew it, could be resumed.

Frik was, amongst other traits, a very patriotic Afrikaner and could be found, on most weekends and public holidays, helping with the Voortrekkers, an Afrikaans alternative to the Boy Scouts. In full dress uniform, carrying a flag at the parade, he was quite an imposing sight in shorts, a short-sleeved shirt over his burly upper figure bedecked with patches for this and medals for that.

Trev, possibly out of devilment but more likely out of sheer thoughtlessness, had forgotten Frik's temperamental oddity when he said to him early one Monday morning. "Hey Frik, saw you out with the Hitler Youth on parade on Saturday - jeez, that's quite a get-up you guys wear!"

Cue the deep-freeze treatment.

CHAPTER 13

CAPRIVI I

This long, finger-like, extension of Namibia, situated between the southernmost provinces of Angola and Zambia and the north of Botswana, is named after German Chancellor Leo von Caprivi (in office 1890 -1894), who negotiated the acquisition of the land in an 1890 exchange with the United Kingdom.

Von Caprivi arranged for the land to be annexed to the then German South West Africa in order to give Germany access to the Zambezi River and a route to Africa's east coast. The annexation was a part of the Heligoland-Zanzibar Treaty, in which Germany gave up its interest in Zanzibar in return for the Caprivi Strip and the island of Heligoland in the North Sea. The small problem of Victoria Falls had, unfortunately, been ignored in this transaction, because this impediment to shipping meant the Germans got very much the worst of the deal; there was and is no navigable route between the west and east coasts of southern Africa.

In the late 1970's and early 1980's it was split into two by the 'Golden Highway', the eastern end of which was being tarred but the western portion between the Kongola Bridge and Rundu, in Kavangoland, was an often severely pot-holed gravel road.

Frik van der Staal had blithely informed me at one of the 1980 month-end geologists' meetings in Windhoek that I should get ready to meet him in Katima Mulilo, the capital of Caprivi, in two weeks' time. He would fly up to Katima's airbase, I would drive from my camp and pick him up, and then we would chat to the regional authorities about setting up a camp to undertake a few months' diamond prospecting.

Frik had spent time as a younger man in the Zambezi Valley and believed there was great potential in the area, but moreover, there was a need to demonstrate to government in Windhoek that multi-national companies such as ours would be happy to work and contribute to the development of one of the country's poorest areas.

"If you set off early Sunday, it's only five hundred kilometres or so, so you should be in Katima by late afternoon. Stay at the Lodge - you won't need a booking - and I'll see you at Katima airport around ten o'clock on the Monday morning." Thus spake Frik.

The Golden Highway was not only the main route from Kavangoland to Katima Mulilo, but the eastern end also divided ground to the north which had been sown with land mines, from ground to the south which had not, and where I had been tasked to prospect for diamonds. This part of the Caprivi Strip lies between the Zambezi River to the north and Chobe-Linyanti River to the south, forming the border with Botswana. It is flat, very sandy woodland in the main, with, in the late 1970's, abundant game, including elephant.

I wasn't quite as trusting of Frik's assurances as I might have been, but equally, I could not telephone the Lodge and our HF radios were all but useless for calls outside of the company. A mobile phone would have been good but they hadn't yet been invented. I hedged my bets and packed up my trusty Land Rover with two tents - one for me, one for Englebert, my co-opted assistant - sleeping gear, clothes, food, water and enough petrol to get me, if need be, to Victoria Falls in the then Southern Rhodesia. This was in addition to my toolbox, spare tyres, towropes and all the bits and pieces needed to survive the wastes of the Kalahari Desert.

Maps of the Caprivi Strip were all but absent, although I did manage to get some early satellite 'Landsat' images before I left Windhoek.

The western end of the strip contained a few secret South African Defence Force camps but Frik had obtained permission from the military authorities for me to traverse this area, provided I did not stop or camp within it. What Frik had not organised, however, was the weather. The day before I was due to depart, there was a massive rainstorm which lasted several hours and whose clouds I could see were heading east, just where I was due to go the following day.

Englebert and I loaded the last few bits and pieces and set off around daybreak. I have rarely driven in such atrocious conditions. Every pothole was filled to the brim with water and in several places, small rivers crossed the road. After the first few times that bow-waves came across the Land Rover's bonnet, and the engine didn't stop, I relaxed slightly, to being merely a quivering heap. I couldn't get hold of Frik, or *vice versa*, so I had little option but to battle onwards. The soldiers at the western gate plainly thought I was mad, but reassured me that someone would come and fish me out if I was in trouble, as long as I stayed on the road. "But hey, boet, that might not be until Tuesday!"

Thirteen or so very weary hours later, Englebert and I arrived at the Lodge. Or, at least, we arrived where the Lodge might one day be. It appeared to be a construction site, seemingly having been abandoned months before. The remainder of Katima Mulilo was dark - power had been cut - so we couldn't navigate anywhere else because we couldn't see anywhere else. We unloaded the tents, put them up, cooked some food on an improvised barbeque and then slept.

The following morning dawned bright and clear and we could see that the construction site was just a collection of round huts - rondavels - in amongst baobab and other trees, on the south bank of the Zambezi River. The Caprivi Lodge sign, which we could now discern, was there more in optimistic hope than actually declaiming a fact. I left Engelbert to guard our tents and set off for the airbase, some twenty kilometres back the way we had come, to pick up the well-rested Frik, and his charter pilot, at this military installation.

To his hearty, "Good morning Tom, had a good time at the Lodge?" I forbore to reply truthfully and simply said that we might be best finding different accommodation. He looked at me oddly, but said very little. The pilot elected to remain at the airbase, where he said he had arranged to stay with some old flying friends, and told us he would organise refuelling, ready for a ten o'clock departure the following morning.

"OK, what's the matter?" said Frik, as we headed into Katima.

"For starters, it took over twelve hours to get here, through rotten roads and some of the worst weather possible," I said. I went on. "Then I find out there is no Caprivi Lodge, there was no power in the town so I could see sod-all, and then I had a poor night's sleep. On top of that, I've had to leave Englebert in charge of our tents and stuff and he obviously isn't local, so the cops might give him a hard time for no reason. I am not a happy bunny."

"Ag, young Tom," said the fount of all knowledge. "It's just one of those things, hey? We'll sort out somewhere to sleep tonight and don't worry about Englebert, he'll be fine."

As was common at that time, the First National Development Corporation, a South African government initiative, controlled most of the trade in the region and operated as a quango, supplying wholesale goods and credit. It was to their offices we repaired to find a contact Frik had arranged to meet through their Windhoek Head Office.

Peter Russell was a slim, fair-haired individual in his thirties - in a slightly earlier age, he would have been District Officer material. Frik explained who we were, what we planned to do, and who we had planned to meet, ending with a request for suggestions on how better to effect a presence in the Caprivi.

Before he responded to this request, Peter asked where we were staying.

"Well," said Frik. "We'd planned to stay at the Lodge, but young Tom tells me that's not really an option."

"Oh dear," said Peter. "No, it's not any option. Really, there's only the Government guesthouse - which I happen to know is full - or we can find you a room in our guesthouse, but it's only the one room I'm afraid. Mind you, it does have two beds!"

I said, "I've brought two tents with me, because I've brought a Kavango assistant to help with any breakdowns and suchlike. Perhaps we could use the one room and pitch the tents in the garden?"

Peter wouldn't hear of it and arranged for Englebert to be billeted in the FNDC staff quarters for the night. I took Frik to the 'Lodge' - he had the grace to look a bit embarrassed - and we moved Englebert and our goods to the FNDC quarters then drove back to Peter's office. I gave Englebert the rest of the day off and some cash for food, but asked him to have a look round and tell me the next day what he thought of Katima.

It transpired that Frik's plans on who to meet were fairly accurate, but the Paramount Chief had been unexpectedly called away, so that left some free time which Peter said he would fill with personal introductions to the various store managers in the town - most of which were owned by the FNDC. He sounded a couple of words of warning.

"This is a fantastic place. I can go off to South Africa with my family and never even think about locking my doors. Theft is just about unknown because the Paramount Chief is very harsh on wrongdoers. But, it does mean that the locals are suspicious of strangers if anything does happen, so perhaps don't bring too many existing employees with you when you come permanently. Also, as you've probably noticed, Tom, this is a very poor area - there's not many jobs outside subsistence farming - so any employment will be welcome but please don't pay your usual wages. That'll only upset everyone because you're liable to create queues of hundreds long, looking for jobs. You'll do best to go to the chief of the village near your camp and ask him to select some candidates - keep him in the loop, and you won't go far wrong."

We had a quick look round the business centre of Katima Mulilo - 'the place where the fire is quenched' - where we discovered a rather splendid public toilet. It was inside a baobab tree, and back in 1980, was complete with a chain-operated flush.

There was a butchery, a bottle-store and a supermarket amongst other essential stores, while the FNDC cash-and-carry supplied all manner of building goods, fishing tackle, ammunition, vehicle spares and a multitude of tools. The local library was well-stocked; I even found a rather rare novel by my late uncle! The hospital was basic, but clean, and there was no end of specialist expertise available from the South African Defence Force Medical Corps.

At the SADF headquarters, Frik and I were introduced to the Kommandant, a fiery, red-haired smallish man with quick, intelligent blue eyes. After quizzing us on our plans, he asked us if we'd noticed the bomb-shelters in a few of the houses.

"Yes," I said. "We have them in Rundu too, in case the other side decide to throw a few mortars about."

"Ag, ja," he replied. "This end of the Caprivi, it's mostly drunken squaddies across the river in Shesheke on payday, letting off steam. We're not at war with the Zambians and I don't want to create an incident, so I just went across one day in a rubber ducky and got hold of their boss man. I told him that if he didn't stop the *blerry* nonsense, I'd get our planes to flatten his camp and we'd make sure there were a few bodies in the wrong uniforms lying about, so he'd be the bad guy if anyone started looking. It's been quiet for months now..."

The Kommandant introduced us to his right-hand men - Lt. Dennis Goldman in Intelligence and Major John Slaughter in Operations - telling us that we should, or rather I should, be in touch frequently with these gentlemen when our work began.

"You never know what's going on," he said. "If there's a bunch of SWAPO on the loose, you don't want to be in their path!"

"Where do you think you're going to set up base?" asked Lt. Goldman.

I hauled out my Landsat photos and pointed to a spot south of the Golden Highway, in the middle of East Caprivi.

I got as far as "Probably somewhere about here..." before Lt. Goldman stopped me.

"Where the hell did you get these? This is a military area and what you're showing us is classified!"

"Well," I replied. "You'd better speak to the Landsat guys in the USA. We just tell them where we want images and they print us off what they have. Sometimes the data is a few weeks old, it all depends on when the last satellite fly-past happened."

"Mind you," I said. "They're not cheap but they're miles better than the old colonial maps - at least we know where we are, most of the time."

Goldman spluttered. "They're miles better than anything we've got," he said.

"Look here, Sir," he said, turning to the Kommandant and pointing to a small cluster of buildings north of the Golden Highway, "that's where we..."

He stopped under the Kommandant's steely glare. "Ah, yes... Any chance we could get a copy?"

We cemented our relationship with the SADF by handing over what we had - after all we could easily get more - and then reaching agreement on what our workers would wear while in the bush. This was a vital point because it would be all too easy, in the supercharged atmosphere of a war, for a patrol to mistake a group of uniformed men for the 'opposition' and open fire. We settled on bright orange overalls and 'Swakopmunders' (a brand of kudu-skin boot) which would have diamond shapes branded into the heel. I arranged to have specimens dropped off with Dennis, for briefing to his troops, before we began work.

After a supper with Peter Russell, Frik and I settled down for the night. The FNDC guesthouse was a small, brick-built three-bedroomed house, with a corrugated iron roof. Our room had two beds.

"Tom," said Frik. "I'm told I snore, quite loudly, so you might want to get to sleep first. I'll just read a book in the lounge for a while, then, when you're fast asleep, I'll go to bed. That OK with you?"

I had heard tales of Frik's prowess in the snoring stakes, and although I wasn't unduly worried, I thought the offer was quite magnanimous, so I accepted, particularly as I hadn't had enjoyed a good night's sleep the previous evening. It wasn't difficult to drift off.

Two hours later, I shot bolt upright, convinced that either the Zambians had restarted their payday bombardment, or that a hippo had somehow wandered into the bungalow.

In the dark, I was a little disorientated but the source of the noise soon became evident. Frik had been unusually modest when he had said 'quite loudly.' The sheer volume in the build-up to each snorting, window-shattering crescendo was almost unbelievable. Had I not been there, I could never have been convinced that it would be possible for a single human being to create such a cacophony without mechanical assistance. What was worse was that he must have deafened himself, because I could not entreat him to turn over, wake up, lie on his front or please, please just stop!!

I ended up sleeping in a chair in the lounge, having first inserted the small foam earplugs which I normally used when undertaking target practice. Even then, the stentorian efforts of my boss could not be entirely ignored as windows creaked, doors shuddered and furniture rocked back and forth. You may believe I exaggerate, but you were not there!

Conversation at breakfast time was a little short from my side. After a few more meetings, again arranged by Peter, came the time to deliver Frik back to the airport and then for me to add a day to my itinerary, just to catch up on sleep. Englebert seemed to have had a much better time of it and was not at all put out that we had to stay a day longer.

He said he'd enjoyed the small town and he thought that the prices of goods were a bit cheaper than in Rundu, but that there were many people out of work. We finally left Katima on the Wednesday and made the long, but much drier, return drive back to our base near Rundu. I planned to return in a couple months' time, but on that occasion, with my own build-it-yourself accommodation packed on a truck.

CHAPTER 14

ELEPHANTS

When Willie, my Scots colleague in Bushmanland, was transferred to a South African diamond mine, his place in Tsumkwe was taken by Ralph, who relocated from the central Farmlands area where he'd been based for a couple of years. Apparently, it had been a good and enjoyable stay, partly because Ralph's wife, Claire, was very keen on horses and gymkhanas, which the German section of the population promoted in most of the small towns in this cattle-farming region.

Ralph didn't altogether share Claire's enthusiasm for the sport but was quite happy to hitch up the horse-box, take Claire and her equine companion to whichever event was current and after helping her get ready, to go and sit in the stands, drink a beer, watch the competitions and listen to the ubiquitous 'oompah' bands.

At the Otavi gymkhana, Ralph had obtained liquid sustenance and was quietly nodding off under a shady tree, listening to the band gallop through some or other marching air, when the old chap sitting in the adjacent chair addressed him in German.

Ralph blinked awake and said, "I'm terribly sorry, what did you say?"

"Ach," came the reply. "You are not understanding German, ja? You look very German."

"No," replied Ralph. "Sorry, my German is very limited."

"No matter, no matter," said the old fellow. "I was just saying ze band is goot, very goot."

Ralph agreed that it was a very fine band, when the old chap went on, "Is goot, ja, but not as goot as ze last time I heard zis music."

"Oh," said Ralph. "When was that?"

"1938, Nuremberg."

End of conversation.

Shortly after Ralph's move to Tsumkwe, the merry throng of junior geologists was added to by a Welshman, assigned to my care and of whom no more shall be said at this time, and an extremely enthusiastic Englishman from a military family.

Martin Wilson turned up in a bush hat, military-type khakis, short back-and-sides, trim moustache and an eagerness one could shave on. He just couldn't wait to get to the bush, a fact only too evident to all and sundry, but especially to Ralph, his new boss. Before Martin's arrival at camp, Ralph managed to get a message through to Tsumkwe, not to be repeated on air or in any manner, on pain of death, for the Field Assistants to pick up as much elephant dung as possible during their daily travels and to store it near the camp guesthouses.

The journey from Windhoek to Tsumkwe was nearly as long as my trip, albeit there was no need to change vehicles because the camp was adjacent to a main gravel road. Martin was in his element all day.

We all used to leave Windhoek early in the morning so as not to be travelling in the bush at night, but had to be very careful of kudu, browsing the pre-dawn dewy grass along the cleared roadsides. These large antelope, up to a third of a tonne in weight, had a nasty habit when startled, of leaping on top of the startling object, usually a vehicle. Vehicle occupant deaths were not uncommon.

The killer kudu, the ubiquitous warthogs, the mandatory stop at Okahandja to stock up on dröewors and biltong, the final pick-up of fresh bread and pastries at Jakob's Kaffee in Grootfontein and then the last two hundred and fifty kilometres to Tsumkwe as the afternoon drew on - all of these combined to deliver a sensory overload for Martin. Added to this was Ralph, discoursing, from time to time, on various issues and in particular, the problems that the elephants in Tsumkwe posed.

"Not intentionally dangerous, you know," he said. "Just mainly a nuisance. Worst thing is, believe it or not, you can't see them because they get covered in dust and blend in. You might hear their stomachs rumbling," he continued. "Next thing, up to the ankles in a pile of steaming elephant poo!"

Martin asked, somewhat nervously. "What do you do if they get a bit close?"

Ralph said, "There's no single answer to that. It all depends on how they're moving relative to you, whether you're in a vehicle...lots of things. If you're downwind, that's not too difficult but don't worry too much - we can chat a bit more once you're settled in."

“Are they around the camp, then?” asked Martin, suddenly realising that this was it, the real Africa, not an idealised or sanitised version and that the wild animals were just that, wild, and it was their environment into which he was venturing, not the other way around.

Ralph said, “Worse than mice, most of the time, but they don’t usually bother with the tents and huts - they don’t smell right or something, so you’ll be fine. Just one thing, make sure that when you go off to sleep, that you keep the hut door well shut, ignore any noises outside and you’ll have no trouble.”

He continued, “If there are elephants about, they generally clear off by daybreak.”

The party arrived at the Tsumkwe camp just as dark fell. Ralph organised help to get Martin’s good and chattels to a nearby one-roomed tin shack - the guesthouse - and then invited him for a barbeque and beers to welcome him to the bush.

In the meantime, in the dark, an army of Field Assistants was carefully laying out elephant dung all around the guesthouse, except for the path. The long and exciting day and the effects of a few beers took their toll and Martin was soon more than ready for bed. After a quick visit to the longdrop toilet, Ralph carefully guided Martin along the path to his accommodation with the aid of a judiciously pointed torch, made sure everything was in order, and bade him ‘goodnight’. On his way back to his house, Ralph made sure a few elephant calling cards were kicked onto the path.

Martin was sure he would have trouble sleeping, but the worry was unfounded because the next thing he recalled was that he awoke as the sun streamed through the gaps in the metal panels of the hut, his corporeal being unmolested by mosquitoes, snakes, spiders or anything else.

He grabbed his toilet gear and carefully opened the hut door onto a vista of elephant dung. Dung everywhere, even on the path that he’d been guided up so carefully the previous night! He looked round, but couldn’t spot any pachyderms loitering with intent, so he hustled off to the guest bathroom to make himself presentable for breakfast.

“Sleep well, did you Martin?” asked the genial Ralph as breakfast was being served in Ralph’s dining area.

“Fantastically well thanks, Ralph,” replied Martin. “And you were right about the elephants. Must’ve been a whole herd of them around the hut in the night, judging by the heaps they left behind - and I never heard a thing!”

Quite how Ralph kept a straight face will never be known, but when Martin found out shortly afterwards what had really happened, he endeared himself to everyone by taking it in the best of spirits. However, he never passed up the opportunity, as time went on, to get his own back! He's still trying, thirty years later.

The area really was full of elephants, as I found out on another visit when Trev was nominally and briefly in charge. To the south of Tsumkwe was the Panneveld, an enormous flat region, dotted with palm trees, baobabs and ephemeral pans which filled up in the rainy season then gradually dried out as the year progressed. The wildlife used the pans as water sources and as the smaller pans became dust bowls, so the larger pans became magnets for all of the animals in the area.

Trev decided we needed to go on a photographic safari, so four of us loaded up two Land Rovers - strangely, for us, forgetting any alcoholic beverages - and planned a tour of the area. Even here, there were cut-lines, but they were really just Land Rover tyre tracks, bending around the occasional large tree, so no real navigation was needed, just a simple plan of which cut-line went where.

To obtain the best photographs, we decided that one of each pair should be in the back of his respective Land Rover and spot game, calling out to the driver when something interesting hove into view and a photograph was warranted.

Giraffes, zebra, wildebeest, impala in profusion, the occasional sable and roan antelope, ostriches and elephant were all out on show that day and the cameras were put to very good use. I was just putting a new 35mm slide film into my camera, in the back of the vehicle which Trev was driving, slowly, when not very far away behind us, a truly huge bull elephant emerged from behind a clump of camelthorn trees. He was not the usual dusty grey but more a blackish grey, and he was evidently annoyed about something, as his ears were flat against the side of his head and he let out a few stentorous trumpets.

I yelled at Trev, "Look behind, there's a monster out there… get the lead out, he's coming for us!"

The vehicle's speed didn't seem to increase so I yelled once more. No reaction. The elephant was now less than a couple of hundred yards away and accelerating towards us, so I hammered on the roof above Trev's head.

He slid the cab's rear window fully open. "Wassamarrer then?"

"Look in the wing mirror, clothears, and get this thing moving!"

Trev looked in the mirror, turned around and retorted, "You might have bleeding said something… thought you were on lookout. Dozy git!"

With that, we drew smoothly away from our irascible elephant, although I did manage one or two good shots as he faded in the dust of our indecorous exit.

A couple of hours later.

Me. "Trev, which direction is camp from here?"

Trev. "North, of course."

Me. "If it's north, and it's now 3 o'clock in the afternoon, why is it that the sun is shining through your side-window, and you're driving?"

Trev. "We're going south?"

Me. "Pillock."

The next day, having actually managed to return to camp safely, if a little later than planned, Trev took me to see a giant baobab tree that his team had found when making a cut-line to the north of Tsumkwe. Baobab branches, if they touch the ground, can trigger new growth and this giant tree had done just that. It occupied a large area of ground and we walked around the awesome trunk and branches, transfixed by its presence.

"Come here," said Trev. "Look at this."

On the tree were carved the words 'John Black, 1880' and a few other inscriptions. This name could be traced to followers of the Dorsland Trekkers - farmers who had left the old Transvaal and Orange Free State areas of South Africa in the 1870's to try to settle in southern Angola.

We were probably the first Europeans to see this tree in over one hundred years - it is now known as the Khaudom Baobab and attracts its fair share of visitors.

We also had an unexpected visitor that day because as we circled around the tree and approached the Land Rover, we could see there were rather large paw prints covering our boot prints. Lion!

"Oops (or similar words)," we uttered, and flung ourselves aboard the Land Rover, half expecting to hear some roar of protest as lunch escaped. Lions are not cute and cuddly, they are rank, they are big, and they haven't heard of the Convention on International Trade in Endangered Species as applied to humans.

CHAPTER 15

CAPRIVI II

A couple of months after my reconnaissance visit, I returned to the Caprivi Strip complete with four Land Rovers, three experienced supervisors, a Mercedes 4x4 truck full of kit required for a camp and a very few experienced employees. We reconnoitered the area I had selected on the previous visit and found a suitable camp site a couple of kilometres from the village of Linyanti.

As had been suggested, I asked for an audience with the village chief inside his *ilapa* (stockade). When it was granted and we met, I explained, in a mixture of English and Fanakalo, what work was intended, where I would like to set up camp, how many temporary positions I planned and how long we would stay in the area. The chief was an amicable fellow and very pleased that employment would be possible for some of his people. He agreed that we could set up camp where I had chosen - mainly because of the partly-operating windmill which would supply water for everything but drinking - and that we should carry on. In the meantime, he would select a dozen or so of his 'best' workers and send them along for assessment as to their suitability. He also asked that I drop in from time to time, just to apprise him of our progress and to let him know of any issues which might affect his people or his village.

The camp-building took a week or so, during which period, fourteen temporary workers were hired, including a cook for me because Solstice, the avid entrepreneur and my erstwhile cook, had decamped with many of my belongings during an unexpected absence from base camp that I had been obliged to undergo. His replacement, Fulai, couldn't come with me owing to family problems.

Apart from wages, all workers were provided with rations; fresh meat, potatoes and onions, together with tinned fish, corned beef, curry powder, mealie meal (maize flour), coffee, tea, tinned milk, sugar, tobacco, jam, beans, soap, washing powder, salt and tinned fruit. They were also provided with beds and bedding in dormitory accommodation, oil lamps, overalls and boots. Our temporary workers were a little overwhelmed with this bonanza, but were informed that rations would only be distributed on a fortnightly basis, so they would have to budget their daily food intake accordingly.

On the whole, these latest additions to the company's personnel worked very well and I dropped in to see the chief after a couple of weeks had passed since their hiring. We chatted for a time, then I went off to my Land Rover, parked outside the reed wall of the ilapa, to return to camp. Sitting under a thorn tree a few yards away, a very old man, clad in a tattered shirt and trousers, watched me intently and called softly, "Boss, you have *tabak*?"

As a matter of course, we always kept a cloth bag or two of 'Dingler's Black and White' tobacco in the dashboards of our vehicles, particularly because it was the currency of trade with any Bushman we might encounter in our work. A bag of *tabak* eased any language difficulties or indeed *any* possible difficulties.

I grabbed a bag and walked over to the old man. "Good afternoon," I said, proffering the bag in a respectful manner, with my left hand touching the inside of my right forearm. "How are you this winter's afternoon?"

"Ah, lungile," he said. "Boss, wena kuluma Fanakalo? Mina kuluma bejaan lo Engliss. (Ah, fine. Do you speak Fanakalo? I only speak a little English.)

I switched to Fanakalo. "You have been here for many years?" I asked.

"I was a boy when the Germans were here after the Big War (the First World War). I worked on the mines in Johannesburg afterwards but I always came back here when my contracts finished. Yes, I have been here a long time."

Interested, I asked, "You remember the Germans well? What were they like?"

"Eish," he said. "They were hard people. If you did not do what they said, they would beat you. But they were always fair. They never beat you for no reason and if they did beat you, they did not try to kill you. Not like some *baasses* in the gold mines…"

We talked for a while, although Fanakalo has quite a few limitations as a language and it isn't possible to delve too deeply into any subject. I did find out that he was all but alone, with most of his relatives having predeceased him, although the chief made sure he was fed and looked after, as much as the chief's limited means would allow. The sun was beginning to set, so I thanked him for the chat and wished him well, then helped him up so he could go inside the ilapa to get warm.

I don't know to this day why I dwelt upon our conversation, but I did, for a couple of days. I then raided the rations store and made up a package of food and tobacco, together with a couple of blankets, charging them to my account.

"Daniel," I called to my cook. "Do you know the *madullah* (old man) who sits outside the chief's ilapa in the daytime?"

"Yes, Mr. Tom," he answered. "He very *madullah*, that one. Has no sons or daughters to look after him and all the grandchildren have gone."

"OK," I said. "Are you going to the village soon - perhaps this weekend?"

"Yes," said Daniel. "I will go on Sunday because you don't like me to bother you on Sundays. Is that all right?"

"That's fine, Daniel. But, please would you take this box and give it to the old man? I was very rude and did not ask his name, so just tell him it is a gift from the young *mlungu* he was happy to share memories with."

Daniel did as he was asked and took the box with him that Sunday. On Monday morning, he handed the box back to me.

"What's the matter?" I asked. "Was the *madullah* not there?"

"No, Mr. Tom, he was there," said Daniel. "You should open the box."

I undid the string and inside the box was an old, small, carved wooden stool with a black and white *motif.*

"What's this, Daniel?" I asked.

"The *madullah* wants to say 'thank you' Mr. Tom. He didn't think that a *mlungu baas* would have time for an old man but he was very pleased that you gave him respect and listened to his stories. He carved this when he was a young man and he would like you to have it, for your house, so you can remember Caprivi when you are also an old man."

I was struck dumb. I must have mumbled something to Daniel, but I can't remember what. Unfortunately, I never saw the *madullah* again, for various reasons, but that stool has travelled with me since that time and I have told this story often. He will be long gone by now, but perhaps a little of his spirit will live on as long as this story is repeated when visitors and guests ask "where did you get that?"

One of our temporary hirings was Benson Mbonzi, a tall, thin and extremely strong man with a striking, very angular face and a fantastic attitude to work. Nothing was too much trouble for Benson, who may have not have been the quickest on the uptake but who was unmatched in his determination to do his best.

We were out sampling one day, Benson being part of my crew, when I spotted some very large animal footprints in the sand. They were unlike anything I had ever seen, but they were not rhino or elephant and we were too far from the Chobe River for them to be hippo. Not giraffe and not buffalo, they were saucer-like, so I thought they might be partially obscured eland foot prints, eland being one of the largest antelope, with the sand having collapsed around the edges.

"Benson," I called, pointing to the prints. "Ini lo? (What are these?)" Meaning, "From which animal?"

Benson hopped off the back of the Land Rover and followed the tracks for a while, eventually circling back to me.

"Boss," he said. "Yena lo nyama (that is meat)!"

On the subject of game animals, my redoubtable Field Officer, Fernando Rurato, appeared late one afternoon with his Land Rover weighed down to the axles with a mass of dripping, bloody, meat.

"Fernando, what the hell have you been up to?" I asked, knowing that the Paramount Chief was fiercely opposed to poaching, but also with the knowledge that Fernando was not a lawbreaker.

"Tom, Tom, is-a no problem," he replied. "You know there is a hunting camp, near Mpopa Falls? Well, today I visit and the peoples there I know from Angola. These big hunters from Italy and USA and other places, they hunt for trophy only and the meat, it goes to the crocodiles. So I say my friends, 'You give some to Fernando for his workers? They say 'Yes' so I bring. Is bad?"

"No, no, Fernando," I said. "This is very good. The men will be happy. Just don't do it too many times or we might get a bad name."

Just before I went to bed that night, having feasted royally on a fillet of kudu, I spied the gaunt figure of Benson, heading off towards his village with half an impala on his shoulders. It was a good night for 'nyama', as the singing of the workforce would attest.

During the time we spent in the Caprivi, we were asked to facilitate a geophysical survey which would give some idea of the depth of the sand cover over quite a wide area, and pinpoint if there were any shallow areas where bedrock could be reached, suitable for road-building. The method chosen was a resistivity survey, which essentially means putting current into the ground at various distances from a generator and measuring the response at the receiver station, sited next to the generator. We located the receiver station on a road, under a shady tree, where sat the geophysicist, Bob Allenby. The electrical input cables were rolled on drums, which we would unroll a fixed distance and attach to electrodes, at which point we would then radio Bob and he would switch on power and record the response. He would then radio back, telling us power was off, and we would repeat the exercise, an incremental fixed distance further away. This distance could be up to ten kilometres from the generator.

Apart from an incident where a couple of hundred metres of cable was removed by a child from one of the villages, the exercise went off quite smoothly, with one exception.

The electrodes were actually old jackhammer drill steels, which were sledge-hammered into the ground in a tight configuration, and their bases wetted with copper sulphate solution, to maximise electrical conductivity and get as much current as possible into the ground. Benson was the chief electrode waterer, which task he undertook assiduously with a watering can. On this particular day, one of the input sites was very dusty with calcrete, a typical road-building material in dry areas of Africa and which soaks up moisture rather quickly. Bob had just radioed and I had repeated for everyone's benefit, "Power on in five, four, three, two, one," which meant we should stand clear, when I looked round and found Benson gripping the electrodes with one hand while trying to use the watering can with the other.

"Boss," he said through gritted teeth. "Lo into yena bamba mina, yena funa bulala mina (this thing is holding me, it wants to kill me!)"

I yelled on the radio "Bob, switch off, now!"

Thankfully he didn't ask questions and Benson was able to let go and flopped into a sitting position in the roadway. We used quite a high voltage in the transmission of the fortunately very low amperage current so Benson was extremely lucky that his heart hadn't stopped.

"Benson," I said. "Are you all right?"

He looked up at me from his lower elevation and smiled. "Yes, boss, mina lungile (I'm fine). Mina aykona funa sebenza ka lo moobi into lo (But, I don't want to work with that dangerous thing there)," he said, pointing at the electrodes.

"All right Benson, aziko indaba, wena sebenza lapa ka mina (no problem, you work with me)," I replied, and helped him up.

We finished the survey without further incident but I am certain Benson thought that there was a malevolent spirit in the equipment and afterwards, he would always try to sit in the vehicle which wasn't carrying the electrodes.

Shortly after the survey was complete, I was having my weekly chat with

Major John Slaughter when he said, "Tom, we have intel that it's going to be pretty quiet here for the next few weeks. The terrs' are grouping up for a push over in Ovamboland. Do you want to do any work north of the Highway?"

"I don't know John," I said. "I haven't planned anything but anyway, it's mined so I can't send my guys there."

John replied. "Well, if you do want to do a bit of work, I'll make a couple of Buffels (bomb-proofed, armoured, Mercedes Unimog all-wheel-drive vehicles) available and a few troops to drive and look after you. It'll keep my guys from going camp-happy and we can do some recce work of our own. They'll check for mines and booby traps so your guys should be quite safe."

I said I would call Frik and ask for some guidance on the matter and give John a reply within a couple of days. Frik was keen to accept the offer. "If the Army will make sure the guys are safe, then it makes sense to use the opportunity, but hey, we've got to keep a close watch and if anything sounds like it might be going bad, pull the guys out."

An expedition was organised. Frik had expressly said that I should not go, but that I should be liaison between the Army and Windhoek, so John and I arranged for a daily update. Rather than me coming into Katima each day, John said I should use the airbase, which was much closer to our camp, and just phone him from there. On the second day of the expedition, I drove into the air base and parked outside the administration building. My usual field attire was khaki clothing and I always made sure my boots were polished, so with my short haircut, I looked quite presentable when I asked the 'troopie' (a National Service draftee) at the desk to arrange for me speak to Major Slaughter at Katima Base. The troopie sprang to attention and said, "Come this way, Sir," and took me into the Ops Room, where all the planned military movements were laid out on maps on a series of large tables.

The troopie rang Katima and John came on-line. "All's fine, Tom," he said. "The platoon commander radioed in this morning and yesterday was a good day, apparently, with ten samples collected. Think our guys are appreciating your lot's contribution to the food."

"Thanks John, I said. "I'll be in Katima tomorrow afternoon - it's payday soon so I'll need to get cash for that - and I'll drop round for an update then."

I then rang off and turned to find the troopie standing stiffly to attention, obviously bothered by something.

"Yes, troopie, what is it?" I asked.

"Permission to ask a question, Sir?"

"Go ahead," I replied.

"What rank are you, Sir? I mean, you're talking to Major Slaughter by his first name, so you must be at least a major, but you haven't got any combats on, so it's confusing for me. Sir."

"That's OK, troopie, I'm a civilian; Major Slaughter and I are just doing some work together."

"Well," he said, his brow furrowing. "If you're a civvie, you shouldn't be in the Ops Room. You might give away our secrets!"

"Don't worry," I said. "You invited me in without checking my credentials, but if you won't tell, then I won't, and anyway, Major Slaughter will vouch for me. Best you escort me out."

A relieved-looking troopie made sure I left the building, and a relieved-feeling me welcomed the bombproofed expedition back to camp a couple of days later. I instructed Daniel to prepare a barbecue for the soldiers who had looked after the teams; most of these young troops were on National Service and a bit of relief from Army food was, I knew, always welcome. Fernando, who had been the senior man in the team, was the only one who seemed a bit disappointed that the jaunt had finished so soon, and without incident.

"Hey Tom," he said, over a couple of beers that night. "These Buffels - can we get some? They *muito* comfortable than Land Rovers, can carry many sample and, *fantástico*, have good cannons. No bad guys goin' to get away!"

I had to dash his hopes - the idea wouldn't appeal to Frik, let alone the Defence Force - and I couldn't begin to imagine the volume of paperwork involved.

As was the case back in Kavangoland, Sunday was my day 'off', meaning that I arranged work so that everyone had Sunday off, to do as they wished, but I was not to be bothered, certainly not before midday unless there was something serious needing my attention.

About nine o'clock in the morning, on one of these treasured days of respite, a knock came to the metal door of the prefabricated hut which served as both my office and my bedroom.

Somewhat grumpily, I opened the door to find one of our Caprivian recruits standing there, looking apprehensive.

"Yes, Moses," I said. "What is the problem?"

He hopped from one foot to the other. "Mr. Tom, I have something to tell you that you won't like, but I can't tell you everything. It wouldn't be our way."

Knowing a little of different tribal cultures, it made no sense for me to try to bludgeon my way through what was obviously a matter of extreme importance for Moses to even bring it up.

"Moses," I said. "Please just tell me what it is that's bothering you. If I ask questions you don't want to answer, that's OK, I'll understand."

He started, hesitantly. "If you go to the stores hut and you check how any things are there, you might find some things are missing."

"Things like what?" I asked.

"Things like blankets, and oil lamps… and some other things."

"But," I said. "The stores hut is locked and the key is here, in my office. I only give the key out when we're giving out rations or when we need more gear for the teams."

Moses looked at me, a desperation in his eyes. "Yes, Mr. Tom, I know that, but all the same, when you check your numbers, they will not be right, and you will get angry and might blame all of us for stealing. We do not steal."

"So," I said, beginning to catch on. "Someone is stealing things from the stores, but it's not possible to tell me who. Is that correct?"

"Yes."

"This stealing is a very bad thing and you are worried I'll blame everyone and might take away your jobs?"

"Yes."

"Thank you Moses," I said. "I understand why you're concerned. One last question. Is the stealing by one person, or more than one person?"

"It is one person, Mr. Tom."

"Again, thank you, Moses," I said. "This isn't easy for you and I'm very grateful for your courage in telling me this problem. I'll sort it out tomorrow morning first thing. You mustn't worry about the jobs of the people not involved, I don't want to lose some very good men because of one person."

I was annoyed with myself. Generally, when a Field Officer or a Field Assistant needed something, they obtained the key for the stores hut, took whatever was required then signed the stock book for the number of items removed. I trusted their integrity and my stocktakes were usually undertaken twice-yearly, so if things had been going missing, I probably wouldn't have picked up this fact unless there had been a significantly higher rate of stock replacement than was usual. Unfortunately, the trepidation which Moses had shown by bringing the matter to my attention, and the normal whereabouts of the key, led to one highly probable conclusion.

Monday morning dawned chilly and bright in the crisp Caprivi winter sunshine.

As was usual, following the daily radio call, there was a 'sick parade' where all those with ailments lined up outside the office to receive treatment. The hypochondriacs were given large, sugar-coated pills containing little more than medical-grade chalk, the malingerers were given quinine tablets to suck on the basis that an anti-malarial prophylactic would serve some purpose and the awful taste would deter future visits, and the truly ill were given appropriate medicines.

Again, as was usual, everyone lined up to hear what work was planned for the week, who would be doing what and what, if any, additional information needed to be disseminated.

I began. "I was checking the stores shed yesterday and it seems as if some items have been taken and not written down in the stock-book. If this is the case, can whoever is responsible please tell me what he took and where the items went to, so I can balance the book?"

There was no answer to this query from any of the Field Assistants, who looked a bit puzzled, or from anyone else. I had told Fernando, the Field Officer, of the issue, but I had not taken the Field Assistants into my confidence, not through a lack of trust, but because I did not want it to seem that I was targeting only the Caprivi casual staff. They were not good enough actors to appear surprised, had I told them in advance of my suspicions.

"In that case, I can only assume that someone is stealing from the stores," I went on. "That leaves me two choices. I can bring the local police in and ask them to investigate the theft. That will not make the chief happy, but I'll talk to him beforehand. Or, if someone has taken the goods, he can step forward and he and I will go to my office for a private discussion." All the Caprivi recruits stepped back, leaving Daniel, my cook, standing on his own.

I asked Daniel to go to my office whilst I set out the week's work for the crew. They were patently curious about what was going to happen but Moses, in particular, looked as though a weight had been lifted from his shoulders. I dismissed them and returned to my office.

"Sit down, Daniel," I said to my erstwhile cook.

"Is it true," I asked, "that you have taken things from the stores shed?"

Daniel looked at me awkwardly. "Yes, Mr. Tom, I have taken some things."

"What did you take and why did you take them?" I asked.

"There are some blankets and some oil lamps - and some spades. I took them because there were so many you would not miss them and when you are gone from here, I would have things to sell. I have them at my house in the village."

"Daniel," I said. "Have you been so badly treated by me that you felt the need to steal? You have a job, you have food and clothing and for the first time in a very long time, you are able to buy things you want. Why have you done this?"

Daniel replied. "No, Mr. Tom, you have treated me well, it is not that. It is just that it was easy, and I do not know when I will next have work when you are gone…"

"Daniel, Daniel…" I said. "I have no choice but to dismiss you. Please gather your belongings and I'll work out your final pay. If you give me back what you have stolen, I won't take the matter further with the police, but I'll have to tell the chief. After all, he was the one who chose you for the job."

A rather sorry short journey later, I paid a call to the village chief and told him what had happened. He was entirely sympathetic to my position, particularly as I had dealt with the matter fairly, in his eyes, but I could sense he was angry that his trust had been betrayed.

It is a matter of some regret to me that Daniel was from then on a taboo subject with the Caprivi recruits and he was not seen around the village, at least during the remainder of my stay in Caprivi. I have no real idea what happened to him, but village punishments for transgressions were known to be severe and I still believe his was of the most extreme nature.

In a postscript to my stay in Caprivi, about ten years later I was driving down Orrong Road in Perth, Western Australia, when I saw a sign which read 'Biltong and Boerewors for sale.' During my ten years or so in Africa, I had developed quite a taste for biltong, the dried meat which is a favourite snack or indeed, often a staple, of South African culture.

I drove into a parking lot next to a small shopping centre and tracked down the butchery which had posted the advertisement. The proprietor was a man in his middle years, ruddy faced and with wavy silver hair.

"G'day," I said, "I'd like a kilo of unsliced biltong - I take it that it's beef?"

"G'day yourself", he replied, "It is. You're not from here are you? You sound a bit more like you're from near my home country," he said, in a fairly distinctive Irish brogue. He stuck out his hand. "The name's Mick, and I've been here going on ten years now."

I shook his hand and said, "I've just arrived in Perth. The name's Tom, and yes, you're right, I hail from Scotland originally."

"And what would a Scotsman be wanting with biltong then?" he asked. "'Tis not something you're known for."

"I've spent a lot of time in Africa, Mick, and I've eaten a lot of biltong there... beef, kudu, ostrich..."

"Good man yourself," he said. "South Africa, was it?"

"Not just South Africa, Mick, but Botswana and South West Africa."

"Oh," he said. "You wouldn't have been anywhere near the Caprivi Strip now, would you?"

"As a matter of fact, yes," I said. "I'd a camp, back in 1980, about fifty kilometres west of Katima Mulilo."

"Bejasus," he said. "D'ye know the butchery in Katima then?"

"I do," I said. "I used to buy all my fresh meat from there. Why, how come you know it?"

"I was working in Zambia, in 1980, in Livingstone, when there was a post advertised for a butchery manager in Katima." he said. "Zambia wasn't getting so good for the ex-pats then, so I went for an interview. Nice place, but the money was rubbish, so I didn't go. Just think, if I'd met you then, we'd be old pals by now!"

I didn't quite follow his logic, but he turned out to be a very good butcher and produced special cuts every so often which he'd phone me up and tell me about. "Just makin' some pickled pork, Tom, tell the missus, and I'll save you a bit!"

He'll be long retired now, but if Mick of the Caprivi reads this, then all I can say is 'Thanks' for all the good food during our time in Perth. There's only one problem, though. Both our boys became, as they put it when young, 'meatatarians', owing largely to the great biltong and its continued provision has cost me a fortune over the years!

CHAPTER 16

OFFICE AFFAIRS

As time wore in in South West Africa, I began to attain a more senior ranking as geologists came and went, until I found myself taking over the position of Deputy Field Manager when Ralph, who had attained the position permanently, went off to England on three months' leave. "To top up the stiff upper lip," as some uncharitable minion remarked.

We had, in our midst, a Field Officer who had been badly wounded by 'friendly fire' during a call-up to the Defence Force. He had been a tall, imposing, black-haired, saturnine fellow approaching thirty years old, with a nose which had suffered hugely from a failed suicide attempt, well before the call-up incident. After the latest tragedy he was confined to a wheelchair, owing to the loss of the use of his legs, but strangely, and perhaps because he appreciated the fact he was still alive and no false sympathy had been or was likely to be shown by his colleagues, his always wicked sense of humour now knew no bounds.

The Windhoek office needed a dedicated logistics officer and the job had been offered to Murray, not solely because he was injured, but because he knew what was needed in the field to keep operations going efficiently and what was a 'try-on' by the person ordering.

When bored or waiting for a delivery of some item or other, he would often wait until one of us had left our office for a while then, using clear sticky tape, he would tack the ends of our telephone handset to its dial unit. The unsuspecting victim would then return to the office, Murray would place an internal call to the sabotaged extension and panic - and bad language - would ensue when the receiver could not be picked up.

One of our British geologists, Bill Reilly, was quite a religious person and whilst never an evangelical type, lived his life according to his lights. His parents had recently divorced and in an effort to bring some calm to the turmoil, Bill had suggested to his father that he might like to come out to South West Africa and try a spot of game viewing. Etosha Pan, in the north-west of the country was a relatively safe, if quite distant, destination and Bill set about making plans. This involved telephoning or writing because fax was in its infancy and email just a twinkle in someone's eye.

Unfortunately, Bill asked Murray - who knew the area well - advice on where to go and where to stay. He also asked Connie, our receptionist, to help him book telephone calls to the various establishments.

A letter arrived for Bill one day, from a hotel in Tsumeb, a copper-mining town to the east of the Etosha National Park, stating that a phone call would be needed to clear up some 'misunderstandings' and that the hotel owner would try to telephone the office on a particular day when Bill had apparently said he would be in Windhoek. Murray got wind of this and arranged with Connie that she should re-route an internal call from his phone to the geologists' communal office, when Bill would be around. A few of us gathered in Murray's office, a corridor's-length away from Bill, waiting by the phone. Murray rang and Connie routed the call.

"Hello Mr. Schmidt, yes, Bill Reilly here," came the muffled sound. "What seems to be the issue?"

Murray, displaying his best German impersonation replied, "Ja, Herr Reilly, we have ze booking for zwei Mr. Reillys here, but it is stating that only one zimmer is required. Is that correct?"

"Yes, yes," said Bill. "That is correct, one room with two beds and one bathroom."

The voice at the other end replied, "But we are not undertstandink. If zere are zwei Mr. Reillys, zere should be zwei zimmer? Hein?"

Bill started losing it a bit and said, "Nein, Herr Schmidt, ein zimmer, bitte." - trying out his limited German. "It is for my father and me."

Murray wound up the volume. "Your fazzer, your fazzer! I sink you are being one of those, ach, what is zer English word, nancy boys!"

Bill apparently went bright red and started gabbling. "Of course it is for my father and me...how very rude of you to suggest otherwise... I demand my deposit back... outrageous behaviour..." and so on, until he could hear giggling on the line, whereupon he replaced the phone on its hook and marched down the corridor.

Really, no-one had suspected Bill's invective vocabulary was quite so encompassing and varied.

I have mentioned before the very continental, if mostly Teutonic, nature of the food available in Windhoek and this extended to the basics of bread, sugar and salt. By chance, at a dinner party one night, I came across large, well-formed sugar crystals which accompanied the coffee and liqueurs. Having established where they were obtained, the next day I headed off to the delicatessen in question and bought a box.

Back at the office, I set about finding thirty or so of the best crystals and carefully divided them up into six lots, one for each geologist, then put them in cotton-wool inside six small cardboard containers, each about the size of a matchbox. I asked Connie to type up a note from me which said, as far as I remember, something along these lines.

'One of the old prospectors from Damaraland came in yesterday with a handful of crystals he'd found in his licence. They're not the tourmalines he was expecting so he wants to know what they might be. I'll send some off to the lab in Jo'burg, but in the meantime, any ideas will be welcome.'

These were duly despatched to each geologist with the mail that was taken by hand when the various Field Officers and Assistants returned to duty after their respective month-end breaks.

It's a well-known fact that geologists have three hands, because when asked a question, they will often reply, "It could be this... but it might be that... then, on the other hand..." I received a variety of interesting and completely wrong written suggestions, people having researched their textbooks, dug into notes and racked their brains.

Trev's reply was verbal and somewhat laconic. "Not sure, not sure... but they brightened up my coffee no end! Pillock!"

CHAPTER 17

THE MAN WITH THE KEY

In the 1980's People's Republic of China, many changes took place to the accepted way of life and a few unique happenings are recorded, such as the visit of Her Majesty the Queen in 1986, or perhaps less favourably, the events of Tiananmen Square in July 1989. Some things, however, simply did not change and, in talking to colleagues of mine who visit China now, have not changed one iota in the period since.

Most of us, I am sure, have bought padlocks at one time or another, usually with rather odd-sounding names, which have been manufactured in China. They nearly always work very well and the very thoughtful makers seem to include at least three keys, in case of the loss of a keyring. This generous gesture was not one found in the China of the 1980's. Or at least, it was not what happened with keys and padlocks during my stay in this mysterious and somewhat forbidding country.

The phenomenon known as The Man with the Key works like this: -

An individual is given the keys to a desk, safe, door, bicycle or whatever, but only ever has one key for the particular item on his or her person at any given time. Any spare keys are carefully hidden, so that only he or she can open or close whatever is locked or is to be locked. No-one else can therefore assume responsibility for that item, or be blamed if something goes wrong.

One sunny day in the City of Linyi, in Shandong Province, several light-years from Beijing and a few more from anything like the cultures I had grown up in, I was summoned by Our Fearless Leader, Geoffrey, recently transferred to China from the depths of the Dark Continent.

"Right, young Tom, time for some exercise! Just nip down to the bank, will you, and get some US dollars? We're going to need a couple of thousand to pay the bills and for your Hong Kong trip."

So saying, he retrieved the multiplicate-copy withdrawal book from his desk. After filling in the amount to withdraw and countersigning the top page at the requisite spot, he then retreated into the depths of his office to attack and eradicate a particularly poorly-constructed sentence in the Monthly Report.

By this time in my stay in the Middle Kingdom, my Mandarin was fluent enough to enable simple conversations, including chatting to bank personnel, so I hopped onto my trusty bicycle, the transport mode of choice for several hundreds of millions of people, and headed down the hill to the local bank.

There were many banks in Linyi, with varied titles such as the People's Bank of China, the Agricultural Bank of China, the People's Construction Bank, and our bank, the Bank of China, which was the only one empowered to handle foreign exchange matters. As foreigners, we were only supposed to use Foreign Exchange Certificates - 'FECs'- for our daily transactions, or US dollars for official payments, but, being far from Beijing and in a place where FECs were about as much use as strings of seashells, we used the general currency, Renminbi Yuan. The bank officials were, after a couple of years of having to deal with us, very understanding about the needs and peculiarities of dealing with Linyi's total foreign contingent of three individuals.

At the bank, the usual pleasantries were exchanged in Mandarin, and I was invited to take a seat and wait until all the form-filling and 'chop' stamping had been completed. As this usually involved at least six people, excluding me, I had come armed with my pipe and a book.

After an hour or so, the chief Clerk, Mr. Yang, asked me to come to the counter, because, as he explained, there was a '*xiao jishu wenti*' - a small technical problem.

"Mr. Lindsay, we have a slight problem. The Lady with the Key is not here."

"Oh," I replied. "Which key is that?"

"The key to the desk," he replied, pointing to a nondescript, battered looking desk, with a very flimsy, but locked, drawer.

"Is there not a spare key?" I asked.

Back came the answer, "No, the Lady with the Key has the key and she is not here."

Foolishly, I asked, "What is in the desk?"

Mr. Yang replied. "The key to the safe where the foreign currency is kept."

I tried again. "Is there a spare key - to the safe?"

Mr. Yang explained, as one would to a child. "The key to the safe is in the drawer; the drawer is locked; the Lady with the Key to the drawer is not here; we cannot get any dollars out of the safe until she returns."

"Oh", I said. "When will she return?"

"Perhaps next month," said Mr. Yang, although as it transpired, my Mandarin failed me here.

Having left the bank dollar-free and gone back to the guesthouse, what he probably said was 'next hour', because the following day we were informed that the funds were ready for collection.

This is only one example of this phenomenon and its insurmountability. If the person assigned to keep the key was not available, then there was no further course of action possible and there the matter would have to rest until his or her return.

Our laboratory workshop was in the grounds of the new Brigade building and I was nominally in charge as I had been trained in new sample treatment methods, or at least, new to China. The lab was equipped with gear imported from various sources and staff had been appointed, including a laboratory manager.

Simon Webster arrived one day, late in from the field, with a sample which he thought could be very important.

"Can you get this one rushed through, Tom?" he asked. "If we're right, it'll change our interpretation of the sediment source and we'll need to relocate that big bulk sample we're starting in Tancheng next week."

"OK," I said, and headed off for the laboratory. The door was padlocked. I asked our interpreter, Mr. Yang Siji, to find out where Mr. Zhou Andi, the lab manager was, and to please have the lab unlocked.

"Ah, Mr. Lindsay," said Mr. Yang. "He has gone to visit his family in Anhui Province. He will return on Tuesday next week."

"Well," I replied. "Who is in charge in his absence?"

"Miss Cong Junhui," replied Mr. Yang.

"Please ask Miss Cong, then, to let me into the lab," I said.

"But Miss Cong does not have the key - only Mr. Zhou," said our normally unflappable interpreter.

I could see this conversation going on for some time.

"Are you sure, Mr. Yang, that there is no spare key anywhere?"

"Perfectly sure, Mr. Lindsay," replied Mr. Yang. "It is Mr. Zhou's responsibility to make sure that the laboratory works properly."

I gave up and booted in the door, to horrified gasps from the assembled throng. They all moved away from this obvious lunatic.

The sample was duly treated and I offered to pay for the repair of the shattered door. Instead, I was given a stern lecture by the Brigade leader on this monstrous breach of protocol. Thereafter, for any lockable entity which came under my nominal charge, the keys or padlocks were issued by me and I made sure that I kept one spare key for each. In my key-safe, in my office, to which I ostensibly had the only key. But… Simon kept a surreptitious spare in his sock drawer!

What happened when Premier Deng Xiaoping wanted the keys to the briefcase containing China's missile launch codes, I will never know.

CHAPTER 18

BUREAUCRACY

China in the 1980's was full of bicycles. There were cars such as Russian Volgas or Zils, 'Bulgarian' jeeps, the occasional Japanese import, American Jeeps (made in China) and the Made-in-China-under-Licence Volkswagen Santana - a Passat by another name. However, the status of the profession of driver equated to that accorded to a doctor or lawyer in the West and, with wages and livelihoods strictly controlled by the State, there were firstly, no cars for sale to private individuals and secondly, no private individuals with either the money to buy one or the licence to drive one. Bicycles were the order of the day.

The choice was surprisingly limited. Flying Pigeon was the country's biggest bicycle manufacturer. Its twenty-kilogram black single-speed models were highly popular and there was a waiting list of up to several years to get one, even if one could be afforded, costing, as it did, around four months' average wages. The Phoenix, another single-speed heavyweight, could safely transport Dad, Mum and sole child around the city and countryside. As the 1980's wore on, nimbler versions grew in number as did the choice of colours, but almost invariably, they did not embrace the possibility of a selection of gears.

I had purchased a Flying Pigeon, a glorious Communist red in colour, to allow me to escape from the confines of the guesthouse and office for a few hours each week, often in the company of Simon Webster, who had brought a Raleigh sports bike with him from the United Kingdom. Geoffrey Waters, the leader and third member of the intrepid 'China' team for Canterbury Diamonds, had also bought a bike, but mostly ventured only to the Post Office in town.

We had all been informed that we had to have our bicycles licensed, as it was the law, so with Simon and I as vanguard, in the company of interpreter

Miss Wang Xiu Lan, we headed off to the bicycle licensing department.

A rather spotty youth greeted us and Miss Wang explained that the two 'foreign experts' - as we were officially designated in our residence permits - required their bicycles to be registered and licensed.

"Very good," said the youth. "Where are their papers allowing them to have bicycles?"

Miss Wang seemed to argue for a while - it's often difficult to separate argument from robust conversation in Mandarin - but then translated.

"Ah," she said to us. "We have a problem. You see, to be allowed to own a bicycle in China, if you are Chinese, you must have written permission from your Brigade leader. You do not have this, so you cannot own a bicycle. This youth is unable to understand that things may be different for foreigners, but as you are the first foreigners he has seen, he is sticking to the rules."

Simon expostulated. "This is my bicycle, which I've had for many years in England. I have the import papers back at the guesthouse, but what exactly is he on about?"

I chipped in. "Well, I was allowed to buy a bicycle at the department store, without papers, so surely I had permission?"

It became obvious that the official was not going to grant any leeway, except he did allow us to use our bicycles to return to the guesthouse, from where the situation was explained to the head of the Second Geological Brigade, with whom Canterbury was affiliated in a government-sanctioned 'Cooperation'.

The following day, armed with letters of permission, with our 'foreign expert' certificates and with Miss Wang in battle mode, we returned.

This time, we simply left Miss Wang to do any talking and explanation. Papers were prepared, we signed where we were told, we stood by while numbers were stamped onto the crankcase of each bicycle and we watched as a small aluminium number-plate was affixed to each frame. We handed over the requisite sum of Renminbi Yuan for all of this.

"Now," said Miss Wang. "What about your drivers' licences?"

"What about them?" I asked. "They're British, although we do have International Licences, but they're for cars, so what have they to do with this office?"

"No," she said, patiently. "Your bicycle drivers' licences. We need to see your British documents so they can be exchanged for Chinese licences."

Miss Wang's English was very good, but as she'd never left China, it was a bit of a shock for her to find that we British did not need such documents. In fact, as we explained, we had no official documents in Britain to do with bicycles at all. Anyone could buy and ride one just about anywhere, apart from certain restricted roads such as motorways. China had no motorways at all at this juncture, so the explanation was a little wanting.

Miss Wang didn't falter. Brandishing our foreign expert documents, she demanded that licences be issued so that we could carry out our work. "Otherwise," she said, "questions will be asked by 'the authorities' as to why the honoured guests cannot use their properly licensed bicycles." It was a bit unfair on the poor youth, but Miss Wang, having given way once, was not about to suffer a second defeat.

Our licences were issued; I still have mine, and my number-plate, just in case.

To say that China was paranoid and bureaucratic in the extreme, particularly in the 1980's, is no exaggeration. However, things had been, on many fronts, much worse in previous decades during the Great Leap Forward when many millions died of starvation and untold numbers suffered 'enlightenment through labour' with mantras such as *'Develop industrial and agricultural production, realize the simultaneous development of industry and agriculture'*. 'Intellectuals' were shunned and vilified, even killed, by the Red Guard; denouncements and punishments for apparently even being suspected of anti-State behaviour - revisionism or counter-revolutionary thought - were both harsh and common.

The 1980's had seen the worst excesses pass, but China remained deeply suspicious of any ideas or causes which inferred that the Communist Party might not be infallible. As the events of Tiananmen Square in 1989 demonstrated, an apparent softening in attitude of the Communist Party could be quickly and ruthlessly reverted.

It was April 1986 and I was about to embark on my first break after three months' solid work. I was also a guinea-pig, being the first of the China team to venture out since our arrival in January. I had booked my hotel in Hong Kong (by telex), my plane tickets had been obtained by the Ministry of Geology and awaited me in Beijing, together with the Ministry interpreter, Miss Wei Lin. I had also been booked into the Ministry-owned hotel for an overnight stay.

After being met at Beijing's indescribably large central rail station, handling upwards of forty million passengers each year, I was checked into the hotel, each floor of which was guarded by a hotel attendant who opened your room for you, on receipt of a piece of paper from reception, and locked the door after you if you went out. These venerable ladies saw everything and everything was noted down.

My colloquial Mandarin was pretty basic, but good enough for the hotel restaurant. It didn't really matter much, because the answer to most of the menu items was '*méiyǒu*' - 'not have'. What they did have was fillet steak - something I had not eaten for a few months - so I dined royally.

Miss Wei picked me up in the morning with a Ministry driver and checked that I had my copy of the Customs list with me. This list detailed what items I had brought in to China in January - radio, books, watch, clothes, desktop computer and so on. Technically, these were supposed to leave China with me when I left, but as I was only going on two weeks' leave, she saw no problem, particularly as she was with me and I had my foreign expert's residence card, as well as my year-long work visa.

Beijing International Airport in the 1980's was a fairly rustic concrete building with none of the glitz and glamour of Hong Kong's Kai Tak or Singapore's Changi airport. Massive, high-ceilinged, echoey, with small dark corridors and incessant, unintelligible announcements over the tannoy system.

Miss Wei hadn't been to the airport before and had in fact never flown, but she guided me to the desk where the exit forms had to be filled in, stating where the passenger was departing to, how long the stay had been in China and the normal immigration questions.

Before check-in, one had to pass through Customs, where there were the usual Red and Green channels. I checked with Miss Wei, who was not allowed to go any further, and passed through the Green Channel, where the Customs Officer asked for the immigration form and my Customs list. He nodded, handed me back my Customs list and off I went to check in. Boarding pass in hand, I turned to wave to Miss Wei, when the Customs Officer lumbered up and indicated I should return to his desk.

There was, it transpired, a problem. I was leaving China but it did not appear that I was taking all that I had brought in because, for instance, there was no computer to be seen. "What else," I was asked, "are you leaving behind to corrupt our citizens?"

Miss Wei blazed in. "Mr. Lindsay is, as you can see, a 'foreign expert'. He is taking a break from work and will be back in two weeks, so he has no need to take anything out which he will require on his return."

Mr. Customs was impassive. "He says he will return, but that is not necessarily the case. If he wishes to leave these goods in China, he must pay six hundred dollars as a 'bond' or he must go back to Shandong and collect them."

Miss Wei translated all of this for me, to which my reply was succinct. "You have my residence card. It clearly states that I am working in Shandong Province, as a member of the Foreign Cooperation Brigade and you can see my visa allows for multiple entries for a year. I am simply taking leave and I will be back - my ticket shows this - in two weeks."

This was batted back and forth a few times but firstly, I did not have six hundred dollars on my person and secondly, even if I had had, he wasn't going to get it. Scotsmen do not surrender money that easily. Lastly, I was not going to take four days to go to Shandong and back.

Eventually a compromise was reached. He would confiscate my residence permit so that I could not return to work unless I first retrieved it from him, which would prove I had returned to China. I accepted, provided that he would give me a receipt. After all, if I didn't return I would only lose a few easily replaceable items because most of what I had declared were company goods in any case.

Then came the nasty sting. Miss Wei would also have to surrender her Identity Card until I returned. I protested that this was very out of line, because I knew Miss Wei would not be able to obtain some of the basic foodstuffs without proof of identity and that she would be at the mercy of any petty official who demanded to see her 'papers'. Miss Wei was, however, adamant.

"It will be all right, Mr. Lindsay. My mother will be able to support me for a short time. My husband also. I will stay at the Ministry and only go out with important people that the officials will not detain."

I could not persuade her otherwise and truthfully, there was probably little else which could be done if I were to leave on my designated flight.

"Thank you Miss Wei," I said. "Please telex Mr. Waters and let him know that some better arrangement for Customs will need to be made before either he or Mr. Webster make the next trip."

With that, I promised to see her two weeks' hence and took myself off through Immigration and into the First Class cabin of one of Air China's Boeing 747's. We only travelled First Class to get the extra luggage allowances, and the cost, compared to a better-known airline, was minimal. The airline's safety record, at the time, was perhaps not so enviable, but we reckoned with the sturdiness of the 747 and the fact that these were new planes that the risks were acceptable.

I didn't see much of the First Class cabin that trip, as the Ministry Hotel food decided to exact its revenge on me and I spent rather long periods in one of the cabin's smallest rooms.

I returned to Beijing as expected and Miss Wei and I retrieved our various documents, the Man with the Key being, for once, present. She had never looked particularly well-fed but now appeared a little gaunt. "It has not been easy," she explained. "The good news is that now we have a procedure, so this problem will not happen again."

At some convenient time, away from prying eyes, I was able to give her a small present for her invaluable help. I don't remember what it was, now, but it was something available in China but usually only from the 'Friendship' stores, so that while it might be unusual, it was not something obviously traceable to a corrupting foreigner. She was somewhat overcome, but this episode served to seal a friendship which endured all my five years in China and for some time after that.

Back home in Linyi, the Post Office was staffed by ladies. Ladies of fearsome mien who brooked no improperly-stamped envelopes, badly wrapped parcels, would-be queue-jumpers or indeed, anything they didn't like. These were the 'Dragons' and were known to all our colleagues.

Simon, all six feet plus of frame, with blue eyes and blonde hair, received a notification that a letter awaited his collection, so off he cycled to the Post Office. Bearing in mind that he was one of only three foreigners resident in Linyi, he, like us two others, had been accepted by most of the city's denizens as part of the circus of Linyi life.

He carefully chained his multi-speed bike to the stand outside the Post Office and sauntered in, complete with notification slip, queued up patiently, then presented his slip at the counter. "Identity papers!" growled the dragon of the day. Simon was nonplussed.

How many other blonde foreigners were there in Linyi with the surname Webster? None. He tried saying so, only to be met with "No papers, no mail." She was adamant, so Simon left, to return another day, to a different dragon, who presented him with his mail as soon as he reached the counter. Dragons obviously have off-days too!

A couple of weeks later, something similar happened to me, except by this time, I knew to take my identity documents. My American aunt and uncle had written earlier to say they had sent me a food parcel - Hershey Bars, jerky, dried fruits and all manners of goodies - so I trotted along to the Post Office. I presented the slip, showed my residence permit and signed where I was supposed to and the friendly dragon - I had done everything properly - returned with my parcel.

"Ah," she said. "Mr. Lindsay, you have another parcel."

"That's unexpected," I said. "Please may I have it?"

"That will not be possible," came the reply.

"Why ever not?" I asked.

"Because you do not have the slip."

"Please give me the slip, then, and I will sign."

"No, you do not understand. There is a slip, but it was sent to the wrong guesthouse. When it comes back from that guesthouse, we will send it to your guesthouse, then you can collect your parcel!"

You can't beat logic, so I didn't even try; I did get my parcel a couple of days later, though.

A couple of years later in late winter, I was sent, together with an internationally-renowned expert on rough diamonds, to the south of China, to catalogue some alluvial diamond production on behalf of the Ministry of Geology, in an attempt to relate this to possible primary source areas. My presence was required on two fronts; firstly, as an interpreter for Richard Wellesley, the expert, and secondly, to input his observations to a computer so that the data would be in digital form and therefore able to be analysed mathematically.

The age of the Personal Computer had arrived and we, that is the China Team, had embraced this wholeheartedly. We not only bought components in Hong Kong and built our own machines, but we continually up-graded the machines with the latest hardware and tried out all manner of software. Richard, to whom an abacus was a relative innovation, needed assistance.

We flew down from Beijing to Changsha in Hunan Province, taking with us with Richard's specialist microscope, a small portable computer and assorted parapharnelia for sorting and classifying diamonds. Changsha City was a rather miserable damp place, all grey concrete and potholed roads; we were unimpressed, thinking that the south of China might have been at least a little warmer, both in climate and architecture, than the wintery north. Our destination was the small town of Changde, to the north-west of Changsha, situated on one of the tributaries to the Yangtze River.

We were met at the airport by representatives of Hunan's 413 Geological Brigade and soon ensconced in our hotel-cum-guesthouse. It was very similar in construction to the Jinqueshan Guesthouse in Linyi; that is, it had large, box-like concrete rooms which were taller than they were wide, with ill-fitting metal window-frames and wooden doors. The bathroom facilities were, as was quite usual in China at the time, running with water from overflowing cisterns. However, Linyi had heating, albeit furnished by large metal pipes through which hot water was circulated three times a day. Changde, being south of the Yellow River - the arbitrary demarcation between north and south China - was, by decree, not allowed such a luxury.

As a concession to the blistering +35° Celsius summers which the south of China can face, there were air-conditioning units fixed above the metal framed balcony door. Richard and I worked out that these units could provide warmth, if suitably adjusted, so we used towels and spare linen to plug all the gaps to the outside and tried to keep warm. This bodge worked well when we occupied our rooms.

Unfortunately, when we left for work each day at the Brigade offices, the friendly room attendants would happily open all the windows to let fresh air in and then mop down the nice concrete floors with cold water. Returning to our icy caves each day was not a highlight of the visit.

Another non-highlight was breakfast, which our hosts insisted on providing for us. The north of China is not a rice-growing area of note, so we were used to 'mantou' - large grey steamed wheat buns, resembling soft cannonballs. The south of China is much more rice-based, so a rice porridge was a breakfast staple. Because we were foreigners and therefore had to be, by conventional wisdom, consumers of dairy products which, at the time, most of China was not, our hosts had obtained dried milk powder - sweetened - which they had the guesthouse re-hydrate and into which raw eggs were dropped. An 'egg-drop' sweet hot milk and rice concoction, flavoured with pickled garlic cloves, is quite an unusual starter to the day. I haven't tried it since.

At the office, we were shown to a room, complete with tables and chairs built to Chinese proportions, that is, small. We had been assigned Mr. Wu Shoucai, a Brigade interpreter, to augment my limited abilities in that direction. Thereafter followed a quick tour of the diamond workings, which those of a nervous disposition, especially with regard to mixing electricity cables and water, would have done best to avoid.

Diamond diggings for alluvial 'stones' are fairly similar the world over.

The diamonds are released from their parent rock - either a kimberlite or a much rarer lamproite - through its erosion by water, or less frequently, by ice. The diamonds make their way into streams and rivers and, because they are quite dense minerals, tend to be concentrated with the larger-sized particles in those rivers, that is, the pebbles and boulders. It's often necessary to excavate and treat over one hundred tonnes of pebbly material to recover just one stone weighing a carat or thereabouts, but at between US$ 1,500 to US$ 2,500 for good, but not exceptional quality stones of that size, it can be a lucrative occupation.

The diamond diggers of Changde, usually local peasants who were supplementing their minimal farming incomes, would form small work units and lease equipment from the Brigade, in return for which the Brigade would pay for the diamonds thus produced, on an agreed scale, minus a rental charge. The Brigade would combine the various productions and then have a 'parcel' sent for sale in Shanghai, no doubt making some profit in the entire transaction.

Richard and I explained to Mr. Wu, who was not a geologist, that to be truly scientific in our quest, the diamonds we were to examine should come straight from the workings in the river and not be tampered with in any way. This was vital so that the full range of sizes, shapes and colours for each unit's production could be recorded before any mixing and consignment.

In general, in alluvial diamond populations, the poorer quality stones tend to be broken up by being mixed with pebbles and boulders during transport and only the best quality stones - therefore those of the highest value - are left. Diamond is the hardest natural substance, but stones with imperfections of various types are fairly easily broken into smaller shards if pressure is applied to those flaws. The physical appearance and the sizes of the individual stones in a diamond population can therefore tell the analyst quite a lot about how far distant the source may be and, if the surfaces of the diamonds are studied in detail, some of the details of the makeup of the host rock may be deduced.

Each morning, several small, white folded paper rectangles - paper 'parcels' - would be removed from the Brigade safe and handed over to us. Under supervision, we would open each one, weigh the contents and, if the number agreed with what was written on the parcel, sign for custody. The same procedure, in reverse, happened at the end of the day.

There were some very unusual stones in several of the parcels.

"Tom, note this down," said Richard. "Yellow cube, dodecahedral growth on each triple face intersection. Never seen this before, ever. Create a new designation - call it castellated growth."

"This one," he said, beckoning me to look down the microscope. "It looks like someone's taken a blowtorch to the faces and melted plastic all over. That's new to me!"

There was a lot of work involved but I was beginning to see some worrying statistical patterns in the data.

"Richard," I said. "We're not really seeing the size ranges we should expect. To me, it looks like someone has sieved the parcels and taken out both the very large and the very small sizes. What d'you think?"

He looked at the graph on my computer screen and said, "Let's give it a day or two more, but let's just check Mr. Wu passed on the message about not tampering with the parcels."

Mr. Wu assured us that he had indeed passed on the message and that we should not worry.

The following day, as we were weighing the parcels before signing, I spotted what I thought were two holes in one of the stones.

"Richard," I said. "Have a look at this under the mike, would you? Something odd here."

He took the stone and looked at it then sat back, his head in his hands. "Somebody's playing silly sods here," he said. "Those are wire dies. You drill holes in a diamond, then pull some metal through the hole to produce a very fine wire. Usually gold or copper. This never came out of an alluvial working!"

We stopped work straightaway. Mr. Wu was summoned. The situation was explained to him. Then I requested that he ask the Brigade leader for an immediate meeting.

To say the meeting was frosty may be a little of an understatement.

"Mr. Liu," I said. "We appear to have a problem. At very great expense, at the request of your Ministry, Canterbury Diamonds has brought Mr. Wellesley to Changde to examine alluvial diamonds. We have been very precise in stating our requirements, one of which is that the diamonds to be examined are not, in any way, to be sorted, or classified or otherwise tampered with before our examination. Unfortunately, we have just come across a diamond which has man-made features on it. This, together with some worrying statistical data, says to us that we are not, in fact, dealing only with diamonds which have been recovered from the diggings. If this is the case, then all our work to date is meaningless!"

Mr. Liu considered this lengthy diatribe for a few moments, then called for one of his minions, with whom he held a *sotto-voce* discussion. He then spoke to Mr. Wu, who spoke to me.

"Mr. Lindsay," he said, "Mr. Liu requests some time to discuss the matter with his subordinates. Perhaps you and Mr. Wellesley can take the day off and we will reconvene tomorrow morning?"

"*Dang ran* (of course)," I said, looking at Mr. Liu as I spoke. "This is a very serious matter and I am sure Mr. Liu would like time to make sure that he is given a full explanation of what has or what has not happened."

We were never given the true story. When we met Mr. Liu the next day, we were told that there had been a 'development'.

"Unfortunately, the diamond buyers in Shanghai have insisted that the parcels you have been examining must be sent for sale immediately or they will not be able to be sold for some weeks. This will inconvenience the payments for the diggers and cause many problems for us."

I could see that this was not a bargaining move - we were not going to see those diamonds again or find out what had actually happened - and Mr. Liu was between a rock and a hard place of someone's making.

"I see," I said in reply. "Well, it seems that there is little to be done. We will, of course, note in our report that there has been an unfortunate timing mishap which will not allow us to make a complete record of the Changde diamond characteristics."

Mr. Liu nodded gravely. "Yes, it is indeed unfortunate. Perhaps if Mr. Wellesley visits China again, we may be able to come to some arrangement which will be of mutual benefit."

"Yes," I thought. "And it'll be a frosty Friday before we waste our time and money coming here again." Out loud, I said. "Thank you Mr. Liu, I will inform the directors of Canterbury of your offer."

After the inevitable farewell banquet, which type of event will be discussed elsewhere, Richard and I set off for Beijing, this time by train. We travelled 'Soft Class', meaning that there were four beds in our compartment, two of which were swung down from the walls, at the appropriate time, by the carriage attendant. Chinese trains were not fast, but they were remarkably punctual and although journeys tended to be long, they were comfortable. The additional equipment we had brought took up a good portion of the available storage space but the Soft Class compartment was roomy and eighteen hours or so passed in reading, playing cards and sleeping. With the occasional trip to the dining car.

The Changsha train pulled into one of the more distant platforms in Beijing Central; Richard and I struggled manfully with our luggage, hoisting it over the forms of innumerable recumbent would-be passengers and through a few platform underpasses, until we reached the turnstile exits to the station.

To exit these monstrosities, we were required to present our tickets to a fierce-looking lady in uniform. In Mandarin, she said to me. "You are overweight. You may not leave. You must pay extra." "Go there," she said, indicating a ticket-booth affair. Richard had, quite naturally, not understood a word and asked me what was going on.

I explained about the overweight comment to which he said, "You might be, I'm perfectly fine."

"No," I said. "You don't understand. What she means is that we have too much luggage for two people. We have to pay extra for the privilege of carting all *your* gear about the place. It's stupid, I know. I mean, who cares what you take on a train, but there's obviously some rule or other and we've broken it."

I was actually quite annoyed with this senseless regulation; after all, we had travelled for a day and a half, on First Class tickets, and only at the end of a journey were we being told that we had too much luggage. However, getting properly ratty with some official needed a bit more colloquial Mandarin than I could summon, so I just paid up and we were allowed out.

To cap it all, the hotel which had been booked for us was a very bad Chinese copy of something in Hong Kong, only the windows had been put in upside-down, so that they opened at floor-level. The rather scruffy rooms looked as though they had been fitted by someone with a very bad hangover - nothing was straight or hung properly - and the restaurant was frankly awful and hugely overpriced. We very quickly decamped to the Lido - a Holiday Inn on the airport road - where we drowned our sorrows in French wine and Australian steak.

Richard summed things up. "Well, that was a pretty pointless exercise. Don't know how you guys put up with this sort of thing on a daily basis. Better take notes though, you might write a book about it some day! Cheers!"

CHAPTER 19

EXPLOSIONS

In 1981, towards the end of my stay in what had become, officially, Namibia, the border war was heating up. Very many more SADF patrols than usual ventured past the camp south of Rundu, looking for or actively chasing insurgents, and I was advised to keep in ever-more frequent contact with the Security Police.

One of the more ingenious but nonetheless deadly innovations was the Improvised Explosive Device - the now well-known IED - which took various guises. The favourite was an empty soft drink can - most usually red and white, although this was by no means proscriptive - placed in one of the ruts of the very sandy roads of the region. This would be attached to a land-mine. How many drivers can resist crushing an empty can, especially if not crushing it means having to change gear and actively wrestle one and half tonnes of non-power-steering equipped behemoth out of deeply rutted tracks? At first, not many, but we all soon learned. As the ruse became evermore widespread, however, the mines would be planted away from the cans, catching out those drivers who were being cautious. Travel, especially near the border with Angola, was virtually impossible.

Other parts of Namibia were also becoming much more dangerous than they had been, when in late 1981, I received an unexpected transfer to the neighbouring but conflict-free country of Botswana. This transfer was accompanied by a promotion, so although I was by no means ready to leave Namibia, I accepted gracefully and ended up on one of the world's richest diamond mines.

Botswana is, in a number of respects, a very fortunate country. Despite being over seventy per cent covered by the Kalahari Desert, under the sands it has coalfields, nickel, copper, gold and diamonds. It has very little in the way of tribal conflict, the exception being that in recent years, a gulf has opened or has been opened, depending on your viewpoint, between the largely Tswana population and the Kalahari or 'San' bushmen. English is the official language and Setswana is the national language; Botswana gained independence from Britain in 1966.

It is testament to the democratic nature of the country's government that apart from Sir Seretse Khama, the country's first post-independence president, who died in office, all of his successors have served their allotted terms and then retired. Not *were* retired by force, as in the unfortunate case for many African countries.

The year after independence, one of the world's largest diamond-bearing kimberlites, Orapa, was discovered in the north of the country by the South Africa-based De Beers Consolidated Mines Limited. Other major discoveries followed within a few years and it was at one of these locations, soon to be an operating mine, that I found myself in late 1981.

My new boss, Steve Greenall, had been in Botswana for a number of years, having gone from the exploration side of the company's operations to Resident Mine Geologist. A couple of weeks after I had gone through all the settling-in procedures, Steve wanted to show me some of the geography of the area surrounding the mine property - flat - and where we might think about looking for any secondary deposits of diamonds which could have come from erosion of the main pipe, before it had been covered in the all-blanketing Kalahari sands.

We were in his Ford F250 four-wheel-drive truck, these being preferred in Botswana to Land Rovers, when he ran over a soft-drink can some litter-lout had left in the track. Steve had been chatting to me as we drove when he suddenly realised the conversation was very much one-way.

He looked left towards the passenger seat when he caught sight of me cowering in the footwell, under the dashboard.

"What the blue blazes are you doing down there?" he asked, somewhat peevishly.

"You just ran over a soft-drink can," I replied.

"What, you wanted me to stop and pick it up?" he queried.

"No, it's just that where I've been the last couple of years, if you ran over a can in the bush, the chances were you'd be enrolling for harp lessons about now!"

Steve laughed. "Well, you're not there now. This is a peaceable place, the cops don't even carry guns and you can just about get a licence for a hunting rifle or a shotgun, but that's it."

To this day, I will not run over a can in the roadway, unless it would cause an accident not to, and if I do, I still cringe inwardly, waiting for the harp lesson to begin. Or for someone to prod me with a trident.

China of the mid to late 1980's did not have a problem with soft drink cans as litter because there almost weren't any. No international companies had yet penetrated the country other than the very few 'Western' hotels in Beijing or Shanghai and in any case, the average disposable income would not have allowed such luxuries. The local soft drinks were sold in glass bottles, all of which had to be returned to the vendor after use, or no more could be purchased. There was a particular sparkling water we three westerners in the town of Linyi, in Shandong Province, preferred, and on any days spent in the field, the packed lunches provided by the Jinqueshan Guesthouse nearly always had a bottle or two for us, particularly during the hot and sticky summer months.

During one such month, I was halfway up a rather prominent limestone hill, which overlooked a large, flat river valley, trying to obtain samples of an igneous rock called a lamprophyre. The hill was riddled with dykes of this rock-type and we were trying to establish if some of the kimberlite pathfinder minerals we had discovered in nearby soil samples could have come from any of these dykes, as they have a hazy genetic relationship to kimberlites. The limestone itself was quarried in a piecemeal fashion by local farmers, who transported great lumps of the stuff in mule or donkey-drawn wagons to the local cement factory, which could be seen a few kilometres away, peacefully polluting a large swathe of the countryside.

I was with three young, English-speaking Chinese geologists, all of whom, when not under the watchful eyes of their political minders back at base, were keen to hear unsanitised versions of life in the West. The four of us had found some shade and were enjoying our conversational lunch when one of the farmers ran towards us and yelled something incomprehensible - to me - in Mandarin. Mr. Liu Gang, our geophysicist, grabbed me and said "Quick, hide in this gulley," pointing to a deep trench behind our lunch spot. I didn't ask why, I slid backwards into the hole, just as a tremendous 'boom' filled the air and bits of airborne limestone clattered around us.

What we hadn't established, before setting out on our little expedition, was that the farmers had an agreement that if they were in the position to dynamite their particular quarry, they would all try to do so at the same time. Everyone but us knew that this would be around noon, on a daily basis, so for the next few minutes we sat tight as various explosions went off and limestone shrapnel flew about the hill. There was an unexpected bonus in that some of the lamprophyres were included in these blasts, so we were later able to obtain very fresh specimens.

After collecting both lamprophyres and wits, we ventured around the south side of the hill, which was a few hundred metres from our lunch spot and which appeared to host quite a wide lamprophyre dyke, visually unlike any of the others we had seen to date.

On closer inspection, it really was quite unusual, with large mineral grains evident, as opposed to the normally rather fine-grained rocks we had seen up to that point. Below us, at the bottom of the hill, there was a large, walled area with some substantial buildings and what looked like armed guards at the entrance gate.

"It's a People's Liberation Army barracks, Mr. Lindsay," said Mr. Liu. "We probably shouldn't be looking at it too much, or they will not like it and chase us away." He didn't add, although he may have thought, "If we're lucky!"

We busied ourselves with our work, collecting, bagging and recording rock specimens, when suddenly, the air above our heads seemed to be alive with hornets. For the second time that day, we all cowered in the bottom of a hole. Mr. Liu poked his head over the top.

"Ah, I see," he said, retreating to his former position.

"There's a firing range down below," he said. "There's some shooting practice going on but there are no sandbags or earth to absorb the bullets, so they're ricocheting from the rocks behind the targets. Best we sit still for a little while."

We did. We sat still for about an hour until target practice was over for the day. Then we climbed down the hill, quickly, and headed back to base.

"Suppose you've been swanning about in the nice countryside," said Simon Webster on my return to our office *cum* living quarters. "You're a lucky sod. I've been stuck in here all day with the aircon on the blink."

I just looked at him, witheringly. "You wouldn't believe the day I've had..."

He didn't. At least, I am sure he thought I was embellishing matters until he had to make a visit to the same hill a few months later, to follow up some of the results.

"They're mad down there," he said. "Blowing up limestone all over the place..." I just looked serenely smug.

CHAPTER 20

POGONOLOGY AND TRICHOLOGY

Beards have come and gone in fashion, and there have been some notable figures with dislikes of beards. Margaret Thatcher is reported to have said she "wouldn't tolerate any minister of mine wearing a beard." Beards have also been taxed from time to time. In England in 1535, King Henry VIII, who wore a beard himself, introduced a tax on beards. The tax varied with the wearer's social position. His daughter, Elizabeth I, reintroduced the beard tax, taxing every beard of more than two weeks' growth. The tax also appeared in the 1750's in Russia, but to make the people shave, because Tsar Peter the First considered beards to be uncultured.

I've had a beard for most of my life since leaving University. Whether this was a rebellion against my clean-shaven, short-haired, tie-wearing student days or just because I became fed up of shaving twice a day on the gold mine I began my career on, I cannot truly remember.

As a man in his twenties in South West Africa, my black beard and my less-than-a-racing-snake physique earned me the nickname 'Savimbi', after my apparent likeness to Dr. Jonas Savimbi, the leader of Angola's UNITA party, fighting for control of that war-torn country from 1975 to 1992. I have never paid a tax on my beard of which I'm aware, but it did cause some discussion when I was posted to the People's Republic of China.

Chinese men are not, contrary to received wisdom, devoid of facial hair but it does tend to be less dense when compared to men from other ethnic groups and shaving is not, for many Chinese, much more than a weekly or fortnightly ritual. Beards are considered by some to bring bad luck, although this is by no means a universal sentiment but often, it is only old men who disport these adornments. Additionally, in a carry-over from the bad old days of the 1960's, for no discernible reason, those who wore spectacles were considered 'intellectual'. I posed a dilemma - a Westerner, in his early thirties, wearing glasses, who sported a beard - how to pigeonhole him into Chinese society?

Most of the time, it made no difference to anything I did, but one particular related incident does spring to mind.

I was out and about in the countryside to the south of the city of Linyi, in Shandong Province, overseeing some bulk sampling near some old alluvial diamond workings. I used to smoke a pipe, preferring a cherry-flavoured Cavendish tobacco or one of the 'Irish' mixtures which were once upon a time quite common in pipe-smoking circles. After a particularly taxing bout of watching other people work, I felt the need for a smoke, so I found a grassy bank, made myself comfortable, pulled out the pipe-smoking paraphernalia and organised my nicotine intake. At about this point, a rather elderly Chinese man appeared from a farmer's hut a couple of hundred metres away and headed in my direction. He sat down next to me and proceeded to engage me in conversation.

"Good afternoon," he said in Mandarin. "I haven't seen any foreigners around here before; in fact, the last foreigner I remember was in Qingdao, about fifty years ago. What are you doing?"

I replied that I was helping the local Geological Brigade look for the source of the diamonds in the Tancheng workings, using some technology that had been developed in the West.

"Ah," he said. "Tancheng. That was a place. I used to work there and every morning the bosses would give you a new pair of straw sandals. Every night, we handed the sandals to an overseer, who would burn them to see if any diamonds had been caught up in them. As if we couldn't have felt diamonds on our feet!"

He delved into the recesses of his padded jacket and pulled out a long wooden pipe, with a small brass bowl at the end. I had noticed, in other areas of the county, the longer the pipe, the older the person.

He looked at me and stroked his wispy beard. "We might be strangers, but you have a beard and I have a beard, you wear spectacles and I wear spectacles and you have a pipe and so do I."

"Indeed," I said. "But you have the advantage of wisdom and experience which perhaps I may acquire one day."

This rather obsequious sally appeared to please him because then he said. "I grow my own tobacco on the farm here, would you care to try some?"

"That would be very nice," I replied. "Perhaps, in that case, you might like to try some of mine? I only buy it, but it is quite good. It comes from Ireland, not England, but it does have a nice flavour. Or at least, I think it has a nice flavour."

We duly exchanged tobacco pouches and loaded our respective weapons. Bearing in mind I was smoking a Sherlock Holmes-type briar and he had a little brass bowl, I didn't use up his tobacco ration for a week in one go, but filled my pipe to about one-quarter of its depth.

He lit up first. "Ah, that's quite sweet, not very strong... very good."

I lit up next and drew in a lungful, at which point, my head exploded. This may have been tobacco, but it was tobacco without any pretence of being cultured or even domesticated. Raw nicotine hit my bloodstream and unadulterated smoke assailed all my cranial sensory organs.

"Quite... (cough, cough) strong, (cough, cough). Unusual (cough, cough) taste...," I managed to wheeze out. "And you make this yourself?"

"Yes," he said. "I've been curing my own tobacco for over sixty years now... I think that's the secret to my long life!"

I thought to myself, "If you can take daily doses of tobacco at that strength, you'll live forever."

The old chap accepted a twist of the foreign tobacco to 'reflect on', or so he said. I suspect he may either have tried to use it as an example to make his home cure a little less primeval, or perhaps he planned to trot out this foreign cissy material when he and his band of old-timers got together for their weekly mah-jongg session.

On a trip to Canada in the winter of 1989, ostensibly to evaluate the solutions to working in the field in very cold weather and to then introduce these to my Chinese colleagues who simply shut up shop from November until April, my beard and I encountered problems.

At minus forty degrees centigrade, one does not stride out from one's heated tent in the morning and take a deep breath, otherwise one will drop dead from frozen lungs. The hood of the ubiquitous parka is designed to allow expelled breath to warm up incoming cold air in order to prevent damage to one's lungs and the system works remarkably well. However, it is advisable to also wear headgear under the parka to keep the whole head warm and prevent inadvertent frostbite. Most extreme cold-weather gloves have a suede patch on the back to allow the cheeks to be rubbed, thereby increasing the blood circulation to these often ignored areas of the face. All of these are sensible means of preventing physical damage to the human body by extreme cold. What is perhaps not so well documented is what can happen when the weather goes from very, very cold to merely very cold.

The day had started out at around minus thirty-six degrees centigrade, according to the thermometer outside the insulated and heated tent which was my temporary home. I dressed for the day, adding a balaclava under my parka hood and after fastening on snowshoes, I headed off with my Canadian colleagues to undertake some work involving magnetometers. These instruments measure the strength of the Earth's magnetic field at any given point and the results can be modelled to show the causative rock type. In this case we were looking for kimberlites.

In the days before GPS receivers were invented, all geophysical surveying was carried out on pre-determined grid lines, so that the coordinates of each potential reading were known and recorded in a book. Now, all of this data is recorded automatically within the combined magnetometer/GPS unit, making mistakes much fewer and increasing the speed at which a survey can be undertaken. Grid work was quite slow, with one operator carrying the magnetometer, pressing the 'read' button and then repeating the displayed number to a second operator, carrying a notebook, who would record the reading in a column adjacent to the coordinates of the reading site.

The weather warmed up considerably during our working day, to a balmy minus sixteen degrees centigrade; I had to push back my parka hood as it was becoming uncomfortably warm under there and my spectacles began to mist up. With work finished for the day, we headed back to camp. In my tent, I stripped off my parka and went to remove the balaclava when pain shot through my face. I had not noticed that without my parka hood, all my breath had condensed on the outside of the woolen balaclava and the bristles of my beard, which had pushed into the wool, were now inextricably linked to this head-covering by a thick layer of ice. After much chipping of ice, accompanied by a sizeable dose of vituperation on the need to work in cold weather, the balaclava and a good portion of beard came free.

Back in China, this story didn't really resonate, owing to the fact that most of my colleagues did not sport a beard of any description, but they did pay a lot of attention to the felt-lined boots which are an important part of working in snow. Not from the viewpoint of winter work, which never succeeded as an idea during the rest of my stay, but simply for keeping their feet warm in their poorly-heated concrete accommodation blocks.

Men in my profession rarely discuss haircuts - not now and not in the past. A haircut is just something to have done when necessary but it's not always a simple affair, particularly if one is in the bush/outback/boondocks for some time and there's no barber nearby. There's always the option of just cutting one's own hair 'down to the wood' by whatever means are to hand, but this can cause the odd strange look when returning to civilisation, particularly if the cut in question was achieved largely without the use of a mirror.

My hair becomes quite curly when long - defined as beginning to flow over the tops of my ears - and if I get all hot and bothered externally, it tends to assume an Einsteinian look which can be off-putting to strangers, so I generally keep it quite short. Working in the remote Caprivi Strip in South West Africa for an extended period meant that, other than trying to find a barber who was used to cutting 'Caucasian' hair, I would have to either keep my hair long or have a buzz cut, the latter option being one I do not like. Apart from the SADF practitioner who had only one cut in his repertoire - scalp showing, with nicked ears a specialty - there was no barber available, so I resolved just to let it grow. However, it became bothersome.

One day, when accompanying Augustino, my truck driver, on a stores pick-up trip to Katima Mulilo, I was bemoaning the lack of a barber, when he announced that he could cut hair and used to do so for the geologists in a previous company for whom he had worked.

"Right, Augustino," I said. "Would you be willing to cut mine when we're back at camp? I'll pay you myself - it's not part of your job."

Augustino was quite happy with this, provided I had the necessary accoutrements, which I did, as I used them for keeping my beard trim. On our return to camp, he began his work after supper. Knowing that wet hair is more easily cut than dry, I had a quick shower then let him loose.

It all became a little Laurel and Hardy-ish. Augustino mentally split my appearance in two and worked on one side of my head, then the other. Unfortunately, there was no immediate congruence of lengths, with one side drying at a different rate to the other, so back he went to the first side, which he then trimmed too short. This went on for a couple of iterations until it could practically go no further without being a dreaded buzz-cut. The exercise terminated - and Augustino paid - I surreptitiously trimmed what was left with my beard trimmer, hoping that the back of my head wouldn't look too odd.

Later on in my career, in Botswana, when working on a diamond mine, keeping a tidy appearance became a little more important, owing to the increase in interactions I was required to have on a daily basis with both mine personnel and the general public. However, there was no gentlemen's barber nearer than Gaborone or, for most of us, Johannesburg, whose other attractions were considerably greater than those few available in Botswana's capital city in the 1980's.

The mine had one weekend in five or six where the normal Saturday morning work was put in abeyance and employees could escape 'early' on the Friday afternoon. The border gates to South Africa closed at around six p.m.; for those heading for the bright lights of Johannesburg, four or five hours drive away, there was quite a rush of traffic on the only road. Saturdays in South Africa back in the early 1980's were really only 'half' days, as far as shopping went, because most shops closed from just after mid-day. Restaurants and cinemas opened in the afternoon and evening, but if a haircut couldn't be secured before noon, it simply didn't take place.

Fortunately, there was a solution to this dilemma, in the form of Marjorie, a very kind-hearted and understanding woman, married to a mining engineer. Roy and Marjorie Bannerman lived in the town built by the diamond mine, although Roy actually worked for the exploration arm of the company. As a couple they had been involved with exploration 'types' for many years and in many locations across the world. Marjorie operated an emergency haircut service for those of us single men with a desperate need for a tidy-up, for whatever reason. She didn't charge for the tonsorial help, save for the tacit agreement that we would discreetly try to ensure that Roy didn't overindulge in his favourite tipple during the odd occasion Marjorie was absent from site. If he did, we were to make sure he got home safely. Roy wasn't by any means a problem drinker, he was just a very convivial person who enjoyed conversations with people from all walks of life but on most days, never touched alcohol.

It was from Roy that I learned an interesting 'wheeze'.

I used to keep three or four different bottles of whisky in my drinks cupboard. One, of the cheapest variety possible - often decanted into an old expensive brand bottle - for those whose taste buds had been shot off in the war and who insisted on drinking whisky with a cola-based soft drink; a couple of different bottles of good blended whisky and a rare malt whisky for the snobs or the genuinely discerning.

Marjorie would, from time to time, drop Roy off for a drink and a chat at my house when she was off on an errand in the town.

"No more than a couple of drinks, Roy," she would say to him. To me, she'd add *sotto voce*. "Go easy on the quantities, would you Tom, he's not the young buck he still thinks he is."

With Marjorie safely out the door, Roy would nearly always respond to my asking him what he'd like to drink with, "Some of that good blend you've got there… you know, the one that's the very light colour. And just a touch of water." His normal tipple at home was a much darker blended whisky, so this ruse meant that when Marjorie returned, she was supposed to think that he'd been good and just had a very watered-down version of the same, as opposed to a full-strength belt of finest J&B. I don't believe for a minute Marjorie didn't know what went on, but as I always limited Roy to just two drinks, he went home happy that he'd ostensibly had a bit more to drink than he'd been told to have and Marjorie was happy to have a contented, if only slightly woozy, husband.

Haircuts in China proved slightly problematic owing to the fact that Chinese hair is generally straight, not curly. The usual techniques employed or taught in Middle Kingdom hairdressing salons just wouldn't work with my hair, so I did end up, on occasion, with some very strange-looking cranial topiary. The issue was partially solved by asking the hairdresser of the day, of whom there are a great number in China, to cut my hair sopping wet. This meant that at least it was roughly the same visual length all over, at least until it dried. My appearance at one of these salons always seemed to draw a crowd, eager to view the rare sight of a foreigner; moreover, a foreigner with a beard.

As part of our remit to introduce new methods of diamond exploration to the Joint Venture, we had purchased state-of-the-art proton precession magnetometers, whose readings could be downloaded direct to a computer. Owing to previous training, I was appointed as the geophysicist for the British side of the Joint Venture and really enjoyed teaching my young Chinese counterparts how to get the best from our top quality Canadian-made instruments. I kept in close touch with the company's Chief Geophysicist, a German fellow by the name of Werner Schmidt, so that any developments in data processing or interpretation could be acquired for our use.

In one telex message, he said that he was coming out to Japan to a conference on seismic surveying and asked, as he would be virtually next door, if he could possibly visit the venture and see for himself how things were going. The visit was cleared by all the relevant bureaucrats, and Werner duly arrived in Linyi by train a few weeks later.

He was a strapping man, over six feet in height, with 'Teutonic' features and closely curled dense auburn hair. This hirsute appearance extended to his forearms, each of which resembled an otter's pelt. Out in the countryside near Feixian Town, he was followed by groups of giggling schoolchildren, all staring at him. Occasionally, one would dash forwards and stroke one of Werner's arms, before returning quickly, scared but unscathed, to the safety of his or her peers. This interest never abated, to the point where he had to lock himself inside our minibus while he ate his lunch, otherwise there were just small hands everywhere.

"Ach, Tom," he said. "I feel like that fellow in your English stories... Culver, no, no, Gulliver! Does this happen all the time? How do you get any work done?"

I explained that his experience was a little more intense than anything we had seen so far, but that it wasn't so unusual, given that this part of China was very far off any burgeoning tourist trail and that foreigners were a new species to most people. Apart from Qingdao, on the coast, where there had been a German brewery at the turn of the twentieth century, and at Qufu, where Confucius was born, this area of Shandong Province had not figured largely in any travel guides before or after the Communist revolution of 1949.

The final word on hair comes from an old lecturer of mine, who, at the 39th and until then, the only reunion of the 1975 Honours class, awarded me an unexpected accolade. Looking around at many of my balding, if not bald, and (mainly) clean-shaven classmates, most of whom, except for me, had espoused the 1970's hippie look back then, he pronounced that I appeared to be the one student who had actually gained the most hair since graduation. I'm happy with that judgement from an Emeritus Professor.

CHAPTER 21

GOLF

Golf, or 'promotion sticks' as one of my colleagues used to call the game, has figured in my life on a rather erratic basis. I learned the basics in Scotland, using my father's old hickory shafted clubs, but only bought my first set when working on a South African gold mine.

Most mines had their own courses, varying from the 'mashie' par-3 pitch and putt level to something much grander. Labour was never an issue and water was supplied from the vital pumping of the mine, so no matter how dry and brown the countryside in the harsh Highveld winters, there were always lush oases in close proximity to headgear and spoil heaps.

It was on one such course, Goldfields West, near the town of Carletonville, west of Johannesburg, where I first encountered wildlife problems interfering with the game.

Somewhat unusually, I had driven straight - I often took a more scenic route around a golf course than many golfers - when my ball crested an uphill rise on the fairway and disappeared from view. My playing partner, Ben Stewart, assured me it would be fine.

"There's a bit of a downslope there, it should be lying right in the middle… lucky shot!"

"That's not luck, that's years of practice," I replied in a huff after he drove off, inflicting a massive slice on the unsuspecting white spheroid. "But we'll need a search party for that one."

After rootling about in the rough for a few minutes, Ben's ball was discovered under a small bush and two shots were used up getting it back onto the fairway, approximately to where my ball should have been. It could not be found. We looked in the sprinkler heads and we looked in a nearby bunker but it had disappeared.

"I couldn't perhaps have hit it a bit further?" I asked despondently.

"Not unless you were Gary Player on steroids," said Ben. "And there's precious little evidence of that so far today."

Just then, a troupe of green vervet monkeys came running out of the bush, one carrying a golf ball.

"Look," I said. "The little sod's nicked my ball!" I gave chase and the monkey carrying the ball half-threw it sideways into the light rough.

"Hah," I said. "I suppose you'll want me to play it where it lies?"

Ben looked at the ball. "You can, if you want. But it'll cost you two penalty strokes. It's not your ball."

It wasn't. It was a nice new ball, though, so I pocketed it and went back to the tee to repeat my beautiful drive. I didn't. I ended up on the green for six, down in eight. Monkeys!!

A little later on in the same game, Ben, who was in light rough, called from across the fairway.

"Tom, not strictly in the rules, I know, but could you come here because I need some help?"

I walked up to him as he fiddled with the clubs in his bag. "What's up - you know I can't give you any advice on what's the right club?"

"I know, I know," he said. "But that surely only applies to hitting the ball? This problem is slightly different," he continued, pointing to a small Egyptian cobra nestling his golf ball in its coils.

"That's easy," I said, as I retreated swiftly from the vicinity. "Poke it with the longest club you've got! Or drop a ball and claim an outside agent or a loose impediment."

In the end, he decided a surgical strike with a three iron gave him the best alternative, dispatching the cobra with one stroke. He didn't move the ball and it wasn't an attempt to hit the ball, so no penalty stroke was necessary, but he did admit to a touch of the 'Yips' in case he had missed the reptile and it had retaliated.

He admitted it was a tricky shot. "Wasn't a case of 'keep your eye on the ball'. More like 'no Mulligans this time, please'."

Blesbok - a variety of large antelope - were another hazard at Goldfields West, as they tended to lie about, chewing cud or whatever it is that antelope do when they are interfering with a tricky short iron to the green. They weren't aggressive or particularly dangerous, they were simply in the way, and would heave themselves up and stagger off when a golfer approached too closely.

This particular antelope species also proved to inhabit many golf courses in southern Africa - with water and abundant food all year round, and no danger of being shot, which antelope wouldn't? They were certainly evident in one of Botswana's newest golf courses, adjacent to a diamond mine a few hundred kilometres west of the country's capital, Gaborone.

The man who had replaced Steve Greenall as Chief Geologist at the diamond mine, one Bob Hill, was a fearsomely keen golfer, having been deprived of the game in his last posting in Angola, where straying outside the work and living areas invited danger. Such as bullets, or land-mines, or both.

At around quarter to four each Wednesday afternoon, he'd announce that it was time to close the office and everyone should get on home. We were all quite relaxed about working past the normal knock-off time of four o'clock, depending upon our workload, but on Wednesdays, there was the mid-week golf competition which Bob could not miss. As I was his elected playing companion - not that I recall volunteering - and therefore his entry-ticket to the competition until he gained membership of the Golf Club, I also had to leave. It wasn't a great hardship.

The tricky third hole on this course was a par three, with the green surrounded by a water hazard, namely a couple of concrete-lined ponds. The security-fenced main road to the mine ran parallel to the fairway, so any hooking meant out of bounds and lost forever.

Bob selected a short iron and gave a mighty heave, hitting the ball very high.

"Did you see it come down, Tom?" he asked. "I lost it against the sky."

"I thought I saw it bounce," I replied. "Looked like it might have hit the water hazard, but that's empty just now, so it could have gone anywhere."

We trudged up the shortish fairway and my ball lay just on the edge of the green. We searched for Bob's ball but it remained stubbornly lost.

"You might as well putt out, Tom," he said. "I'll just attend the flag then go back and hit a provisional and you can see where that one goes." So saying, he marched up and pulled out the flagstick. A ball popped out onto the green.

He looked at the ball, then looked again. "Stone the crows, I don't bleeding believe it. Look, that's my ball isn't it?" he queried. "My first ever hole-in-one and I didn't even see it happen!"

I agreed it was his ball, so his card was marked accordingly and his bar-bill that night was quite a bit larger than usual. Bob's handicap was lowered accordingly, which didn't worry him unduly. To have his name - eventually - in gold letters on the clubhouse Roll of Honour was a reward with no price attached. He and I are both long gone from that part of Africa, but perhaps one day we'll go back and have another game, for old times' sake. Another hole-in-one? Not in a month of Sundays.

Australia has some magnificent golf courses and I've been lucky to play on a couple, of which 'The Vines', to the north of Perth in Western Australia, was quite special. However, it paled into insignificance when I received an invitation to play in the Royal Gidgee Creek Open, held in the shire of Upper Gascoyne in outback Western Australia.

For a start, it was a requirement that the log book be signed when arriving, which was precisely that. A log, with a flat area whittled out of it, on which one wrote one's name in marker pen. The competition was limited to twelve entrants, all of whom must have worked in diamond exploration on Gidgee Creek sheep station.

The fieldhands at one of the camps under my control had devised a nine-hole course in a flattish bit of country. The fairways were relatively rock-free areas, albeit with abundant, deep red, desert-polished small stones and pebbles. Only the largest boulders had been relocated. The 'greens' were circular areas on the red earth, swept free of stones. In the middle of each green, an old tent pole and a piece of flagging tape served as a flag, sitting in a hole lined with an (empty) beer tin. Tees, which could be used at all times, were small cylinders of hosepipe.

There were one or two tricks to playing the course, the first of which was not to hit the ball - a standard golf ball - too hard, or there was the strong probability that it would land in a rocky area and ricochet off, never to be found again. Kangaroos, particularly for the first foursome to tee off, could be a bit of a distraction as they awoke from their dozing under shady bushes and took off in all directions. Putting, unlike on true oiled sand 'browns' where a route to the hole could be indented with a putter, was a difficult exercise, with too heavy a stroke resulting in the ball shooting off the green for several tens of yards. There was little doubt, players in this competition had to be at the top of their game!

Footwear was optional - many choosing to play in bare feet or 'thongs' (flip-flop sandals) - and the dress code was, well, the best word would be 'relaxed'. Clubs, unlike on a normal golf course, were shared between foursomes and it was often a case of choosing the least badly dented and chipped implement with which to strike the spheroid.

Refreshments consisted of beer, with water for the wusses.

Despite all the unorthodoxies of this invitational game, concentration was intense and rivalries were fierce. The various Australian factions - Queenslanders, South Australians, West Australians and those from the Northern Territory - sorted out their tribal differences and formed alliances. Steve Greenall and I, being Poms, were partnered against a couple of diehard 'ocker' fieldhands and the 'sledging' more often associated with Ashes cricket produced some of the usual witticisms.

"Geez, you're about as much use as a one-legged man in an arse-kicking competition!"

"Is that how they putt in Pommieland? Why not use a snooker cue instead?"

"That was a fine sweep-stroke!"

The foreign contingent did not win the Royal Gidgee Creek Cup - yes, a ceramic mug with 'RGCC' written on it - but we did enjoy the barbie with yet more beer, afterwards. The photographs are memorable, but the sheer enjoyment of such a surreal day is difficult to relate. A perfectly normal recreational sport, played in the harshest of conditions, with a varied bunch of convivial reprobates for company - that was a game of golf!

CHAPTER 22

WEATHER

The 4 am flight from Perth to Paraburdoo on Ansett Airlines isn't the sort of flight where you chat to your neighbour. He's quite possibly six-foot odd, covered in tattoos, has the tail-end of a monstrous hangover and he's going back to work at one of the iron ore mines after a two-week bender.

Many Australian mines work the FIFO system - Fly In Fly Out, or as it's also known, Fit In or **** Off - and when possible, the commercial flights are timed so there's a minimum of disruption to the numbers of bodies available for work. The iron mines are in the Pilbara region of Western Australia and in high summer, these are not the place for anyone of a nervous or delicate disposition. The heat is magnified by the red-black of the haematite ore and outside the air-conditioned offices and accommodation, it's just dry, dusty, and unbelievably uncomfortable. It's not much better in winter, either, just a few degrees cooler. Those who choose to work in this region of Australia are as rugged as the countryside in which they toil.

It was April 1996 and I was aboard the flight, together with a trainee geologist, Carl Wright, heading for one of the company's exploration camps. Ordinarily, I would have driven from Perth, but it was a two-day drive there and the same back, and I didn't have the free time available. I wanted to introduce Carl to his new boss, Helen Simpson, and to see for myself how Helen was doing in this, her first independent command.

We were met at Paraburdoo by one of the fieldhands, John Early, in one of the ubiquitous Toyota 'utes' - a pick up (utility) truck - beloved by those in the Outback. They could be Nissans, too, but the mighty 'Tojos' (nicknamed after Japan's wartime Prime Minister Hideki Tojo) were the weapon of choice.

"G'day, Boss Man", said John to me. "This the baby geo?"

"G'day John," I replied. "This is indeed Carl Wright, late of Melbourne Uni and a week in the Perth Office."

"Carl, this is John Early, field hand extraordinaire and camp darts champion. Don't bet against him!"

"We have to pick up anything in town, John?" I asked.

"Nah, she'll be right, Tom," he replied. "We're only thirty k's away from here, so the cook's pretty happy."

We loaded our gear - swags, suitcases, some camp equipment and the all-important mail - onto the Tojo and set off for the camp, sited, as most were, next to a billabong from where water could be drawn for laundry, showers and, after going through the purifier, for drinking and cooking.

I hadn't been to this camp before but it was all neatly laid out with the accommodation tents far enough apart, but not too far, the cook's caravan and lean-to mess tent nicely positioned, the stores tent in a tidy state and the generator behind a bunded dirt wall to minimise noise and also to contain any diesel spill. There was no rubbish lying about and altogether the camp was a credit to its inhabitants. There wasn't a great deal of vegetation in the vicinity except for some eucalypts near the water; off to the west lay some small undulating hills and to the east, the looming bulk of the iron formations.

Helen was out in one of the two-man sampling crews and, apart from John, the only other people in camp were Carol, the cook, and Dougie, the helicopter engineer. The outback of Western Australia is very sparsely populated, with roads extremely few and far between, so we employed the services of a contract helicopter company to allow us to sample this fairly barren and largely inaccessible terrain. Helicopters are inherently unstable aircraft, so our contract stipulated that all the pilots had to have at least one thousand hours on type, and that each helicopter would be accompanied by a qualified engineer. We generally used the workhorse of the Outback, the Bell Jetranger 206, a two-bladed single-engined machine with a carrying capacity of five, including the pilot.

The engineers varied a lot; some would be strictly professional, attending only to the helicopter at start-up and shut-down for the day, whereas others would help ferry fuel to strategic sample-pick up points, take rubbish to the nearest disposal point and be a general help around camp. Dougie was one of the latter variety.

"Hey, Doug," I said. "How's things with that airborne bucket of bolts you keep patching up?"

"Yair," he replied. "If that bunch of hoons you call a crew could just let a man have some peace, and stop all this sampling malarkey, she'd be fine!"

I said, "Stop whingeing, you'd think you were a Pom the way you keep going on!"

Motioning behind me I said, "Meet Carl, he's the new geo going to be working with you for a while."

"G'day Carl," he said. "You been up in a rotary wing before? See, that's what we engineers calls helicopters. These uneducated types," he went on, glancing in my direction, "calls them 'choppers'."

Carl said, "No, I've never been in a helicopter."

Whereupon Dougie replied, "Let's get some coffee and I'll run you through the safety procedures - kind of important - eh?"

We went to the mess tent where I introduced the fabulous Carol. Bush cooks tend to be very good at their job, otherwise they are not cooks for long.

As one apocryphal tale goes, a cook had complained to the geologist that the fieldhands were less than complimentary about his efforts. The geologist assembled the crew and asked, "Alright, who called the cook a bastard?"

To which the reply was, "Who called the bastard a cook?"

Carol, on a normal day, conjured amazing meals from basic ingredients and on a good day, what we ate could have graced any of Perth's finest restaurants. Her prowess was appreciated by one and all, and Carl, from a gastronomy viewpoint, was very fortunate indeed to start out his bush career in the care of the equivalent of any of today's best-known TV chefs!

He and I spent the next few hours in the office caravan, where I outlined how to organise and manage adequate sample coverage, cost-effective helicopter movements, staff duty rotas and most importantly, how and why to liaise with landowners to cause minimum disruption to their work.

Helen returned to camp in the early afternoon and took Carl off to introduce him to the rest of the crew and to put him to work offloading samples from the helicopter. I used the opportunity to test the camp's newly-acquired satellite telephone to call home and assure Sue that all was well.

"Have you been listening to the radio?" she asked.

"No," I replied. "What's up?"

"There's a Category 3 or 4 cyclone coming in over the north coast, could be heading your way!" she said. "They don't know if it will turn that far inland yet, but you might want to check - in any case, you're going to get wet."

I finished the call and then tried, on radio, to get through to Perth Base but the reception was shocking. The helicopter came in with the last sampling crew but before the engine was shut down, I asked the pilot, 'Bing' Crosby if he'd heard about the cyclone.

"Yeah, mate," he replied. "But they reckon it'll probably touch down out towards Onslow, so we might get a bit gusty and wet, but we should be OK." He went on. "I'll park 'er so she's facing into the wind."

The weather didn't deteriorate noticeably as the afternoon went on, but the satellite phone suddenly shrilled. I answered.

"Tom," said my boss, Steve Greenall. "You know about the cyclone?"

"Yes," I replied. "But the last update we had, it was going to hit at Onslow so we'll be on the fringes."

Steve said, "No, that's just been changed - we phoned the military airbase and they're now saying touchdown will be much further east, so you're going to be right in it by nine or ten o'clock tonight!"

"Understood," I said. "I'll get the place evacuated and we'll overnight in Paraburdoo. "Don't think we're going to be able to move everything, so we'll take the most valuable bits and batten the rest down."

Steve replied, "Do what you can, but get the people safe, that's the most important thing."

He asked me to let him know, if at all possible, when we had the situation resolved and rang off with a "Best of British, you'll need it!"

I spoke to Helen and briefed her on the situation, then suggested she get her team together to strike as much of camp as possible. Carl and I were supernumary, so we were delegated to organise accommodation in town, get the vehicles fuelled, and otherwise, keep out of the way.

I used the satellite phone again and got through to the sergeant at the Paraburdoo Police Station.

"G'day," I said. "Tom Lindsay here, Outback Exploration Company, we've got a camp about thirty k's north of you." I went on. "We're planning to evacuate camp and come into town - will that cause any problems?"

"Strewth mate," he replied. "If you can get into town in the next ninety minutes that'll be fine, otherwise stay where you are, 'cos I'm locking the place down."

He continued. "You want me to book you into the motel? There's plenty of rooms."

I said, "That'll be good, ten rooms if that'll work, otherwise as many as you can get and we'll worry about who's sleeping where when we get there."

I let Helen know the latest news. "We've got forty-five minutes at most to get out of here, so Carl and I'll finish getting the utes and the truck fuelled and we'll start loading the gear, that OK?"

"Fair enough," she said. "Also, just ask Bing what to do about the chopper, will you?"

I found Bing packing his kit. "What d'you reckon, should we take the helicopter to Paraburdoo or go further south to Meekatharra or Carnarvon?"

"Nah," he replied. "Don't forget these things fly at a hundred knots and are meant to go through the air, so she'll just shift into the wind."

He continued. "We'll just make sure she's full of Jet A1 to give her weight and leave 'er be."

Shaking his head, he said, "Taking 'er to Paraburdoo might mean she'd get smacked about if she was parked up next to other machines and one got loose."

Well, Bing was the pilot and in charge - I was the client and it didn't really matter to me if the helicopter was the worse for wear, I'd just ask for another one!

The tents were dropped flat, then rocks, bedframes and heavy items placed on top of them. Chairs and tables in the mess tent were folded and stored under the caravan and then the tent folded and stored in the same place. The helicopter was fuelled. Valuables, radios, office files and whatever else was deemed important and portable were loaded onto the vehicles, along with personal swags, and the convoy set off.

Although Australian field-hands are not, in general, noted for their sensitive natures, it was obvious there were nerves about and none more so than when we arrived in Paraburdoo and checked in at the motel. Rooms had been booked as promised, so we dumped our swags and bags and made for the pub restaurant.

Being the most senior, I ordered a round of drinks as menus were scrutinised. The inevitable 'true' stories about cyclones picking up trucks, cows, houses and the like were all being aired by those who had firsthand knowledge, or so they claimed, mainly with the objective of scaring the inexperienced contingent. That first round of drinks vapourised, so I ordered another, saying "that's the last one on the house, guys!" That didn't stop the rate at which alcohol was being consumed, but it did mean my budget wasn't going to take too big a hit.

The television in the corner of the bar was on and all eyes were glued to the weather updates. It was an almost one hundred per cent certainty that the eye of Tropical Cyclone Olivia would pass over or near the camp, meaning either little potential damage, or the chance of the strongest winds ripping the camp apart. Paraburdoo could be likely to suffer gusts in excess of two hundred kilometres per hour, so we were in a frying pan and fire situation. At least our 'fire' had solid walls!

As soon as I had eaten, I claimed fatigue, having been up for over eighteen hours, and left for my room as the wind began to increase markedly and the odd rubbish bin left its moorings. Most of the crew stayed at the bar and continued to help Australia's National Debt decrease.

I fell asleep immediately and only awoke at around seven o'clock the next morning, with the sun coming in through the partially closed curtains.

"Funny," I thought. "I don't remember a tree in my door when I came to bed!"

Halfway through the room door was the snapped-off middle section of a small palm tree, looking somewhat out of place in the general décor. Power was on, so I had a shower and dressed, then ventured, with some difficulty, outside.

There was debris everywhere, but remarkably little major damage that I could see. I wandered into the breakfast room - the same bar as the previous night - and the television showed a trail of destruction at Pannawonnica, a town to the northwest, where over fifty houses had been severely damaged. It seemed that Paraburdoo had escaped quite lightly, with wind gusts of only up to one hundred and forty kilometres per hour.

Helen rounded up the human wreckage and, after checking with the police that we could travel, the vanguard, including Bing and Dougie, set off for camp.

It was possible to see that there had been a camp, because the cook's caravan and the office van were still standing, albeit the worse for wear, the generator was fine and the helicopter was sitting where it had been left. Apart from these larger items, there was simply a sea of bits of prospecting gear as far as the horizon, up in the small scrubby trees that were scattered around and in the muddy, and overnight much larger, billabong.

Bing and Dougie inspected the helicopter, which had some water pooling at the base of the main rotor housing, but whose engine started at the first attempt. Carl and I undertook some aerial reconnaissance, while Helen directed rescue operations and apprised Perth Base of our situation over the HF radio in one of the utes.

The largest piece of intact debris we could find was a plastic 'Esky' - a cool box - about five kilometres to the west of the camp site, otherwise there was just a backdrop of bits of camp equipment everywhere.

Back at camp, everyone worked to Helen's plan based on getting the cook's van working, restoring generator power, resurrecting the tents, and then salvaging equipment. I left for Perth the following morning, as planned, leaving behind Carl, whose introduction to the rigours of bush life could scarcely have been more dramatic.

"Oh well," I thought. "If he copes with this without too much trouble, he'll be fine."

His first monthly report stated that he had spent two weeks on 'cyclone debris collection detail', which is probably unique in the annals of geological career starts. It hasn't seemed to have dented his progress at all.

CHAPTER 23

BANQUETS

As anyone who has been to China on business will attest, apart from interminable meetings whose apparently sole purpose is to test patience - don't expect one set of meetings to produce anything worthwhile, these are just the warm-up rounds - the real business often begins with the banquet. Often, many banquets. One of the rules of protocol is that if you are invited to a banquet, you are expected to reciprocate - not in some distant future, but within a few days, or even the next day.

These are very stylised affairs, with a very precise protocol, although back in the 1980's in the very rural areas of China in which I worked, the worst excesses were mostly avoided. Nonetheless, it didn't take long until the words 'Mr. X would like to invite our British friends to a banquet' would send a frisson of quivering through the combined stiff upper lips of the Canterbury Diamonds' China Crew.

My first introduction to these trials took place in Mengyin, a diamond-mining town in Shandong Province, to where I had been consigned for a couple of days on my own, by the Supreme Being to whom Our Fearless Leader reported. The whole contingent of Canterbury was involved in a protracted meeting with various 'authorities' in the city of Jinan, capital city of the province, but it seemed, as the junior delegate, that I could be spared this tedium.

This Supreme Being, one Harry Ashe, sent me off in a Volga, complete with an interpreter and a very fierce-looking, but actually very witty and compassionate, eminent Chinese lady scientist, Madame Cong Weiwei.

"Don't let on you have anything to do with the Saint Kilda Corporation - remember you are a Canterbury Diamonds employee," said Harry, ushering me off to two days of constant external scrutiny and internal self-doubt, with me assessing each reply for veracity.

The problem was that the Saint Kilda Corporation was a company based in South Africa and in the political climate of the 1980's, therefore, it should not deal with any Communist country, or it would face untold problems in South Africa, where communism of any description was banned. Additionally, China should not be seen to have anything to do with a 'representative' of the bastion of apartheid. This was solved on a personal level by each individual having two passports, making sure that one passport was used only for China and the other only for South Africa, and on a company level by operating out of a shelf company based in the United Kingdom. The subterfuge was quite obviously seen through by the Chinese but 'face' had to be preserved for all concerned.

Mengyin was, to my eyes, in terminal decline as a town, but I was assured that it was really quite a prosperous place. Grey and off-yellow concrete apartment complexes were scattered between office buildings, all looking forlorn and strictly utilitarian. The guest house was typical Communist style - a grim, high ceilinged concrete monstrosity of square rooms with ill-fitting windows and doors and highly dubious plumbing.

The journey had taken a good six hours, so Madame Cong suggested that I 'rest' and that supper would be at half past six. In deference to my supposed fatigue, having flown in from London a day or so previously, I was informed that rather than have a proper meal, the guesthouse would supply supper for me to enjoy on my own, as we would have a very early start the following day.

I sat alone in the massive, cold, white-tiled dining room at a circular table designed for at least eight and various dishes were placed in front of me by smiling, if slightly nervous, staff. They couldn't speak English and I couldn't speak Mandarin, so we were equal on the communications front. I recognised chicken, prawns and rice but the various fungi defeated my knowledge and I was pretty sure there were sea-slugs hiding in a pile of some green stuff. However, the *piece de résistance* was a plateful of deep-fried scorpions.

I looked at them and they looked at me. I counted them - twelve - and I'm pretty sure they counted one of me. I slugged down some beer. No, they hadn't scuttled off, they were fairly dead. I slugged down more beer.

At this stage of Canterbury's relationship with the powers-that-be in China, ground rules were just being established and we were trying very hard not to cause unintended offence through ignorance or boorishness. Such as not appreciating traditional delicacies.

"Thanks Harry," I thought. "Just what I've always wanted."

I was fairly sure that the scorpions had not just been carelessly tipped on to the plate, but that they had been carefully placed there and someone would check if the foreigner had actually eaten any, with a report to go off somewhere if they had been refused. So I ate one. Then slugged yet more beer and had another. Honour being satisfied, I went off to bed.

After a fitful sleep, I was shown around the diamond mine. 'Somnolent' would best describe the activity I saw and the state of the treatment plant made me wonder if any diamonds could possibly be recovered. However, I kept these thoughts to myself as we trudged around, with our interpreter Mr. Yang and Madame Cong doing their valiant best to answer the technical questions I asked.

Madame Cong explained, as the tour drew to a close, that the manager of the guesthouse was very pleased to have a Scottish guest and that he would very much like to provide a special meal for us before our departure. "Thank you," I said, through gritted teeth, wondering what had become of the last Scotsman to have ventured here.

"You may not know, Mr. Lindsay," said Mr. Yang, "but in Shandong, we have very special scorpion farms. Much of the ground is very hard and it is difficult for things to grow, but in many farmers' yards, they are able to dig pits and grow scorpions for sale at market."

"I believe I had some for supper last night, Mr. Yang," I said. "Certainly an unusual dish."

Lunch was partaken in the same edifice in which I had eaten the previous night, but I had obviously passed some or other test, because there were quite a number of people both at our table and throughout the restaurant. Madame Cong was a jovial hostess, explaining what each dish was and inviting me to try some of the more unusual delicacies. We chatted about Chinese food, which I enjoyed cooking (true) and about living in the United Kingdom (not very true, as I hadn't lived there for over ten years).

"We have noticed you are very good with chopsticks, Mr. Lindsay," she said. "You must have practised a lot?"

"I first came across Chinese food when I was at university," I explained. "I developed a great liking for the very different tastes from our usual food, so I thought I'd try to use the implements of the culture."

"Well," she said. "You are a very good ambassador for cultural appreciation, so here is something you may never have tried before." With that, she took the serving chopsticks and placed a morsel of a newly-arrived dish on my plate.

This was a scorpion's distant relative, a rather large, fat cricket, minus legs. It had been flash-fried but to be honest, it wasn't the most appetising thing I had ever seen. So, mentally cursing Harry once more, I grabbed the insect with my chopsticks but couldn't manage the whole thing in one. There's not much worse than half a cricket on your chopsticks, except perhaps half a caterpillar in the remainder of your apple, but the moment passed and thankfully, the meal was at an end.

We set off on the return to Jinan, with at least two-thirds of the Mengyin party happily replete with Shandong delicacies. On arrival, we found Harry and the others gearing up for a banquet. "Not a chance," I said to myself. Feigning tiredness after a long drive, I was able to beg off attending and disappeared to my room to find some carefully squirreled away cheese and chocolate. However, I didn't get off entirely lightly as there was a return banquet the following night, hosted by Harry.

Seating at a banquet is very important. The principal host, the master of the banquet, sits at the centre of the main (usually round) table - the seat of honour - facing the entrance to the room. The seats on the left hand side of the seat of honour are second, fourth, and sixth in importance, while those on the right are third, fifth, and seventh in importance. In a grand banquet of many tables, the table of honour is the one furthest from the entrance. The tables on the left hand side of the table of honour are, in order of importance, second, fourth, sixth and so on, and those on the right are third, fifth and seventh. Guests are seated according to their status and degree of relationship to the master of the banquet.

Drinks are very carefully arranged in front of each guest with glasses in decreasing size, left to right. It is the custom, when joining in a toast, to use the same drink as the person toasting unless it is stated early on that there is an aversion to a particular drink. This is usually couched in language such as "I'm afraid I really have no appreciation for..." or words to that effect, implying some cultural or taste deficiency on the part of the decliner.

The last, very small glass is usually reserved for a clear white spirit - *bai jiu* - often known as *mao tai* after one famous brand of this distilled sorghum drink. *Bai jiu* was, back in the 1980's, of varying quality, but of one almost unremitting taste, which, to our untutored palates, was reminiscent of rather unpleasantly decayed and somewhat rancid vegetables. The first glass at any banquet took a herculean effort to down in one, as the salutation was nearly always *gan bei* (empty glass). Glasses two and onwards became progressively easier to swallow until, eventually, a numbness set in.

Bai jiu did, fortunately, have one major saving grace and that was it tended not to create hangovers. However, combined with the copious quantities of garlic often present in Chinese food, it did produce an utterly vile-smelling miasma which would emanate from one's pores the day after the banquet.

Harry, being a very important guest but having no taste whatsoever for *bai jiu*, would occasionally appoint one of his minions to respond to toasts so that his Chinese counterparts could indulge in their fair share of the noxious liquid. There are no prizes for guessing who was called upon to undertake this duty. After my recent encounter with scorpions, I thought that I might be spared. A forlorn hope.

"Don't worry, Tom," he would later say in a fatherly way. "It's all for the good of the company!"

"Never mind the company, what about my liver?" I muttered.

China in the 1980's was emerging from the appalling atrocities fomented by the Great Leap Forward, the Red Guards and the Gang of Four. When it came to banquets, these were seen as occasions to dispense with the general austerity in which many people were forced to live and to bring out 'delicacies' never seen on a regular basis. Coincidentally and rather unfortunately, Westerners were believed to eat mainly protein so a banquet tended to be very heavy on strange and exotic lifeforms.

A few examples spring to mind. Terrapin soup, where the animal was removed from the shell and cooked, with the head and shell being replaced in the resultant broth as though it was swimming. The giveaway was the little stumpy legs in one's soup bowl.

Fragrant roasted duck was rather pleasant, with the possible exception of when the duck's bill and tongue were given to the guest of honour; even the feet were chewed.

Thinly sliced whole lake fish, with a small tomato in the fish's mouth. The issue here was that the fish was still alive. This was probably no more 'barbaric' than eating fresh oysters, but it was a great deal more graphic because the creature gradually expired in front of one's eyes.

Flash-fried sea-slugs have all the consistency and taste of uncooked pork crackling, but were all too often presented as a delicacy.

Plates of fried sparrows - with feathers removed but otherwise served entire - as a crunchy entrée, were not a particular favourite of mine, I have to admit.

There were many more oddities - to a Western palate - but some delights such as toffee apple slices, moon cakes and in the winter, what is called in

Malaysia, 'steamboat'. This particular dish is slightly similar to a fondue but uses a charcoal brazier set in the middle of the table, heating a broth in which various meats and vegetables are cooked. The practice was said to be Mongolian in origin, but wherever it originated, it was always a welcome sight at a banquet.

Many prawns were from farmed sources and certainly, in the 1980's were becoming much more available to the *pǔ tōng mín zhòng* (ordinary people), so they were staple fare in any banquet. Prawns were generally served and eaten whole, with heads and feelers on, with the inedible chitinous bits either spat on the floor, or rarely and more genteely, placed on a side plate.

A small incident bears re-telling, when, much later in my sojourn in the Middle Kingdom, I attended a banquet with Harry's replacement, Harry having been promoted to some directorial plane. Ken was a rather impatient blunt-speaking Yorkshireman who had his way of doing things and who didn't really wish to understand Chinese culture. Circumlocution did not appear in Ken's lexicon.

He was seated to the right of Mr. Jian Tuo, the Chief Geologist of the brigade we were visiting. I sat to Mr. Jian's left. Mr. Jian was a very amiable fellow, a geologist's geologist with no obvious political aspirations, who normally dressed as though he was just off to the field, no matter what the occasion. He had a great sense of humour, very buck teeth, smoked incessantly and was prone to burping loudly when nature demanded.

Mr. Jian had just begun to dismember a large prawn in his mouth, the feelers waggling about in front of his lips, when Ken requested me to ask a question. I just looked at Ken, signalling him to wait a moment.

"Don't mess about," Ken said, *sotto voce*. "Just ask the question." I complied.

Mr. Jian turned to Ken and answered him directly, energetically spraying him with bits of prawn shell and leg as he masticated while talking. I translated.

Ken looked at me. "Timing could have been better," he muttered as he brushed bits of prawn off his suit jacket.

I think it's fair to say that Ken and I never really got on. I don't appreciate 'straight talking' as a mask for rudeness and he didn't like smart-alec juniors who were not prepared to jump at his beck and call.

As a last word on the subject of banquets, we were paid a visit by a member of the British Embassy in Beijing. Bill Campbell was the Agricultural

Attaché or some similar title and a career diplomat of over twenty years' standing. After the inevitable banquet, we were standing on the balcony of our 'games room' - a bedroom we had fitted out with a TV, video player and hi-fi system - chatting about China in general and his job in particular.

"Not a bad banquet, Tom," he remarked. "Not too much grog or silly speeches."

I agreed. "Yes, it was fine as these things go but that's the fourth we've had this last couple of months."

"Four?" he asked.

"Four." I confirmed.

"That's about what I have to get through every week in Beijing," said Bill.

Some diplomats really earn their pay.

CHAPTER 24

COOKS II

When I began work in China in the mid 1980's, the city of Linyi, in Shandong Province, housed three foreigners, of whom I was one. Our home was the Jinqueshan Guesthouse on the banks of the Yi River and we occupied the third floor on the west wing of this concrete accommodation block.

The management and staff had had one or two foreign visitors in the past, but we three were to stay for just under three years all told, by which time we were part of the furniture. However, in January 1986, we were very much an unknown quantity.

Our dining room was a small, windowed concrete box, open to the elements much of the time, quite close to the large main kitchen. I have vivid recollections of sitting at the table, wearing a fur hat and a sheepskin waistcoat, trying to eat some rapidly cooling vegetable with chopsticks manipulated by gloved hands.

The cooks had been told we ate strange things, mainly protein, and they did their manful best to try to keep us happy. We struggled for a while with food which lost all vestiges of warmth between the kitchen and the table, but then came Chinese New Year and a trip away to Qingdao, on the coast. The hotel we found wasn't especially grand, but the menus had a printed quasi-English translation for each dish. We tried out the various choices and purloined a menu for our return, so we could point out what we liked and what we didn't. Gradually, we converted the guesthouse cooks to our 'Chinglish' tastes.

Sometimes, things went a little awry such as the first time we requested *zhá tŭ dòu tiáo* - hot chips - and a bowl of succulent potato slivers arrived, doused in about a kilogram of sugar! The ladies who cleaned our little dining room were also gradually convinced to shut the door after tidying the table, and between mealtimes, so that what little warmth there was did not immediately leak away.

As the weather became warmer, the variety of food increased, fresh fruit adding a welcome change to the staples of hawthorn pastilles, elderly bananas and mandarin oranges.

I was appointed as honorary Catering Manager - CatMan - for the Brits and would spend much of my 'free' time sourcing hard-to-get items such as cheese, red wine, olives and chocolate. Dairy products were almost unknown in China at that time, but one of the country's most northerly provinces, Heilongjiang, produced an Edam-like cheese which could occasionally be obtained at a 'Friendship Store'. These stores, like the 'GUM' stores in Russia, were for the Party faithful or for foreigners, where hard currency could be exchanged for otherwise unobtainable goods. They only existed in the larger cities, but as we each visited Beijing or Jinan every three months or so, the CatMan would plan foraging expeditions for the individual who was travelling.

Our Fearless Leader, Geoffrey, was particularly fond of a glass or two of red wine at the weekend and in one Friendship Store which we happened to be in together, he came across a French bottling that he particularly liked. Chinese red wine was best avoided, owing to its mainly syrupy nature. All the items were carefully stacked behind counters, or in glass showcases, away from grasping hands, so he asked the assistant if he could look more closely at the three varieties of French red wine on display. She carefully handed them over, one by one.

"Look, Tom," he said. "This is a 1973 - that's a really good year for this vineyard; this 1978 and 1983 aren't quite in the same league but they're much more expensive. Wonder why that is?"

I asked the assistant if she could explain the price difference.

"Of course," she said. "The cheap wine is very old, so we cannot charge much for it. If you want to buy some, we can make a special price because no-one wants to buy it."

Geoffrey took a micro-second to digest this information and then immediately ordered three cases, obtained at a twenty-five per cent discount because of its antiquity.

"First time I've ever paid this little for this vintage - hope it's not corked!" he said. It wasn't.

Later on that year, Geoffrey's fiftieth birthday loomed and our Chinese colleagues wanted to give him a special celebration, which he wasn't quite dreading, but in which he wasn't too eager to participate.

"Come on, CatMan," he said. "See if you can suggest something which'll be a little unusual and won't kill off too many more liver cells."

I thought for a while then suggested that perhaps we might introduce our colleagues to a barbeque - hosted by Geoffrey and prepared by me.

"D'you think we'll be able to get enough meat and so on? Chickens shouldn't be an issue and we can always get fish, I suppose," he said.

I said I'd look into the possibilities and we agreed to chat more extensively later that week. I sought our Mr. Yang Tuo, our interpreter, who had spent time in Africa in the 1960's and was well-versed in the funny ways of westerners.

"What meats are you thinking of, Mr. Lindsay?" he asked. "There's a farm run by minorities not far away where we can obtain beef, and the guesthouse will be able to get pork ribs and chickens."

"If we get any of these that'll be fantastic," I said. "We can cook potatoes and we can make fried rice; there's plenty of vegetables to make a few different dishes, and as long as we have beer and soft drinks too, it could be very good. We'll need to make some actual barbeques - you know, with fuel drums cut in half?"

Mr. Yang promised to make enquiries and was as good as his word, coming back a couple of days later to say that everything was possible. I discussed the issue with Geoffrey and Simon.

"These guys don't know what a barbeque is," I said. "I'll happily do all the meat preparation and cooking but I'll need a hand getting the rice and veggies sorted. If you, Simon, could handle the booze side of things, I reckon we could give the guys a real treat and we don't need to buy any of the dreaded *bai jiu*," I said, looking at Geoffrey.

The matter was settled apart from the guests. We made a rough list, then added half as many again for civic dignitaries, then a few more for good luck. Geoffrey undertook to speak to his opposite number, the Brigade leader, to finalise the guest-list and also to ask if assistants could be provided for Simon and me.

The barbeque became all-consuming. Cooks Number 2 to Number 5 - all young geologists - were assigned to me. Barmen Number 2 and Number 3 were assigned to Simon. Those not assigned to cooking and bar duties would help with serving food and drinks. The event would be held in the grounds of the Cooperation Brigade. Barbeques were constructed, charcoal was obtained, guest invitations were sent out - the fervour is difficult to describe. Around one hundred guests, including the various cooks and bartenders and general hangers-on, were expected.

Two days before the actual event, the beef arrived. As two entire freshly-slaughtered hindquarters. I set about butchering these in the Brigade kitchens - the guesthouse facilities couldn't spare me enough space or time - and putting the slices of beef into large enamel bowls of home-made marinade. The pork ribs arrived, were defrosted, cut to size and they too were marinated. Fortunately, the large concrete store-rooms, even in summer, were cool enough to make deep-freezes or very large fridges unnecessary.

The following day, the chickens arrived and were part-cooked in the large woks in the Brigade kitchens. The meat in the marinades was turned and the seasonings checked.

Then barbeque day itself arrived. My assistants lined up in the kitchen.

"Cook Number 2 and Cook Number 3 - scrub the potatoes and then cook them in salted, boiling water for no more than 10 minutes. Cook Number 4 and Cook Number 5 - prepare the rice in the big wok and then add the vegetables." This latter instruction caused chaos. Cooking rice was easy; adding vegetables to the cooked rice was unheard of. I had obtained tinned mushrooms, tinned peas and tinned sweetcorn - fresh vegetables would consist of blanched bok-choi - but I only found out that morning that something I took for granted was absent.

"Please, Mr. Lindsay," said Cook Number 4, Li Feng. "We cannot open so many tins."

"Why ever not?" I asked querulously.

"It takes a long time to open them," he said.

"Nonsense," I replied. "Give me a tin opener, I'll show you!"

Li Feng passed me a screwdriver.

"No, no," I said. "A tin-opener."

"That's what I've given you," he said. "That's how we open tins!"

I looked at him askance. I went to my little pack of knives, sharpeners, corkscrews and other tools and pulled out a cheap can-opener, one of those with twin handles and a large butterfly nut, which cuts off the top of a tin can. I demonstrated.

It's difficult to quantify the astonishment that ran through my assistants when they saw the ease with which I was opening cans. I soon had a line of assistant cooks, assistant barmen and many others, all eager to try out this marvellous invention. We quickly ran out of cans. This totally unexpected happenstance solved the issue of 'acceptable' gifts I could give to my Chinese colleagues. I never returned from leave thereafter without at least a dozen of these useful little items in my luggage.

We worked on through the morning, chopping, cooking, mixing, boiling and preparing. Outside, the barbeques and charcoal had arrived, as had the seats.

Geoffrey was in charge of seating arrangements. The concept of informality was entirely new to our Chinese colleagues, who set out the seats in serried rows. Geoffrey explained and re-set the chairs in loose groups of four or five. As soon as he left the scene, proper order was restored. The tussle between cultures went on good-naturedly throughout the afternoon.

I gathered my troops. Simon did the same with his volunteers.

"We have three barbeques. I will take charge of Number 1 with the beef. Cooks 2 and 3, you have Number 2 Barbeque. Cooks 4 and 5, you have Number 3 Barbeque and the woks. I'll help you with any problems, but the main thing is to cook the food but not to burn it. On Barbeque 2, we'll cook the pork and the chickens, and on Barbeque 3, the potatoes. We'll start cooking a little later on Barbeque 3, which will give you time to reheat the rice and get the bok choi ready. Don't panic and make sure you have plenty of clean warm bowls to place the cooked food in. We'll light the barbeques soon, to give them time to get to a proper temperature."

Simon's merry band were being instructed in how to pour beers, deal with too-fizzy soft drinks and to keep wandering hands from filching bottles of '*balandi-jiu* (Chinese brandy),' a favoured route to instant intoxication.

A few moments later, as the barbeques were lit, we were off!

The charcoal reached operating temperature, the guests began arriving and the bustle increased to manic levels. Soon, the smells of cooking meat began to waft around the courtyard and within an hour or so, the most-honoured guests began to fill their plates, followed by the lower orders, some of whom had to be forcibly dissuaded from making off with barely-cooked chickens and potatoes direct from the barbeque grids. Informality may have been a difficult concept to impart, but when alcohol had dissolved any lingering reservations, there was no stopping our newly liberated colleagues.

The cooks cooked and served, the bartenders coped admirably and predictably, one or two speeches were made, but then spontaneous singing broke out in one or two areas of the courtyard and the evening dissolved into one of rarely-seen public happiness for most people. For once, they had a good supply of food and drink, they were among friends, or at least good colleagues, and they were enjoying being treated, with no *quid pro quo* expected. We lost Bartender Number 2 for a couple of hours, but he'd been at the *balandi-jiu* and had then found a nice corner to collapse in and sleep it off.

The important guests departed after murmuring some very genuine thanks for a new experience, and the rest of us began tidying up, sufficiently at least for the evening.

"Well," said Geoffrey later on, when we'd returned to the guesthouse. "That was pretty good, CatMan and BarMan - thanks for all the work. Don't think our colleagues have ever eaten so well. Tell you what, when Harry is out here in a couple of months, how about we do the same thing again? I mean, the guys know what to expect now, so it should all go off without a hitch."

We did in fact do exactly that. Harry, our big boss, was impressed that we'd developed a pretty fair camaraderie with a notoriously reticent culture and possibly even more impressed that the expected *bai jiu* did not make an appearance. Whether this bridge-building translated into his grand strategy for the company was for him to know and for us to find out in due course. However, for the remainder of my time in China, whenever Geoffrey's birthday was approaching, there would always be the not-so-subtle quizzing of whether or not Mr. Waters wanted to hold a party? He invariably did, so off we went on the rollercoaster yet again.

CHAPTER 25

COCKIES

It was after nine o'clock at night when the telephone rang in our Perth house.

"Tom Lindsay," I said.

"Tom, it's Stefan, we've got a big problem." Stefan was my senior geologist in the Pilbara region of Western Australia, a first-generation Australian of Hungarian parentage, with a great deal of field experience, so his calling me meant that something serious was amiss.

I said, "OK Stefan, fill me in." Then I asked, "Do I need to sit down?"

He replied. "You might want to; it's the owner of Bull Creek Station, he's threating to shoot down the survey plane if it comes near his station again!"

He went on. "Seems like they were mustering down the south end of the station when the MagSurv plane went shooting through the muster and the cattle went every which way."

"I've got to say," he muttered. "I've never seen a cocky as mad as this before - think I was lucky not to get shot meself!"

Geological exploration often involves the use of airborne geophysical surveys. These surveys measure various properties of the Earth - its magnetic field, the radioactive background, changes in the strength of gravitational pull and other physical attributes - which are differently affected by different rock types.

Specialist companies are contracted to undertake this work, which can often take several months to complete and which can cover hundreds, if not thousands, of square kilometres. Outback Western Australia has either sheep farms or cattle farms, either of which can be many thousands of square kilometres in area, so a single survey might require flying over one or more stations.

Cattle stations, in particular, conduct periodic 'musters' where the animals are herded into fenced areas prior to inoculation, marking or shipping to market. Each muster involves a great deal of planning and when taking place, frantic activity using bull-buggies (cut down and bush-toughened 4WD vehicles), motorcycles and helicopters, all of whose movements are coordinated by the man or woman in charge.

So that survey flights - usually in small, twin-engine planes, but occasionally using helicopters - do not interrupt a muster, a representative of the survey company will liaise with the station owner - the 'cocky' - to find out when and where musters are planned and plan the flights accordingly.

"OK," I said. "But surely Spike (MagSurv's liaison officer) checked where they'd be mustering?"

Stefan replied. "Yair, he did." He continued. "Only problem is, Spike spoke to the cocky's missus and she gave him the wrong place and dates - she was a week out!"

"Are you sure?" I asked. "I know Spike's good, but it could be he made a mistake."

Stefan said. "No, Spike didn't make a mistake, he copied everything down and he's got a mud-map she drew with the campsites and dates marked."

"That's going to cause us grief if we try to tell him his wife was the problem, not us," I said. "Let me think about it and I'll get back to you tomorrow but in the meantime, phone him - if he'll speak to you - and say you've given the message to Perth and you're waiting for a reply."

I continued. "Tell MagSurv to stand down tomorrow; if need be, I'll fly up to Port Hedland and we'll go and sort things out once I've spoken to the boss in the morning."

Next morning, I spoke to Steve Greenall, my boss and the man in charge of all of Western Australia for our exploration company.

"What a cock-up," he said. "Is Stefan sure that Spike isn't just covering up?"

I replied, "He is, but I won't know for certain until I've spoken to Spike and seen the mud-map, but you've got to admit, he's been doing this job for years with no reports of anything like this."

"OK," said Steve. "I'll clear it with Head Office, but you get yourself up there and if you're happy it wasn't Spike, tell the cocky we'll pay to help re-muster, just try to limit the cost." He continued, "If it was Spike, then MagSurv can pay the lot!"

Steve agreed with me that blaming the cocky's wife wasn't going to do much for us, even if we were in the right, so I would try to appease him and reduce the tension.

I got on the radio to Stefan. "I'll be up in Hedland this afternoon, any chance you can pick me up and we'll go see Spike tonight and the cocky in the morning?"

I explained briefly what the plan was and Stefan assured me that I would be collected.

"The cocky's spitting nails, Tom, it could be a bit tough, just so you know!" he warned me when he picked me up.

Spike was indeed in the right, as was obvious later that evening, after looking at his notes and the hand-drawn sketch map he produced.

He confided to me. "Listen, the cocky's old lady seemed a bit distracted when I was speaking to her, that's why I asked her for the mud map."

"That's fine, Spike," I said. "We're not going to try to lay the blame on anybody, we're just going to say something unexpected happened, and we'll do what we can to make it right."

This area of the Pilbara, centred on the small historic gold mining town of Marble Bar, is not as red and oppressive as the areas around the iron mines, but it is still very remote, covered in spinifex grass, and in the season, the Sturt Desert Pea. This town set a world record of one hundred and sixty consecutive days of 100°Fahrenheit (37.8°Centigrade) or above, from 31st October 1923 to 7th April 1924. It boasts the 'Ironclad' Hotel - a building fully covered in sheets of corrugated iron - built in the 1890's and still going strong.

The station homestead lay a few kilometres away and next morning we parked up by the cattleyard where the cocky, Mal Pearson, could be seen checking cattle in the pens.

The first thing I noticed was that he was in his bare feet amongst all the cattle dung and the second was that he was a person of the large, very solid, very muscular variety. We waited until he'd finished and then called to him.

Stefan said, "Hey Mal, g'day - this here's Tom, the boss man from Perth, he wanted to meet up with you about the problem with the muster."

Mal squinted at me, offered a hand the size of a small shovel, and commenced to cut off the blood supply to my arm, or, at least that was what it felt like. The vice slackened.

He grunted, "Well, at least you've got the guts to come here - let's get in the shade and you tell me what you're gunna do, 'cos if I see that plane again, I'll put a hole in his wings!"

We sat on the homestead's verandah.

I said, "First thing, we're, that's the company 'we', very sorry about your muster getting stuffed. Did you manage to pen any stock at all, or did they just disappear?"

"Nah," he said. "We were mustering just shy of a thousand head, and we only got a couple of hundred after that idiot pilot cut us up!"

He went on, "It's not just that he cut us up, but I've got to pay the jacakaroos and the chopper pilots for nothing, then I've got to pay them if we muster again and anyway, I've lost me slot with the cattle buyer."

I let him ramble on for a while then said, "Listen, Mal, we can't make everything right, but obviously there was a communication problem and we'll cop that."

"How much d'you reckon it'll cost to re-muster that same area?" I asked.

He thought for a bit and said, "Well, they've not all gone back to where we drove 'em from, so they're closer than they were, but it's still gunna be eight or nine thousand dollars, I reckon."

"OK," I said. "I'll find eight thousand dollars for you within the week, you set up a new muster and we'll keep out the way until you tell us that you're done. That seem fair?"

"What?" he said. "You're gunna pay me the money I lost?"

"That's right," I said. "The muster was messed up - let's leave it at that - but we can wait a while to fly the south section, so what about a deal?"

"Jeez," he said. "I ain't never met a bunch of geos like you lot. Last mob that broke me fences down tried to tell me they'd have fallen down anyway from the termites. Yair, course you got a deal!"

With that, he yelled in the general direction of the kitchen, "Mary, these here geos need a wet - get us the billy on, would you, love?"

He went on in a softer voice, "Mary said that that feller from the plane mob was here a couple of weeks ago, but her sister down in Carnarvon 'ad just bin diagnosed with cancer, so she were a bit out of sorts that day. Daresay she might have been a bit short with him."

We parted, a little later, if not exactly bosom buddies, at least on good terms, and with Mal saying, "Any of your fieldies need to stay out here if it's too far from camp to work easy, there's a few rooms out the back you can use any time. Hoo roo!"

On a much bigger cattle station, some three hundred kilometres to the south, we had been given reluctant permission to camp provided we followed

'The Rules'. The station co-owner, Greg Bradford, had had several bad experiences with prospecting outfits and his partner, or at least the partner's wife, was a very strong environmentalist, who would have nothing to do with mineral exploration companies, believing them all to be ravagers and plunderers of the Outback.

As a consequence, 'The Rules' came into being - two A4 sheets of strict requirements - to which I had to sign agreement before I could allow Julian, my geologist, to set up camp. To be fair, there was nothing surprising in the document and our normal operational practices would have covered all the strictures, but I signed it and gave my word that we would do our best to meet or exceed its intent.

Greg, who had obviously heard all the weasel words many times before simply said, "Yair, you bloody better. I can't stop you prospecting, but I can kick you out the campsite and lock all the gates and make it real hard for you to work if you don't!"

Julian briefed his crew before the move on to Barlee Creek Station and there was no possible chance of any misunderstanding. We also made sure that any visitors to camp, such as the company mechanic, or the truck driver who came by on a monthly basis to upload our samples for the Perth treatment laboratory, knew and understood we were dealing with a particularly prickly individual. Instructions were given for anyone departing Perth for the camp, to first phone the homestead and ascertain if any mail or small items could be picked up for the station, thereby saving on their transport costs and, often, time.

Over the next few months, Greg and his wife, Belle, came to understand that we were determined to be good neighbours and a wary acceptance, eventually veering towards quite a decent friendship, developed between the station and the explorers.

Greg and his partner had also acquired the adjoining station, Upper Warra, nearer the main gravel road into the area and which had a much more substantial farmhouse and outbuildings. Greg and Belle had moved their base there, leaving the Barlee Creek homestead for their sons to occupy. The combined area totalled over twenty thousand square kilometres and Greg patrolled the windmills and fences from the air in his trusty high winged, single-engined Piper Cub.

He would occasionally 'buzz' the camp on his way around the properties, just having a look-see, and loaned us a short-wave radio so he could let us know if any mustering was taking place owing to a windmill having dried up, or whatever other reason he had for moving cattle.

Towards the last couple of months of 1994, this southern Pilbara area was getting rather warm. The teams were getting through copious amounts of drinking water each day and the helicopter was beginning to find lifting off, particularly from ten o'clock onwards and with a full load of four sampling crew and several forty-kilogram samples on board, almost impossible. The air at ground level was too hot and therefore too 'thin' to afford the blades much lift, so a decision had to be made on when to strike camp and declare exploration closed for the year.

I happened to be on one of my routine visits to the area and was in camp when Greg came on the radio, asking if anyone was receiving.

"G'day Greg," I said. "Tom here. What's up? Over."

"G'day Tom", he replied. "Just thought you might want to know, temperature in the shade here at the homestead just cracked fifty degrees (centigrade). Hot enough for a Pom like you? Over."

"Thanks, Greg," I said. "Where there's no sense there's no feeling, so I'm OK, but I'll let Julian know. Think we'll probably have to just stop the work anyway. The chopper's taking a lot of strain and the guys are stressing out, so I expect we'll be on our way out in a couple of days. Thanks for the heads-up, we'll be in touch. Out."

Julian and I discussed the situation and we agreed that the conditions were pretty much intolerable for the fieldhands; the helicopter pilot, Nigel Rush, thought that there were about to be serious safety issues with the heat so that was it for the year - time to strike camp!

The helicopter departed the next morning, taking off in the cool air and heading for its home base in Melbourne, a three-day journey away. Perth was alerted that the camp was on the move and that space should be made ready in the office yard to receive all the gear.

I was determined that the camp-site should be left as we had found it and for two days, we dismantled tents, packed the two caravans, raked back the pebbles which had been moved to provide flat bases for the tent groundsheets, picked up any and all litter (there was very little) and restored the site to its former glory.

The crew left late on the second day, heading to overnight on the three-day journey south to Perth at a station we had worked on previously and whose owner, John Bytchuk, was very kindly disposed towards us. I stayed a little later, paranoia at work, checking that Greg would find no fault with our tenancy of his land.

Eventually, I climbed into my Tojo station wagon and headed for the Upper Warra homestead to report to Greg that we were done for the year.

"Jeez," he said, catching sight of me as I came through the homestead garden gate. "Just go leap in the tank, you Pommy bastard, before you come in here!"

I hadn't given my appearance much thought, but it seemed that I was an apparition covered head to foot in red dust, with sweat rivulet trails down my finely chiselled features and a not very prepossessing mien or aroma. I duly cleaned up a bit and accepted a bottle of something cool and refreshing.

"That's it, Greg," I said. "We're done for this year and you probably saw the guys on the back track to Clover Downs."

"Yair," he said. "I reckoned you'd have to be out of here soon, it's hottern'hell down here, so she'd have to be pretty bad at the camp."

With that, I thanked him and Belle for their hospitality and putting up with us for the last few months. He said, "When you first came in, I reckoned you was the same as all the other outfits, but I gotta say, you and your guys are something else. You haven't caused any trouble, you lived by The Rules, you treated us decent and you're welcome back any time."

I left for Clover Downs Station and then onto Perth the following day, but thought rarely of Greg over the next few weeks, other than sending a Christmas card to him and Belle.

The telephone rang at home, sometime in February 1995.

"Roleystone 2265," I said. "Tom Lindsay here."

"G'day you Pommy bastard," came the gravelly voice. "Greg here, Upper Warra, how're you doing?"

"I'm fine Greg," I replied. "To what do I owe the honour?"

"Had the partner's wife here last week," he said. "Nosy old bat, greener than a three-day dead 'roo, she wanted to see where you lot had camped, 'cos she reckoned you were the scum of the Earth and would have stuffed up the area."

He went on. "I told her I'd checked and as far as I was concerned, you guys were the best I'd come across and that the camp-site was clean as a whistle."

Apparently, this redoubtable lady had then commandeered a bull buggy and had gone off to investigate for herself. She returned some hours later and confronted Greg in the office.

"So," she said. "They're a good mob are they? How'd you explain this then?" she said, thrusting a tomato sauce bottle under his nose. "Filthy swine, they can't be trusted as far as the nearest bar!"

Greg took this diatribe personally, as he had not only spoken on our behalf, but had also inspected the campsite after our departure.

"Show me on the map," he asked. "Where'd you actually go?"

The partner's wife pointed to a spot and said "Here! It was about ten kilometres from this gate," she said, indicating a notation on the map. "Off to the left, a couple of hundred metres."

Greg apparently retorted. "You addled sticky-beak, that's one of our mustering campsites, the exploration mob was up here," he said, pointing to a spot equidistant from the gate but in a direction several kilometres at right angles to her 'find'."

After a pause, he went on. "Thought you'd want to know the story - ended all right for us, 'cos she hopped it back East quicker than she'd intended. I'm all for looking after the environment but that one even complains when we burn old fence posts; says we're depriving the termites or some greenie bulldust."

I said, "Thanks for letting me know, Greg, I'll tell the crew when we start-up in a month or so - that'll give them a laugh. Before I go, how's the water situation? It's getting a bit dry down here."

"It's not good," he said. "Most of the billabongs have just about had it and the feed's pretty scarce, so we need a storm or two soon otherwise I'll have to ship some stock down south quicker'n I'd planned. Hope we see you soon, hooroo."

What Greg didn't tell me was that he had written a letter to my boss, Steve, in which he commended the entire crew for being entirely cooperative and good-neighbourly and that he, Greg, would be happy to stand up at a Cattleman's Association meeting and say, for once, there was a decent exploration outfit working in the outback.

This was unexpectedly welcome news for the company, which, like many others, constantly had to fight the stereotypical negative profile of a prospecting company, created and reinforced by the plethora of fly-by-night operators who infested the business in Australia. As I recall, this end of the industry Greg described as being "full of fellas' flasher 'n a rat with a gold tooth."

CHAPTER 26

CHINA MEETS AUSTRALIA I

Sue and I, who had been conducting a long-distance courtship via letter, married when I left China at the end of 1990 and in early 1991, we set off for Australia and the fair city of Perth. I had been told that I could expect to begin work the day after our arrival, as it was the company's annual two-day strategy meeting, so Sue and I gave ourselves three days in Kuala Lumpur, which is in the same time zone as Perth, to get over jet-lag.

I had worked for my new boss, Steve Greenall, once before, in Botswana in the early 1980's and had visited him in Australia a couple of times on break from my duties in China, so it was fair to say that we got on quite well. He and his wife, Jenny, met us at Perth Airport and after a quick Sunday lunch at their house, they took us to our temporary hotel accommodation via a sightseeing tour. I had been to Perth twice before, so I had some inkling of what to expect, but it was a completely new vista for Sue.

Perth is a small, but quite magnificent city, split as it is by the Swan River. Building is not allowed on either foreshore in the centre of the city, giving a very spacious feel to the area. The Central Business District on the north bank has one or two taller buildings but the various architectural styles complement each other, rather than compete, and the sweep down to the Swan foreshore is gentle, with views over South Perth and east to the WACA ground, the airport and the blue-green escarpment yet further out. At the western end of this green space, on the north bank of the foreshore, a bluff rises up to the aromatic eucalyptus and wattle-strewn expanse of Kings Park. To a casual visitor, Perth looks inviting; to those intending to stay longer, it is a welcoming host.

The next day flew by in a buzz, for me at least, at the company's offices near the airport, and that evening both Sue and I joined the meeting's participants for dinner. The following day was also quite hectic, but the Managing Director, the Human Resources Director and the Chief Financial

Officer all flew to Darwin in the afternoon to repeat the same strategy exercise at the regional office there. There was nothing formal planned for the evening, so to make up for largely neglecting my new wife, I suggested a meal in our hotel's restaurant, one with a very good reputation, or so I had been told.

The tables were very elegantly decorated, the mood was one of subtle but understated quality and the menu appeared rather impressive. We ordered and chatted of this and that over our drinks, Sue being very keen to find out what we should do in the way of more permanent accommodation. Starters came, were eaten, and the table cleared for the next course.

My steak arrived, I picked up my knife and fork and promptly landed head-first on my plate, snoring. I knew from experience that when flying east for any distance, Day Three was always my worst day for jetlag. If I didn't get to bed by two o'clock in the afternoon of that day, I would fall asleep wherever I happened to be. In the excitement of a new wife, new job, and new country, I had thought that the Malaysia stopover would have taken care of this problem, but I had badly misjudged. I was not drunk or drugged, I was severely jetlagged. That's the truth, Ossifer!

Sue was fine, because she had been able to take the odd nap when not looking round Perth, so was much more acclimatised than I was. However, that didn't prevent her from having to propel a half-asleep husband from the restaurant to our room, whilst having to endure knowing smirks from the staff and patrons. I apologised, or at least I am pretty sure I muttered something in the way of an apology, because when I awoke the next morning, Sue was still there and hadn't taken the first plane back to the United Kingdom.

I left for work, leaving Sue to begin sourcing stores where we could obtain the essentials for furnishing a rented house until what we already had would arrive from Britain. I didn't have very much to contribute to our new household, having lived a bachelor life in serviced accommodation in a number of countries, but Sue had a few possessions which we had consigned from London the previous week.

Next to the hotel was a very pleasant Swedish-themed restaurant, part of a small chain in Western Australia. Arriving back at the hotel on Wednesday, I suggested that rather than show our faces – or at least not my face - in the hotel restaurant, we go next door and enjoy a smorgasbord dinner.

Australian seafood varies quite a lot in its taste and texture, depending on whether it has been sourced from the cold currents emanating from Antarctica or from more tropical, warm-water regions. Fortunately, the selection laid out in the smorgasbord covered all bases and soon we each had a plate full of delicious prawns, oysters, caviar, pickled and smoked fish and a mixture of salads. I said to Sue that Steve had suggested that with the meeting over, that I take much of the following day off and that we explore the various suburbs, shopping centres and malls and begin to think about where we might like to rent a property.

Sue was happy with this - Jenny had taken her into the city centre the previous afternoon - and she had a few things she wanted to show me. Soon came the time to recharge our plates so Sue got up from our booth, which had high-backed bench seats, and went off to the buffet table. She returned, having found an unusual delicacy from the East Coast of Australia - Moreton Bay Bugs, a form of slipper lobster - and I got up to follow her example.

What transpired next is probably best told by Sue.

"Tom got up to go to the buffet table, but with the high chair backs, I could only see his head. I was busy with this strange bug creature when I saw him coming back. Suddenly, he stopped, and began talking in tongues, gesturing behind me. He jabbered away for a couple of minutes then came to sit down. I felt very uneasy. Here was my new husband who, the night before, had collapsed at dinner, and who was now talking in gibberish to some invisible entity behind me. I was at the other side of the world from my family, I didn't know the country or anyone at all, really, and my husband seemed to be an undiagnosed lunatic. It was very unnerving."

"Sue, "I said. "Please get up, I'd like to introduce you to Mr. Liu and his team. I worked with them and Richard Wellesley - you remember Richard - in China. I'm really surprised to see them here, but they're on a visit to the Argyle Diamond Mine and are overnighting in Perth."

Sue had never heard me speak Mandarin and it just so happened I'd caught sight of some faces I recognised as I returned to our table. Having left China only a couple of months previously, my Mandarin was still reasonably good and I hadn't given it a second thought as I greeted this group of *lǎo péng yǒu* (old friends). Sue looked at me oddly. I introduced her to Mr. Liu and his minions, chatted briefly, then we both sat back down.

"Honestly," she said. "You might have warned me. I thought that after last night that you'd really gone completely doolally." I'm never sure how to answer that sort of assertion. Does being a geologist make you mad, or is it because you are mad that you become a geologist?

This Chinese connection was to surface on a couple of occasions later in our stay in Australia in the 1990's, portions of one of which are stamped indelibly in my memory.

My former boss in China wanted to bring some Chinese geologists to Australia to show them kimberlites in the ancient and very deeply weathered regions which give the Outback the pervasive red colour with which many people are familiar. The visit was all teed up - Geoffrey would meet them in Melbourne, tour the company's head office and laboratories there - then fly with them to Perth. I would arrange the Western Australia leg of the trip.

I called Geoffrey. "How many are in the party, what exactly do you want to do with them and how much time have you allocated? WA's a pretty big place, so we'll probably have to charter a plane, but my crews are all a few days' drive from the nearest kimberlites, so I'll need to organise ground transport too."

"There will be four geologists," he said. "In addition there'll be an interpreter, you and me, so all told seven, until we leave for the Northern Territory and you go back. I've provisionally allocated four days in WA, but we can go one less or more – you'll know best."

He went on. "They really want to see how the kimberlites look when they've been altered so much by all the old tropical weathering – they think they may have something similar in a couple of the southern provinces, including Sichuan, so they're keen to take photos and perhaps a few samples. Don't worry, I'll arrange any paperwork!"

"OK," I said. "Leave it with me and I'll get you an itinerary by the end of the week."

Steve, who usually wasn't keen on any sort of formal function, let alone one where an interpreter was involved, decided to be absent on the probable dates for the visit.

"You speak the lingo," he said. "After your horror stories about banquets, there's precious little chance I'm going to eat sea-slugs and the like, so it's me for the Outback! You sort it out."

I discussed the visit with Sue, explaining that the visitors wouldn't be able to stay in any of the current camps because where we needed to go was where we'd been camped the previous couple of years but now, we were nowhere near that spot.

"How many did you say there were coming?" she asked.

"Probably eight, including me and a pilot," I said.

"Why don't you see if John and Petra will let you use the shearers' quarters at Clover Downs? They're not being used right now, so if you offer them a few dollars and provide some food, I'm sure they'd help. They could do with the money, the wool price being as low as it is, and you'd practically be on site. You could probably get a ute from Julian's camp to do the ferrying about."

This was a great suggestion, so I called Clover Downs Station. John and Petra Bytchuk had become great friends to all of the company personnel working on or around their sheep station, partly because they worked their 30,000-hectare property themselves, with no outside help, never complaining about the unending, backbreaking effort they had to put in, and partly because their hospitality was boundless. Unfortunately, good wool prices, or even wool prices which allowed break-even were long gone. John, unlike some, had not squandered the good fortune of a few years earlier, but the tanks were close to empty.

"G'day, Clover Downs Station," came the rumble of John Bytchuk, former 'roo-shooter and current supporter of the Fremantle Dockers AFL team. This latter development was mainly to annoy Petra, who was a die-hard West Coast Eagles fan.

"G'day John, it's Tom here, the Pommy geo from Perth."

"Yair Tom, how's things with you? Had a couple of big storms here last week, just as well, think the sheep were down to eating rocks, there wasn't a blade of grass anywhere. What's up, you coming to pester us again?"

"Well," I said. "Sort of. There's a mob of mainland China geos want to visit those kimberlites on Gidgee Creek but I'm having a bit of a problem sorting out where to stay and the like. We might stay in Carnarvon and, if it's OK, fly in to your strip and then fly out again, but I'll need to send a ute over from Mount Augustus way."

"Hang on," said John. "When're you thinking of coming? Reason is I'm goin' to have the brother-in-law here soon to help with a bit of fencing, so you can borrow me ute if that helps?"

"That'd be really good, I was thinking of abut ten days from now," I said. "There's something else… any chance of us renting the shearer's quarters for the night? It would save the charter back to Carnarvon and the Chinese guys would get an experience like they've never had."

He chuckled. "Yair, I reckon we could do that, long as the Chinese blokes don't mind roughing it a bit. I mean, the quarters are clean enough, but she ain't the Ritz!"

We chatted a bit more and I suggested a reasonable price for renting the ute and for the accommodation. He said, "I'll talk to Petra, but that sounds pretty fair, 'specially if you'll supply the grub. Best give me a call a day or two in advance, just so we get the numbers right and the strip's not flooded or anything, but yair, lookin' forward to seeing you."

Next, I phoned Gidgee Creek Station, owned by an Aboriginal group and run by some of its members, the Murdoch brothers. The kimberlites we wanted to see were mostly on this station, but there was no airstrip or potential accommodation. Although Jason, the elder brother, could be a bit prickly with outsiders, we had been good neighbours on the property and had helped him on a few occasions, the most recent being the helicopter ferry of a seriously ill girl to Carnarvon, around four hundred kilometres away, or a half day's drive.

"Gidgee Creek Station, g'day."

"G'day," I said. "Can I speak to Jason please, it's Tom Lindsay here from that prospecting outfit that was camped up at Sunshine Bore."

"Nah," said the voice. "Jason's not here, just me, Jarli, and some other fellers. What you want, Tom?"

"I just wanted to ask if it'd be OK for me to bring some visitors to have a look round those rocks we were working on? Would be in about ten days' time."

"Yair, that'd be OK, Tom. We'll be doing some dipping an' that but nothin' down that way. Any chance you could bring us up some mail order stuff if we get it sent to the office?"

I replied. "That'd be fine Jarli, as long as it's not too big, 'cause I'm flying up to Clover Downs by charter so there's not a lot of room. Could you just let Jason know, though - I don't want him chasing me off the property!"

"No worries, mate," he said, and signed off.

Some of the peculiarities of dealing with delegates from mainland China in the 1990's, owing to the various arcane rules to which they were subject, should perhaps be explained before going further.

Before leaving China, each (male) participant was issued with a suit, two shirts, belt, tie, two sets of underwear and socks and a pair of 'city' shoes. If there was only one overseas visit made in twelve months, the suit and shoes had to be returned. If more than one visit was made, these items could be kept. I never found out, mainly because the subject would have been considered indelicate, what female visitors were issued in the way of 'official clothing'.

There was also a cash allowance given, in US dollars, but this came with not-so-gentle encouragement that it be spent at a Friendship Store or at the airport before departure, ensuring that the currency remained in the People's Republic of China. The upshot was that most mainland visitors usually arrived with Chinese gifts and cigarettes but nothing in the way of funds. Their hosts were unsubtly required to ensure their charges didn't starve or be left to wander the streets.

The itinerary was duly arranged and the delegation arrived in Perth at the appointed time, late in the afternoon from Melbourne. I dragooned in a couple of colleagues to provide transport from the airport to the hotel and then came the welcoming banquet at a recommended Chinese restaurant. It may seem patronising at this point in the twenty-first century to appear to assume that our visitors would only want Chinese food, but back then, many Chinese, on their first foreign trip, had great difficulty with 'Western' food and cutlery. One interpreter had confided in me that his party's individual digestions could not cope with 'all these lumps of meat'. In addition, salads were all but unknown in China, owing to a country-wide predilection for fertilising vegetable plots with 'night soil', that is, human waste. How anyone could eat an uncooked vegetable was simply beyond imagining.

The banquet details are lost in the mists of time, but one of the visitors, Mr. Zhang Peiyuan, was very taken with a photograph Sue showed him of our then only son, sitting in his high-chair, wearing a baked bean foundation cream, topped with a yogurt hair-do. I knew Mr. Zhang and his somewhat erratic English very well from many train journeys together in China. He was very prone to exclaiming, after a beer or two, '*wǒ you yī gè miàn hóng* - 'I have a red face' - then laughing loudly. In our eldest's case, Mr. Zhang pronounced, with a snort, "he has a red face!"

The following morning, plans started to go awry. John phoned from Clover Downs to say that they'd had a massive storm and that the airstrip was under water. We would not be getting to the Outback today.

"There's no way you're gunna be able to land anything on that strip until tomorrow morning at the earliest. Sorry, Tom, but either you wait or perhaps forget this part of the trip."

I couldn't really not make an effort, so we compromised. I said to John that we'd fly to Carnarvon that afternoon and that I'd get hold of him the following morning to see whether we could land or not. If not, then we'd just go on to Tom Price, an iron-ore town in the Pilbara proper, where the next charter, coming in from Darwin, would pick the visitors up.

Our office manager, Boyd Watson, re-arranged the timing of the charter flight from Perth and booked us accommodation in Carnarvon, on the coast, about nine hundred kilometres north of Perth. There was no mail for either Clover Downs or Gidgee Creek, but we packed a couple of 'Eskies' with frozen and perishable food for the planned stay at the shearer's quarters.

The flight up the coast was very scenic, leaving the vineyards north of Perth and then flying over low coastal scrub and farmland all the way to Geraldton, about half-way to the day's planned destination. Some way beyond Geraldton, there is the barren expanse of Shark Bay and Monkey Mia - wide, shallow inlets of clear blue water with sandy islets and spurs.

These warm, salty waters are home to one of Earth's oldest lifeforms - stromatolites. These rock-like structures are built by single-celled cyanobacteria (also known as blue-green algae) which form colonies, trapping sediments and forming small, cauliflower-like structures which 'grow' upwards. The Shark Bay colonies have been dated at between 2,000 to 3,000 years old, but they are similar to fossilised life forms found on Earth up to 3.5 billion years ago.

Apart from a banana plantation or three, the seafood-processing plants and the 'One Mile Jetty', Carnarvon is really a jumping-off spot for the Ningaloo Reef and the watersports available along the coast. It's not at all an unpleasant little town, but it's not hugely remarkable either. After a couple of hours' flight, we landed at the airport close to the town centre.

Geoffrey and I quickly organised a couple of taxis while our pilot, Max, organised the use of a cold store in which to keep our Eskies. Once at the hotel we arranged to meet at six o'clock for dinner. Mr. Gao Fang, the interpreter, came up to me.

"Xiao Lin da zay (Young Lindsay)," he said. "Perhaps tonight we not have so much protein, just simple meal, please?"

I replied. "I will see what can be done, of course. Until later, then."

Geoffrey and I asked at the reception desk and there was indeed a good Chinese restaurant a few hundred yards away, so we phoned and booked for the eight of us.

It was a typically tropical evening as we walked along to the Golden Swallow; the light was fading slightly in the warm, moist air, then rather suddenly, darkness fell. We went inside, where a table was made up for eight people, but as we sat down, one of the party, Mr. Guo Wei, started chatting excitedly to the waiter. Apparently, some of the calligraphic wall hangings had been drawn by a distant, but famous, relative of Mr. Guo's and he was asking if the waiter knew who had bought them, and where?

The owner appeared and then chaos ensued. Happy chaos, with much smiling and gesticulating and the usual torrent of vernacular Mandarin.

Mr. Gao approached. "Please excuse us, Mr. Waters and Mr. Lindsay, but this owner," he said, gesturing behind him. "He has met Mr. Guo once before and is very amazed to see him here. If you will permit, we five will have supper with him."

Geoffrey and I naturally said that we would be very happy for our Chinese guests to have supper with the owner – it meant less stilted conversation for either of the groups – so we left them to it. Much plain food was consumed, we noted, although Geoffrey remarked that the per-capita alcohol consumption seemed a bit higher than on previous occasions. The decibel level rose steadily throughout the meal.

Rather later than planned, we re-grouped and headed off for bed to gather strength for what the morrow might bring.

CHAPTER 27

COOKS III

Thoughts of barbeques almost inevitably bring memories of the 'Lucky Country' and 'throwing another prawn on the barbie', although meals in the bush camps there tended to be more organised and largely without copious alcohol. The field hands often weren't much interested in socialising at the end of another gruelling day, they just wanted good tucker, a couple of beers and an early bed.

Bush cooks generally had to be good at their jobs, or they could be not-so-nicely instructed by their erstwhile colleagues to stay on break indefinitely, but by and large, those who lasted at least one field season would have gained a measure of respect and could be sure of another job when work restarted after the annual 'Wet'.

One such individual was a stocky, muscular ex-biker, tattooed every which way, named Wally Turnbull. Wally had a monster of a beard and long, braided, black hair. His intimidating physical appearance was coupled with a fairly monosyllabic style of communication and a commitment to his person and his workplace always being fastidiously clean. Woe betide any fieldie appearing in the mess tent without having changed out of work clothes and having had a shower. If they didn't move at the yell of "Out", they had a short lesson in backwards flying. No-one ever needed a second lesson.

Wally used to put up a chalkboard menu for each meal, announcing what was available and what, if any, choices there were, particularly for breakfast. I was studying the board one morning.

"Hey Wally," I said. "What're these 'ding snags'?"

"Jeez, you Poms," was his reply. "You know what a snag is, right? It's a sausage."

"I know that," I said. "But to me, a ding is something that happens in minor car accidents. So how can you have an 'accident sausage'?"

"Nah," he said. "A Frog's a Frenchman, right? A Pom's one of you Britishers. A Ding's an Italian. So, Italian sausages for breakfast."

Wally's food was always good, if not greatly imbued with flair, but he was constantly trying to improve his repertoire and the exploration crew respected this, even when they couldn't pronounce his latest creation.

"What's this steak 'poivre' stuff then, Wal? Sounds like 'Steak Pooftah'! Learnin' that from that Froggie cookbook you're always lookin' at? Tastes all right, but." Wally's replies to these sorts of comments were generally unprintable.

When our eldest son was around six months old, my mother-in-law came out to Australia to visit us, and, in an inspired moment, having first checked with my geologist that it would be OK, I asked Sheila if she'd like to go on a trip for a week or so to visit the Outback and to stay in one of my camps. The one where Wally was the cook. We'd all go. Sheila was game for anything, so, with the venerable Toyota station wagon loaded with bush kit, and many packs of disposable nappies, the expedition set off northwards from Perth.

It was a long way, enlivened with an overnight stop in the metropolis of Meekatharra, a small gold mining town in central Western Australia, but we eventually arrived at the camp, set on the banks of a billabong close to the slopes of Mount Egerton. The crew were finishing up for the day as we arrived, but were happy to help install us in our respective tents. Sheila was introduced to the contingent - her name lent her instant kudos - then we let the crew get cleaned up for supper, as prepared by the inimitable Wally.

Sitting around the camp fire later on, Sheila having been introduced to drinking beer from a can, Sue and I were a little concerned that Sheila seemed to be involved quite heavily in all of the conversations. When Sue attempted to intervene, she was told, quite politely, to "Leave 'er be. This is like chatting to our mum or gran - she's good stuff, your mum!"

So, we left her be, as Agony Aunt to the happy company of a half-dozen or so of rough, but very good-natured fieldhands. They would see she navigated her way to her tent safely.

The next morning, the geologist, Dave Fletcher, and I were on radio call when one of my other geologists, Julian Maber, came on-line asking to speak to me. Julian was running a camp about three hundred kilometres away to the north and was on his own that week because his understudy, Lawrie, was in Perth on break and not due back until Thursday, three days hence.

"Victor Juliet Bravo mobile three, receiving, over," I said.

“Tom, I’ve got a family emergency at home - I need to get to Perth quick. Can you get someone to cover for me? Over,” asked Julian.

I thought for a moment and said to Dave. “Is it OK to leave my family here - I can cover for Julian for three days until Lawrie gets back?”

Dave was quite happy with that suggestion - Wally would be in camp each day, as would Frank, the helicopter engineer - so it wasn’t as if my family would have to fend for themselves.

“Julian, just organise a flight with Perth Office and get yourself down to Carnarvon now. I’ll be up at camp this afternoon. I can look after things until Lawrie gets back. Over,” I said.

I spoke to Sue and Sheila, explaining the emergency nature and they, being practical people, were not put out whatsoever. After all, they’d be well looked after and could just relax with the infant Lindsay, who would probably appreciate the lack of bouncing about on rutted gravel roads. I left for the north.

The billabong was a quiet place, the peace interrupted from time to time with the screeching of flocks of green budgerigars or pink and grey galahs, and too far away from the coast to worry about crocodiles. On the second afternoon of my absence, Sue took her sketch pad to a gravel bank in the water, while Sheila sat in the shade of eucalyptus tree, reading to her grandson from time to time. This was in the Outback spring, so the weather wasn’t too hot and the flies only very mildly bothersome.

A hairy figure shambled down from the camp, bringing a little table and a box containing cups and saucers, teaspoons, plates and a tablecloth. Wally didn’t say anything, just set up the table and crockery and walked back up to camp, re-appearing a few minutes later with a tray complete with teapot, scones, cream and jam.

“There you go, girls,” he said. “Afternoon tea inna bush.”

Sue spoke. “Wally, that’s very kind of you - whatever made you think of this?”

Apparently, he blushed a bit - always difficult to tell under his beard - and said, diffidently, “Just fort you’d like a bit o’ proper tea an’ that.”

After I’d returned from the north and we subsequently returned en-masse to Perth, the ladies decided they really wanted to say ‘thanks’ to the crew, and in particular, Wally, for looking after them so well. The crew wasn’t a problem - wine, beer and a big card would do the trick - but Wally was a little more difficult. In the end, given his desire to better his skills and extend the range of his cooking repertoire, they bought him a lavish and expensive Italian cook book, suitably inscribed. It could have been sent through the weekly mail which those returning from break always picked up at the office, but I had to return to the area shortly afterwards, so I volunteered to deliver the package and to ensure that the bottles of wine and beer were handed over.

I gave the beautifully-wrapped present to Wally, after the alcohol had been distributed to the crew; he looked a bit puzzled.

"What's this then?" he asked.

"It's from Sue and Sheila, for you," I said. "Look, there's a card..."

He read the card then slowly and carefully opened the wrapping paper. He read the inscription. "Jeez, Tom, the girls didn't have to do this. It's a bloody beauty," he said.

A voice from the assembled masses called out. "Whatcha got there, Wal?"

Wally proudly held up his new recipe book for all to see.

"There you go, Wal," cried the same voice. "Told you, you couldn't bloody cook! Now maybe we'll get some real food," said the heckler, disappearing out of the tent rather smartly.

CHAPTER 28

CHINA MEETS AUSTRALIA II

The morning after the Carnarvon Chinese Dinner, I managed to get hold of John Bytchuk who said the airstrip was nearly dry; if we were to arrive from twelve o'clock onwards, it should be perfectly fine. We headed off to the airport mid-morning and I gave Max the GPS coordinates for the Clover Downs airstrip.

"Mr. Gao," I said, before boarding the small twin-engine Cessna. "Please explain to our guests that we're now heading into a very lonely part of Australia. There are no towns on our way to the farm where we'll stay tonight. There are no people and only a few cows and sheep. There's only one road, but I doubt we'll see much traffic on it. All we'll see from the air is red soil, with some, mostly dry, rivers with eucalyptus and thorn trees along the banks. There's no reason to be concerned, but I can understand that some members may be a little nervous."

Mr. Gao nodded. "Yes, thank you, I understand. I will tell my colleagues."

I sat at the rear of the plane, to allow the visitors the best views of the Shire of Upper Gascoyne in the seventy minutes or so of flying time the journey would take.

"Mr. Lindsay," said a worried-looking Mr. Gao, after about an hour. "You said this would be lonely part of Australia, yes?" I nodded. "But this *very* lonely. Will there be people at the farm? You are sure?"

I reassured Mr. Gao that all would be well. As we approached the Clover Downs airstrip a few minutes later, the corrugated roof of the old homestead building flashed in the sun and I could make out a couple of vehicles near the windsock. I pointed these out to him and he relaxed a little. There was a lot of water lying about but John hadn't blocked the strip with a truck, which he would have done had there been a problem, so Max lined up and we touched down on the graded gravel.

The engines stopped, Max gave me a nod, and I opened the rear door and let down the steps. John was standing there in his battered Akubra hat and dust-stained clothes, looking, as he always did, the epitome of an Aussie stockman. Big, muscular and generally weather-beaten around the edges. He was in his early forties.

"G'day Tom," he said. Gesturing to the very similar-looking figure standing next to him, he went on. "This here's Trev, me brother-in-law, just up to give me a hand for a couple of days."

I shook hands with both, then introduced them to our visitors as they emerged from the plane. The Chinese delegation looked round, but could see no obvious buildings.

"Gents," said John. "Let's jump in the utes and get over to the homestead. It's just there," he said, pointing to buildings in a clump of trees a kilometre or so away. After pushing the Cessna off the runway to a small parking area, we loaded up the utes with people and belongings and set off for the buildings.

Clover Downs is an old station, and the original stone farmhouse, built in the 1800's, John now used as a storeroom and a schoolhouse for his children. With the money he'd made from 'roo shooting before getting married, he'd bought the station with a mortgage and he and Petra had built a new brick homestead over the years. This was set in well-watered lawns, with large shady trees planted by the first settlers.

Petra was, as always, a gracious and welcoming hostess. Despite the rigours of station life, she was always lady-like, both in demeanour and appearance. However, woe betide he or she who crossed Petra - that was not a good idea - for she had a steel interior and would not accept foolish or bad behaviour. After the introductions, we handed over the food we had brought to Petra, and the beer, wine and soft drinks to John, to be put in the cold room. He was very keen on a particular brand of the amber fluid - Swan Gold - so I had made sure to bring a case or two with us.

Only one of the Bytchuk's four children - Catherine - remained on Clover Downs, as she was too young to yet go to boarding school. Trev's wife and two children had come along on the trip and together with Petra, they had prepared a light lunch for our contingent.

Before enjoying the food, we took ourselves off to the shearer's quarters and arranged who was sleeping where, making sure everyone knew where the toilets and showers were located. I commented, in passing, that if our guests wished to change out of their travelling clothes, this would now be a good time. Mr. Gao translated, but only Geoffrey and I put on more workman-like clothes and boots before joining everyone in the garden for lunch. The Chinese visitors remained in their suits and city shoes, although one or two ties were removed.

Petra had been told about the sorts of foods the visitors would like, so she had made sure everything was not only 'finger food' but light on protein. John called me over.

"Right, I've cleaned up me old ute and put a couple of mattresses in the back. It's got rails so nobody should fall out, but just tell 'em to hang on if the road gets a bit bumpy. You goin' to drive, I hope?"

I said that I would indeed be the driver. "I'll call in at Gidgee Creek, just to let Jason know we're around, but I reckon we should be back well before dark. We're just going to go past the old campsite a couple of k's and walk around there for a bit, then visit that digging on your north boundary, just off the road."

Lunch over, we climbed aboard the Gidgee Creek Explorer and set off on the thirty or so kilometres of rough track leading to the kimberlites. Geoffrey passed the initiation test of managing to both open and close some typical 'cockies' gates - concoctions of wire and wood of which Mr. Rubik would be proud - and we reached the station. Unlike Clover Downs, the Gidgee Creek buildings were stacked on a hill-side, with not a great deal of shade. I could see quite a bit of activity down at the yards, so I asked Geoffrey just to sit tight with the visitors, while I said hello.

As I approached the yards, I could see Jason had spotted me. He walked towards me, looking a bit thunderous. As he got closer, his brow cleared and he yelled. "Whatcha' doin' here mate? You shoulda' told me you was comin' and I'd have got you to pick up the mail."

"G'day, Jason," I said. "I did speak to Jarli and tell him - when you weren't here what, about ten days ago?"

Jason looked around and yelled at Jarli. "Hey, you - you forget to tell me Tom was comin' up?"

Jarli looked at the ground. "Yair, must have forgot," he said.

Jason looked disgusted but turned back to me and went on. "No worries. What you doin' with John's old ute then? Your fancy wagon bit the dust or what?"

I explained that I was only here for a very short visit and that I had some visitors from mainland China. They didn't understand English very much -

"Bit like Jarli then," muttered Jason - but they were keen to see the rocks we'd been working on.

Jason was visibly excited. "What, these're from real China? Get them over here, mate, let's introduce them to some real Australians. You got a camera, Tom? I want a photograph. We'll call it 'Yellafellas and Blackfellas on Gidgee Creek'."

He laughed uproariously as we made the introductions to him and his crew and we took photos, the Murdochs obviously delighting in the presence of some 'real foreigners', even dressed as they were, in city clothes. It was difficult to gauge the Chinese reaction to being gently manhandled into position by lanolin-smelling, blood-covered (they had been castrating lambs) native Australians, but the whole episode seemed to go over very well and we departed amidst much handshaking and backslapping.

Although the later examination of the kimberlites appeared to be interesting to our guests we formed the impression, compared to the other experiences the trip had thus far brought, that it might have been a bit humdrum.

Back at Clover Downs, the extended Bytchuk family had prepared a 'barbie' - heavy on the protein for the Western element - but with a few innovative variations on rice and noodle salads for the Eastern guests. The Swan Gold flowed freely.

Catherine took our guests to the schoolhouse, and, with a very good understanding of how strange it might seem, explained how the 'School of the Air' worked.

Mr. Gao was in his element. "So, you have teacher where?" he asked.

"Some are in Carnarvon, some in Geraldton, some are in Perth - we mainly use Carnarvon. My written work gets picked up once every two weeks by the mail truck, when I get back my past assignments and any new material. Every day, we have to be on the radio at a certain time for classes."

John and Petra had decked out one of the rooms in the old homestead for this purpose, complete with a proper desk and a blackboard (Petra took her duties very seriously) and the vital HF radio. There was no 'I'll do it later' attitude allowed - education was the key to a good life - and all that the Bytchuk parents asked was that their children studied to the best of their abilities. All four have done well in life thanks to this firm but fair parental guidance.

Back at the barbie, Mr. Gao had a few more questions.

"Mr. Bytchuk, you say have over three thousand sheep, correct?"

"That's right," said John.

"So," Mr. Gao went on. "We not see any big house for sheep. Where they go to at night?"

John explained that the sheep were largely left alone and that much of his work was to ensure that there was water and food for them in whatever part of the farm they occupied. The farm was divided into quarters and he would move the sheep from quarter to quarter as forage became exhausted. The sheep slept wherever they happened to be at the time and John would check up on them regularly each week, making sure there were no wild dogs in the area and that all the windmills supplying water were working. If a windmill was down, he would have to fix it himself.

This elicited much fast Mandarin and shaking of heads.

"Mrs Bytchuk, where you go for shopping? You take bus or car?"

Petra said that usually, she went once a month to Carnarvon by car as there was no bus. The journey took four hours there and four hours back (Petra wasn't a slowcoach behind the wheel), mostly done in one day, but she would occasionally overnight if there were school matters to be discussed.

"Sometimes," she said, "If we're short of something, I'll radio the store at Carnarvon and the mail truck will bring out food if it's coming here more-or-less directly."

The rigours of life in the Outback were becoming clear to our Chinese colleagues, and they were highly fascinated by this hitherto unknown existence. There was one special surprise I wanted to deliver and I asked Mr. Gao to ask his colleagues to follow me. We trooped out of the garden, me with my torch, a few hundred metres down the entrance track.

I switched it off and said, "Look up."

A night sky, unpolluted by light is one thing. A sky with no man-made pollution is something I never encountered in China. The southern hemisphere night sky, seen from the Outback, is utterly magical in its brilliance and the five Chinese men stood entranced for many, many minutes.

We didn't have to say anything, we just returned to the barbie and our desserts. I believe that the Chinese contingent went to bed that night thoroughly happy, if a little bemused, by what had been an extraordinary day in their lives.

We departed the next morning for Mount Tom Price, an iron-ore mining town to the north-east, as planned. Both the Clover Downs residents and the Chinese visitors had seen a little of lives well beyond their experience to date and both were genuinely sad that the short visit had to end. Catherine, in particular, produced some very special anecdotes for the School of the Air not only immediately, but for some time after, because she and Mr. Gao established a 'pen-pal' correspondence.

At Tom Price, the touring party were met by the Darwin charter and, after much shaking of hands and protestations of gratitude, they took off north, while Max and I turned southwest for Perth.

"Friendly little guys," said Max, apropos of nothing. "You lived there, Tom, is that right?"

"Five years, man and boy," I said. "I'm often asked what it was like and the fairest I can say is that it was interesting. There were no pubs or clubs or any ways to get away from work, apart from running or cycling, but I learned a lot about geology and computers and a whole lot about communism. It sounds fine on paper, I suppose, but you wouldn't believe the control the State has."

"So, Oz isn't so bad then?" Max asked.

"Max," I said. "Oz is a fine place; there's a bit of nannyism but we don't mind that - it's for the good of the many. Anyway, I'm in Oz because Sue and I chose to emigrate and our boys will have some of the best shots at life, growing up here."

Max said. "Yair, know what you mean. I was thinking of moving to Asia at one time, but Oz is all right. Only problem for me is that I'm making a small fortune out of this charter business."

"What do you mean, problem?" I asked.

"Problem is, I started out with a large one," he laughed, having suckered another Pom.

CHAPTER 29

DOWSING

"Berthus," I announced. "We'll have to move camp in the next month or so - the travel distances are getting just too far." My new Field Assistant, Berthus Rothke, a bank-teller in his previous job, looked at me. His change of career owed everything to a few drinks after work with my colleague Trev Callaghan, one of the bank's clients. So far, he was proving very able.

"Have you picked out any sites then?" he asked.

"I've got a rough idea," I said. "I'll need to go and have a look, but we'll probably have to drill a couple of holes at each likely site, just to see if there's water. This camp is really good, the water's only twenty metres down and it's as strong as ever, but who knows what it'll be like twenty or thirty kilometres away?"

Berthus hesitated, then said. "I don't know if you believe in *wasser dowsing*, Tom, but I used to do it on the farm."

"Dowsing?" I asked. "With sticks and wires and so on?"

"Yes," he said reprovingly. "With one twig from a special bush."

In the United Kingdom I knew that hazel was used as a divining rod, but hazel didn't grow in the semi-desert of northern South West Africa.

"OK," I said. "Any chance you can show me here? I don't know what bush you're looking for but there's lots of varieties about the place."

"Let's see," he said. He went off with a panga in hand and reappeared half an hour later with three 'Y'- shaped twigs from different bushes.

"I'm not sure which will be best," he explained. "I'll try each one to see if any will work finding one of those buried plastic pipes from the big overhead tank. They're all full just now, so let's have a go."

With that, he lightly grasped each of the two short segments of the 'Y' with both hands, letting the twig rest gently between his upturned palms and his curled fingers. The longer part of the 'Y' was almost horizontal.

Berthus walked towards the buried pipe with Twig Number 1, crossed over, then came back.

"Nothing," he exclaimed in disgust. "Let's try this one - it looks more similar to what we had on the farm," he said, picking up Twig Number 2.

This time, as Berthus approached the buried water-line, I could see the horizontal part of the twig was jerking, mostly downwards. After he crossed over where the line was, the twig gradually returned to the horizontal. He repeated the exercise a couple of times and pronounced the twig satisfactory. Twig Number 3 also produced similar, if slightly muted results.

"Surely," I said, "It's just that you know where the water-line is and you're unconsciously twisting it in your hands?"

"No, Tom," he said. "Why would I want to do that? If my old man paid someone to drill a water-hole on the basis of a trick, I'd have got a hiding. I'm not saying every time I got a response we drilled water - may be that sometimes it was too deep for the drill rig - but I was right over fifty percent of the time."

"Fair enough," I replied. "Can anyone do this, Berthus?"

"I learned from an old German man in Gobabis," he replied. "My father and my brother tried at the same time, but they couldn't make the stick work, so no, I'd say that it only works for certain people. D'you want to try?"

Berthus showed me how to hold the twig. The arms of the 'Y' rested on my palms, lightly gripped by my curled fingers so that the horizontal portion was horizontal, but not so tight as to be able to make it move and with a slight tension applied to the end of each 'Y' by my thumbs.

I walked towards the buried pipe. The twig leapt in my hands and the horizontal portion went vertically downwards. I walked backwards and the twig went quiet again. Back and forth I went, getting the same response each time. I was excited.

"Hey Berthus, this mumbo-jumbo really works!" I exclaimed.

Berthus looked at me solemnly. "Try it somewhere else", he said. "Just to be sure that you're not sub-consciously 'fixing' things."

I spent the next hour going all round the camp, getting a similar response every time I came near buried water. I was a convert. Berthus was clearly happy that I now believed in this phenomenon, but cautioned me that what I was looking at was really a two-dimensional response, given that the water-lines were buried just below the surface of the sand. What we really needed to work out was some way of associating depth with the movement of the twig.

The easiest way of achieving this was to look at past borehole records and at what depths water had been struck, then to go back to those sites and see if the responses could somehow be calibrated.

We did work out a rough calibration, based on how far from the borehole the twig began to respond, but it was very rough. The best news was that we did in fact find water at the chosen new campsite, drilling in an area where the strongest responses were achieved both from Berthus and from me.

Before we actually moved camp, we had a visit from the Deputy Field Manager, one Henk Vermuelen, a gentleman of Dutch, not Afrikaans, extraction. Although Henk had been on long leave when I had arrived in South West Africa, we had, over the intervening period since his return, formed a very good working relationship which had also become a personal friendship. Henk was, apart from being a geologist with quite a wide experience of southern Africa, a pyromaniac.

Before any of his visits, I would arrange to have a huge stack of firewood placed outside my house so that after supper with everyone, Henk and I would sit outside, ostensibly discussing work but in reality, seriously damaging the contents of a bottle of the good whisky which he would always bring with him. The cost of this whisky was a fire which could be seen from the moon. Henk didn't just want to keep warm in the chill desert night, he wanted to self-toast!

During one such occasion, I casually mentioned my new-found skill in water divining. Henk was unimpressed.

"Don't believe in that *kak*," he said. "It's all trickery."

"No, no, it isn't," I said. "I was a bit sceptical at first, but it really does work. I'll show you in the morning." This being somewhere approaching three a.m., that time wasn't very far away.

"Right," said Henk, looking nauseatingly fresh and alive, a few hours later. "Let's see this black magic of yours!"

I produced the twig which Berthus had tested as being the best and duly undertook the water-line demonstration, followed by visits to one or two other locations where everything worked perfectly.

"Give me that thing," said Henk. "I'll try for myself." He was shown how to hold the twig and off he set. Nothing happened. Several times.

"Told you," he said. "It's all trickery, doesn't work."

"OK," I replied. "You're as strong as me, how about you hold one arm of the twig and I'll hold the other. If you can feel me pushing or twisting, you push back."

“Fair enough,” he said. The two of us approached the water-line and the twig began its downwards movement.

Henk muttered. “You’re twisting the thing.”

“Fine, you twist back then.”

Henk couldn’t. As much as he tried, the long arm of the ‘Y’ was going vertical.

“Stop,” he said. “I don’t know what’s happening, but I don’t like it, far less understand it!”

The subject was never discussed further between us, although Henk didn’t object to my using my dowsing ‘gift’ to find water, particularly to add to his whisky at night, in front of the usual conflagration.

What I did do, after the success of finding water at our new camp, was to establish if I could do the same thing with wire, as I had seen on British TV some years previously. I discovered that two brazing rods, each bent into an ‘L’ shape and held loosely by the short arm of the ‘L’ but parallel, in vertically clenched fists, would cross as I approached water and uncross as I went away from the point of strongest response. Fencing wire worked fairly well, as did unwound wire coat hangers. Brazing rods were, however, the best.

In Botswana, a couple of years later, I was working on the wellfield which supplied one of the country’s major diamond mines. Botswana is drier than much of Namibia, being almost totally covered by the Kalahari Desert, with, in the 1980’s, only three dams to supply water to the major towns of Lobatse, Gaborone and Francistown. The country’s newest diamond mines lay far from these towns and depended almost completely upon artesian water. Careful management of the wellfields abstracting this scarce resource was a major part of the work of the Geology Department in each of the mines.

We were drilling a couple of observation boreholes on the fringes of the sedimentary basin which formed the wellfield (the aquifer) for the mine, so as to check if there was any recharge of this aquifer by rainfall. Often, there is no relationship between recent (i.e. rainfall) and fossil water, because many aquifers have an impermeable upper layer, which means that continued abstraction of fossil water will ultimately result in the total failure of the aquifer. At the time, one of the ways to check the recharge rate was to compare the oxygen isotope ratios from the possible sources and the aquifer in question, over a few years, so we needed to access these sources by drilling.

Drilling can be, pardon the pun, a boring occupation. Hours are spent watching a drill rod slowly inching its way downwards, followed by a few moments of excitement when something new is encountered. Water drilling is, however, nearly always exciting, because when an aquifer is struck, the sound of water rushing up the drill stem presages a scene like those old photos of the California oilfields with 'gushers' spewing forth. In this case, one tends to get wet, not dirty.

To while away the time not spent logging the drill's movements, I cast around for some bushes from which to cut a dowsing twig. When I had a couple of candidates, I spent some time seeing if they were of any use and to do this, I used the water bowser as a focus. Many types of drilling need the drill bits to be flushed to keep their cutting edges clear and cooled down, so even when drilling for water, water has to be pumped down the hole as drilling progresses.

One of the twigs displayed an impressive response to the bowser's contents, so I wandered around with it, trying to establish if there were any areas where a heightened response might indicate water near surface.

The bowser's driver, one David Wasetso, looked on as this obviously deranged person, supposedly his boss, emitted yelps of excitement from time to time.

"Mr. Lindsay, "he said. "What are you doing?"

"Looking for water," I replied.

"There's plenty of water in the bowser," he pointed out, helpfully. "And soon, there should be some coming out of the drill."

"No, David," I said. "I'm trying to see if there is strong water underground. This stick will tell me where there is water down there and it should tell me where the best place to drill will be."

"Mr. Lindsay," he said, patiently. "This place is called the Wellfield, so there's going to be water everywhere, isn't there?"

I couldn't really argue the point, so I just said, "I'm only trying to see if this stick method works as well here as it did when I was in Namibia. It seems to."

David was intrigued, as were a couple of labourers sitting in the shade of the bowser.

"How does it work, then?" he asked. I said that I didn't really know, but when it worked, the stick would jump around on its own and point to the water source.

"Can I try?" he asked.

"Certainly," I said, handing him the dowsing twig and showed him how to hold it.

David went about fifty paces from the bowser and walked slowly towards it. Nothing happened for about forty paces, then it suddenly twisted in his hands. He flung it away, with a look of fear in his eyes.

"I don't like that, Mr. Lindsay, it isn't right. It's witch-doctor stuff..."

I couldn't convince him that there was no harm intended or likely from this demonstration, so I snapped the twig in half and went back to being bored, which mollified him somewhat. However, he didn't put it out of his mind and word got back to his colleagues at the mine, some of whom asked me to show them. They thought it would be good for their cattle-posts as a quick way of finding water, instead of spending lots of money drilling dry holes based on optimism.

I tried to put any demonstration off, but my supposed prowess eventually reached the ears of Mike Sindibe, one of the Mining Engineers. Mike had spent some time in Scotland, training with one of the earthmoving companies of the time, Blackwood Hodge, and anyway, he was my next door neighbour in the Senior Flats.

He cornered me in my office at the mine. "Come on then, *sangoma*, what's all this about you being able to find water?"

"Mike," I said. "It's just something I can do, but probably so can lots of other people. They just need to be shown how."

Mike was insistent I show him so I said he'd have to find me a couple of brazing rods, with which, being an engineer, he returned in a few minutes' time. We went to a patch of empty ground outside my office where I knew a water pipe had been laid and I proceeded to undertake the usual demonstration. Quite soon, a crowd had gathered, each eager to see me not only doing my 'party trick' but also keen to try for themselves.

It was at this point that a cavalcade arrived outside the office block, consisting of the General Manager, the Mine Manager and several high-ranking Government officials, all on their way to the open pit to view the mine in action. It was quite amazing to see a crowd disperse like smoke in the wind, leaving me in an empty space, looking somewhat vapid, with a couple of wires in one hand.

Fortunately, time did not permit these exalted beings to undertake a cross-examination of my activities so I escaped unscathed. I expect they probably thought 'geologist' and left the matter there. We were, after all, people to whom rocks told stories, so querying odd behaviour simply wasn't necessary.

In the very, very dry continent of Australia, finding potable water for the outback sheep and cattle stations is big business. For many of the cooler months of the year, the billabongs and creeks will contain water from the cyclonic thunderstorms which happen in autumn, but in spring and summer, these can often run dry. There's a lot of artesian water all over Australia, but it's frequently very salty or very alkaline, so is not suitable for sheep or cattle over the long term. Fresh water is a must.

John Bytchuk, of Clover Downs Station, was chatting to me one day when he happened to ask if I could have a look at his South West 'paddock' and see if there was anything geological which might indicate that fresh water might be obtained by drilling.

"Not that we can afford to drill, right now, but if we get a few spare dollars, I'd really like to get a bore in here, so we can shift the sheep around a bit more," he said.

I had the geology map of the area with me, albeit that it was a large-scale map and not much use for detailed investigations, but I opened it up and asked John where he was talking about.

He pointed to a spot. Fortunately, it appeared as if there were some ancient sedimentary rocks there, as opposed to granite or gneiss which, although they often contain water and retain the water in cracks and fissures, frequently have only low volumes available and are quickly pumped dry. Sedimentary rocks of the right sort, such as sandstones, can be sizeable aquifers, with long lives.

"OK," I said. "D'you have any brazing rods in the workshop?"

"Yair, got those," he said, looking puzzled. "You got a problem with the radiator on your truck or what?"

"No," I said. "I use them to find water." I explained my 'party trick'.

"Strewth Tom, does that really work? You're not leadin' me up a gum tree are you, mate?"

I persuaded him to get a couple of rods and off we went to the 'paddock', several tens of kilometres away and a few thousand hectares in size.

"So," I said when we reached the vicinity. "Any place round here would do, would it?"

"Yair," said John. "Anywhere would be fine."

I looked at the geology map and worked out the general coordinates of where the sedimentary rocks should be and fed then into my GPS. We were only a few hundred metres from their outcrop, so we parked up and I unshipped the trusty brazing rods.

We probably walked a few kilometres in a grid pattern until I thought I had the best responses mapped out, giving each one a GPS position. It became obvious that these responses formed a decent circular pattern, coincident with a shale outcrop. Any water-bearing sedimentary rocks would be trapped beneath an impermeable caprock - the shale - so holes drilled in this area would be likely to produce water.

"I can't give you a precise depth estimate, John, but I'd guess anywhere between fifty and ninety metres and you should start seeing water. Might be a bit better if you went deeper, but that's about all I can say right now."

John was mightily pleased with this, although his personal efforts with the brazing rods came to naught, but as he'd said, he could not afford to drill at that time.

A few months later, the company began a drilling programme on the neighbouring station, Gidgee Creek. We drilled quite a few holes in an unsuccessful search for kimberlite, but some encountered water, which I'd let the owners know about and which they asked me to leave uncapped so they could be used. Just as we were about to leave the area, I radioed Steve, my boss in Perth.

"Any chance you'll authorise a hole for John at Clover Downs?" I asked. "It'd be pretty much on the way out for the rig and we wouldn't want to go more than about ninety metres at most."

John and Petra were recognised as having been exceptionally kind to our company, having frequently put people up, loaned us vehicles and generally looked after us in this remote area. It was not unheard of for exploration companies to assist struggling farmers once in a while and I really believed this was one of those occasions. Steve agreed.

"Keep it below a hundred metres and one day and it's OK by me."

I called in at the homestead, where, in advance of Saturday's forthcoming fixtures, John was bemoaning the fact that 'his' Fremantle Dockers AFL team had been beaten by the Collingwood Magpies the week before.

"Well, you're not going to see tomorrow's game, so you won't get the chance to see them lose again," I said.

"What d'you mean?" said John. "Is the satellite going to be off?"

"Nope," I said. "I mean you're going to be standing next to a drilling rig in the dry paddock. The rig's on its way from Gidgee Creek now and if you can let the guys use the shearer's quarters, they'll drill you a hole tomorrow."

John spluttered a bit. "Mate, the guys can stay here, no worries, but I can't afford to pay for any drilling."

"Let's just say that this is a 'trial' hole," I replied. "You don't say anything and we won't, but we'll foot the bill. Mind you, the rig can only be here the one day and we've got to keep the depth down, but I reckon we have a good chance of getting you that water."

For once, he was nonplussed. Petra, gracious as ever, said "Tom, that's very good of you, but won't you get into trouble? After all, it's not as if the company is actually working on Clover Downs right now."

I smiled at this hard-working couple. "It's OK Petra, I've cleared this with the boss and he reckons that if we can help, we should, so unless you have any objections, we'll move the rig onto site in the next couple of hours and start drilling in the morning."

A drilling rig is a noisy beast, particularly one which uses a percussion bit to hammer through the rock. Apart from the noise of the hammer, the compressor which drives the whole affair is constantly roaring and the engine delivering power to the rotating string of rods contributes to an assault on the senses. Even with ear-defenders, it's mind-numbing.

John couldn't have cared less. He was transfixed, examining the chips coming out of the hole as the bit powered downwards. I gave him a commentary on the rock types we were encountering.

"That first brown, metallic-looking stuff is ferricrete - it's not really a rock, but the effects of tropical weathering on whatever rock was there."

"The greyish stuff is shale - that's what I was hoping to see, because any water will be below that."

"Oops, that green stuff is dolerite - it could be good, it could be bad, depending on how thick it is."

Hitting dolerite, a very hard igneous rock, slowed down the drill's progress. If the dolerite was a sill - a flat lying slab of injected molten rock - it would be an even better cap rock than shale. If it was a dyke - the vertical version of a sill - then we might have to abandon the hole.

The sill was around six metres thick, but it took two hours to get through, then we were into sandstone. "Stand by John, if there's water here, we'll see signs soon," I said.

No sooner had I said that than the chips coming out of the hole were damp to the touch. We were drilling dry, so this was a good sign. However, there was no immediate indication that a lot of water was evident.

Pete, the foreman driller, looked at me. "What d'yer reckon mate? Give 'er a couple more rods?" he asked.

A standard rod is six metres long and we were at seventy-two metres depth.

"OK," I said, "Let's see what happens."

The bit went down very quickly in the sandstone then Pete yelled "Stand clear!" as water fountained out of the borehole. He had felt, through the rods, the inrush of water as a major aquifer was pierced.

John danced around, wet as could be. "You've done it, you've done it... you and your ******* brazing rods!"

Pete settled everything down, then did a test to see what the flowrate might be. From memory it was somewhere around twenty cubic metres of water per hour, but steady. It would take quite a lot of work to equip the borehole with a windmill and pump, but as John undertook borehole maintenance on a daily basis, he had both the equipment and the expertise to finish the job off at his leisure.

Clover Downs Station that night was a scene of celebration as a 'barbie' was lit and the coolroom was raided for beer and wine. The drill crew were given a hero's reception and went to bed, eventually, as very happy, if slightly inebriated people.

A few weeks later, John phoned me at home. "Just thought you'd want to know," he said. "I registered the new well with the Water Board and the Geological Survey - it's called Lindsay's Bore. It's flowing real good."

There are not, unfortunately, too many happy endings in life and although this borehole undoubtedly helped John and Petra to keep Clover Downs Station a going concern, it couldn't prevent John from succumbing to cancer a couple of years later. Still, a bit of pseudo-science generated quite a lot of happiness and brightened up some lives, so the 'mumbo jumbo' does have its uses. And it continues to work.

CHAPTER 30

EQUATORIAL GUINEA

Fernando Po, the butt of so many schoolboy jokes, is now Bioko, a small island in the Gulf of Guinea, just one hundred kilometres south of mainland Nigeria, in the armpit of the outline of Africa. The city of Malabo, the capital of Equatorial Guinea, sits in the north of the island, at the base of a rather impressive tree and shrub covered volcano, rising to around three thousand metres above the sea. The majority of the town, formerly Santa Isabel, is of Spanish design and must have contained, in its heyday of Spanish colonial rule, some marvellous buildings, most of which have now fallen into disrepair. It the only country in Africa where Spanish is the co-official national language.

Equatorial Guinea is physically in two locations, because some two hundred kilometres to the south-east, on the African mainland, sandwiched between Cameroon and Gabon, lies the region of Río Muni, occupying the bulk of the 28,000 square kilometres of the country.

My Spanish-speaking fellow geologist, Jane Alexander, and I had boarded the Swissair Flight to Malabo in Zurich, together with one of the then government's Deputy Ministers. I was a little nervous as I did not have a proper visa - simply a letter of introduction, signed by some or other government Minister.

The Deputy Minister had assured me in the Zurich departure lounge that this was absolutely fine and that he would take care of any issues. "After all, Senor Lindsay, I represent the government, and you are coming as a consultant to one of our *importante* clients."

I wasn't terribly reassured when he jauntily went off, clad in his trademark Texan cowboy clothes, to First Class, while Jane and I turned right on boarding, into the delights of Economy Class.

"Are you sure he'll even remember we're here?" I asked Jane, who had made this trip once before.

"Ah," she said. "He's a bit of an oddball, but he generally seems to get most things done. Or at least he did, on my last visit."

After an otherwise unmemorable, but longish flight, we arrived in the early evening at the country's International Airport. In 2001, this was a fairly rudimentary construction, consisting of a tar runway and some broken-down, leaky, brick, corrugated iron and wattle and daub structures. Most of the passengers on board were destined for the plane's next stop in Cameroon, but a still-sizeable number made a frantic rush, in the midst of a tropical downpour, for the steps to the tarmac and the rickety terminal building.

Our erstwhile mentor had obviously been freely partaking of the undoubtedly excellent liquid refreshments and was yelling at all and sundry to get his bags. We gently reminded him that we needed his assistance to navigate Immigration, so more yelling ensued at some hapless officials, I obtained an entry stamp in my passport and we managed to rescue our bags from evil-looking 'porters' who were trying to manhandle our luggage for an exorbitant fee. The Deputy Minister departed in a cavalcade of expensive automobiles and flashing lights and we were left with a company guide who took us to the guesthouse.

The *importante* client was a British group helping the government to manage the development of the recently-discovered oil fields off the coast. I had secured a contract from their infant minerals division to devise and run a small diamond exploration programme on the mainland, near to an area within Gabon where kimberlites had been discovered a couple of years earlier.

The well-appointed guesthouse was located in a fairly run-down area of Malabo, but, with the exception of the President's accommodation, just about everywhere in Malabo was in the same state at that time.

A few days' preparation for the trip then followed, including visits to the Ministry, where credentials were inspected, guarantees given that all help would be afforded and statements made that everyone was terribly excited about the exploration work. While Jane finished off the last few issues needing our attention, I was despatched to the mainland capital, Bata, together with a high ranking official (HRO), to secure transport for the venture. The ex-Russian Army aeroplane which took us over the Bay of Biafra wasn't designed for comfort or quiet, but we made the crossing without incident. I'm still not certain the pilots were entirely sober - the enthusiastic singing of Russian folk songs and clapping from the cockpit was a little disconcerting - but they got us up, and more importantly, down.

There were no car-hire companies operating in the country at this point in its history, so, clutching (or rather, hiding about my person) a rather large and grubby wad of Central African CFA Francs, I inspected a few candidate vehicles that the HRO had selected.

My total lack of Spanish and his sparse command of English didn't really help, but the sorry parade of dilapidated and superannuated wrecks we were shown didn't inspire me with confidence that we would reach anywhere, let alone return.

We eventually settled on an aged Mitsubishi Pajero - British readers will know this as the Shogun. This particular Spanish name has an unfortunate onanistic connotation which the vehicle gamely lived up to. After some haggling, principally because the Pajero wouldn't start so we could test-drive it, the price was knocked down to something approaching merely eye-watering, a new battery was secured, and we retired to a mosquito-infested residence for the night.

Eventually, after a delay owing to Jane's becoming too friendly with a salmonella bacillus, the merry convoy - the Government had made a new Land Cruiser available for the HRO and his minions - set off for the interior, along the only tar road then existing. The HRO had been assigned by higher powers to smooth our way with any officialdom, to make sure we were set up as planned and then he would return to civilisation to do whatever his day job required.

We eventually reached the little town of Nsork in the south-east of Río Muni which was to be our base of operations. We had been assured there was electricity, at least on three occasions a week, so our plan was to rent a house and from this base, venture out on a daily basis to the work area, through the middle of which ran a reasonably-surfaced logging track. The overnight accommodation might have better suited someone who actually enjoyed mosquitoes, a sagging mattress on a broken bed, no electricity and no running water, but I just wrapped myself in my sleeping bag, sprayed tropical strength insect repellent on any exposed extremity and hoped things would get better in the daylight.

They didn't.

We picked up some last-minute provisions, loaded the vehicles - we couldn't leave anything at our temporary accommodation or it could have been 'liberated' - and set off. Five kilometres from Nsork and twenty-five from the beginning of the work area, the road ran out.

"Ah," said the HRO. "There is a little problem."

"Not so little," I thought.

"Excuse me, Señor," queried Jane, in Spanish. "What has happened to our road? Are we on the correct road or have we taken a wrong turning somewhere?"

It became obvious that we were neither on the wrong road, nor had we taken a wrong turning. There was no road. Well, there had been a road in colonial times, but it was long overgrown and the logging company was simply clearing the bush and small trees, together with repairing bridges. However, they had stopped when they reached just beyond the village where some then-currently-important politician had been born and were unlikely to start work again for a few weeks. No matter what the HRO wanted. We returned to Nsork and the Palace of Broken Beds.

The HRO went off to speak to some local authorities while Jane and I discussed matters. We agreed that having made the journey to Nsork, there was no point in abandoning the whole project without trying to achieve some of the objectives, although it was becoming painfully obvious that most, if not all of the advance information, had been obtained from individuals who had told the Ministry what they thought the Ministry wanted to hear, rather than the truth.

The HRO returned. Through Jane, he said, "I have hired some porters to take your food and essentials and tomorrow we will walk to your area. There we will find you accommodation and when everything is settled, I will return to Nsork and then to Malabo."

We didn't argue, we simply asked what accommodation we were likely to find - 'something suitable' was the answer - and we pointed out that our suitcases were not the best things to be portered through the jungle. We said we would be happy to go with a minimum of personal gear, which we would put in our rucksacks, but that we would need to stock up on more non-perishable food, bottled water and the like. Arrangements were made to lock up our suitcases in a room in the Palace, to which we would have the only key.

Privately, Jane and I agreed we would give the arrangement a try, but if it was simply too difficult to operate, we would retreat to Bata and talk to the principals in Britain. We did have a satellite phone with us, but with not knowing when we could charge it up again, we decided to limit its use for the time being and to call only when the way forward was clear. There was no cellphone coverage in Nsork and even had there been, there were no reciprocal arrangements between our service providers and any organisation in Equatorial Guinea.

After another night of feeding mosquitoes, we set off to the road's end, from where we geared up, loaded the various porters and set off on our stroll in the jungle. The path was roughly half a metre wide, bordered by tough, scaly grass which itself quickly gave way to the rain-forest proper in which giant trees towered over a dark forest floor. There was bird life but very little in the way of obvious other denizens of the jungle, save for one or two 'whoops' which were, apparently, some species of monkey. It was tough going as the path wound its way through a hilly landscape in a sticky, sweaty, almost thick air.

The 'bridges' over the frequent rivers were usually one or two planks wide at best and possibly might not have passed a Safety and Health inspection by even the most easygoing of inspectors operating under the influence of drink or drugs. The lack of landscape in the jungle was also a little disconcerting. Even where there were hills, the height of the forest canopy obscured anything unless it was a truly massive mountain.

After a long, weary and blister-inducing march, we arrived at the village of In'kumi, Somewhere-in-the-Jungle, Río Muni. The village of some hundred souls existed in an open grassy space in the jungle, and sloped gently down to a fairly strongly-flowing river, the N'kem. Houses - mostly mud huts - were scattered within the open space and chickens, small pigs and children ran about.

The HRO consulted his minions, who consulted the village minions, who consulted the village powers. After some time, while Jane and I recovered somewhat in the shade of a mud hut wall, the HRO gathered us together.

"My friends," he said. "I have secured you a house to stay in and my cousin, Diosdado, will be your liaison with the village chief. He will help you select workers from the village and will make sure all is done to your satisfaction." With that he introduced us to his cousin and to the village chief, after which we inspected our quarters. Mud walls, corrugated roof, three rooms (not including the pig-pen), broken beds, no power or water, very rickety long-drop toilet at the edge of the jungle and chickens all over the place.

Jane said. "Thank you Señor, for your help. One small question. We had planned to work from Nsork, as you know, so our food supplies are limited. How do you think we should go about getting more supplies?"

“Ah,” said the HRO. “Diosdado will arrange to send bearers to Nsork when you need food and they will bring it back. Now, I must go, if I am to get back to my vehicle tonight and not be eaten by the jungle animals!”

With that, he took his leave of us, and set off with his minions in tow. The HRO may have been a Space Cadet for some of the time, but he didn’t lack stamina or resilience. He did promise to arrange that the Pajero would be kept under lock and key in Nsork until it was time for us to leave and that he would send a porter back with all the details and keys. He kept his word.

Jane and I approached Diosdado. “Please introduce us to the owner of the accommodation, so that we may make arrangements for payment for the use of the house, and to find some people to help us with food and laundry.”

As it transpired, the owner’s relatives and close friends were drafted in to help make the otherwise empty house habitable for the foreigners, a lady cook-cum-laundress was found and we set ourselves up in what we nicknamed the In’kumi Hilton. Jane and I had had the forethought to buy a few padlockable trunks so we stowed our gear away in these, along with the various valuables and important kit, such as the satellite telephone.

Our cook, well-intentioned though she was, seemed to have acquired her culinary skills from the ‘drench it in oil and fry it’ school of cuisine. Fried rice is very pleasant, from time to time. Fried rice which is accompanied by fried, tinned luncheon meat, all in an oil bath, isn’t terribly appetising.

There wasn’t much local produce to be had. No chickens were for sale - we never found out the real reason why not - eggs were scarce and the ever-abundant pigs never ended up as roast pork at any time during our six weeks in In’kumi. The local fish were very small and bony, but were available for a minimal cost. Bread didn’t exist; neither did potatoes. There was some cassava, the infrequent avocado pear and the occasional lump of bushmeat, the latter of which we avoided at all costs. It was more than likely that it been gaily swinging through the trees prior to its sudden demise. Small ‘duiker’-type antelope were occasionally caught - and almost recognisable - but butchery skills weren’t high on the list of priorities for the In’kumi villagers. Catch it, gut it, take off the skin and either roast it over a fire or chuck it in a pot were the two principal styles of cooking.

The lack of running water for basic ablutions was quickly solved for us. Diosdado escorted us down a well-trodden path to the river. “Here is the ladies’ area,” he said, pointing to a small gravelly beach. “The man’s area is over the little hill just there. No-one will bother you - when they see you coming down to bathe, they will go back to their houses until you are finished."

The In'kumi villagers were as good as their word and we were never spied upon or otherwise made to feel uncomfortable during our stay as guests in their village.

Exploring for diamonds can be fairly basic menial work, involving the collection of up to forty kilograms of sandy material - the sample - from sites in the riverbed where kimberlite pathfinder minerals are likely to be concentrated. The sample is washed through screens to provide a uniformly-sized product, which is then sent to a treatment facility where the few grams of minerals of possible interest are concentrated, prior to being shipped off for analysis in a specialist laboratory.

In'kumi didn't have a treatment facility, so we built one.

Concentrating heavy minerals, such as gold, involves swishing material around in a prospector's pan, removing the 'light' fraction until only the gold and a little extra heavy residue, often iron or manganese minerals, is left. Concentrating kimberlite pathfinder minerals is little different, except that a sieve is used and this can be done by hand or by the use of a jig. A jig is a mechanical device which imparts not only some vertical movement to the sieve but can also impose a swirling motion to the sample. The simplest type of mechanical jig is a so-called 'Zambian Jig', requiring only manpower to make it work. The sieve sits in a cradle suspended from the end of a fulcrum, which is itself attached via a bolt, at its centre, to a vertical post stuck firmly into the ground. The sieve is lowered into a drum of water, the man-powered end of the fulcrum is gently agitated, whilst simultaneously being slowly lifted clear of the water. A 'pancake' is formed in the base of the sieve, which, when it is up-ended on a flat surface, will, if the sample is positive, reveal a small circle of concentrated black, red and green minerals in the centre. This concentrate is carefully scooped out and dried, before being packaged for shipment.

Plans for a Zambian jig had been given to a factory in Bata, but as we were now deep in the jungle, it would take some time for the two units we had ordered to arrive. The sieves had been part of the porters' loads so the essential equipment was on site. Communicating through Diosdado, we chose a flat, unused, area close to the river at the bottom of the village and asked that the vegetation be cut back to give us room to work. The assistance of a couple of helpers was secured and work began.

The fulcrum and vertical post were easily made from large bamboo poles taken from large clumps of the plant which grew prolifically along the riverbank. The bolt on which the fulcrum pivots was fashioned from a hardwood branch and the cradle in which the sieve sits was custom-woven by a maker of fish-traps. Water containers of different depths and girths were obtained from the village, then we were ready.

To test this *ersatz* version of the machine, I had some density tracer beads - small plastic chips of different densities which simulate pathfinder minerals - placed in a mock sample and then the sample placed in the sieve. The sieve was lowered into the tub, the fulcrum then jiggled up and down in short strokes for a few minutes before being lifted slowly from the water, all the while being tapped to impart vibration and aid the settling of the densest minerals to the base of the sieve pancake.

Then came the truth-test when the sieve was upended on a flat, tarpaulin-covered tabletop. Success! The orange, yellow and blue tracers made a neatish circle, right in the middle of the pancake, albeit with one or two outside the centre. After calibrating the apparatus in terms of time submerged, optimum sample thickness within the sieve and the length of the fulcrum stroke, we were set to take on all that the exploration programme could deliver.

The programme had been planned on the basis of such maps as were available for the area - none of much use - and what could be discerned from aerial or satellite photographs. Ideally, we wanted to collect samples whose results would lead us to areas where kimberlites were being actively eroded by a river, thus depositing pathfinder minerals into the stream, where they would be concentrated behind boulders or in other 'traps'. In a simple explanation, after the first phase of work, we would have positive and negative drainages and we would follow the positives in succeeding phases until we found the source rock. The original plan called for a coverage of roughly one sample per ten square kilometres, to be modified as necessary by what we found in the field.

This approach works well in many and varied geographical locations. It doesn't work so well when there are no tracks or paths, let alone roads or navigable rivers and when actually getting to the planned sample point, towards which the ubiquitous GPS is directing you, requires significant and sustained physical effort.

Our hired guides and sample collectors had mostly never ventured far from In'kumi into the jungle; frequently there were no hunters' trails and we had to make our own paths, often hacking through areas of dense riverside grasses and thickets of a palm-like vegetation with particularly wicked barbs. The record was a couple of hundred metres in three hours of chopping, swearing, bleeding, sweating and general misery.

Then there were the patches of one of the unsung delights the jungle provided; these we termed 'El Squidge'.

El Squidge was swamp; a muddy, foul-smelling, not-quite-liquid, not-quite-solid mass, with scrubby thin trees and no sensible way around. We had long grown accustomed to being wet for most of the day as we waded through streams or as the rain - hence the reason for the term rainforest - pelted down through holes in the canopy, but the feeling of having one's boots removed from one's feet by some squishy malevolence was not particularly pleasant. Occasionally, patches of El Squidge did coincide with known paths and the hunters who used these trails had hacked down a few branches here and there to form a wooden walkway across the morass. Unfortunately, neither Jane nor I were small, barefoot, lightly dressed and incredibly nimble, so we would continue to sink as we struggled forward. Luckily, only once did we come close to a terminal disaster, but I wouldn't recommend an El Squidge experience for anyone's bucket list.

Our merry band of samplers and guides were incredibly tolerant of their two lumbering visitors, but would occasionally, and disconcertingly, drop all the gear and hare off after some unsuspecting jungle denizen to grace the cooking pot that night, leaving us in some spot in the jungle with a GPS for company and no idea when they might return. Return they would, but it was a matter of some concern for us, which we made known. To little avail. We might be paying for their services, but food in the pot now took precedence over food in the pot some days or weeks hence, when payday came around.

There was also the matter of communication. Jane spoke English and Spanish; Diosdado spoke Spanish, English, Bubi and Fang; the workforce spoke some Spanish, some French, mostly Fang and I trailed behind with English, French and quite uselessly, Mandarin. I developed 'Frespanglish' which served me well.

Our little treatment workshop continued to function well, so Jane and I would often split up and collect samples from different locations on the same day. We started out close to In'kumi, but as our teams grew more expert, we decided to tackle the far reaches of the planned area and move gradually back towards the village. On some days, these far reaches would involve round trips, on foot, of up to forty kilometres just to collect one sample. Jane and I rapidly became fit and we planned on how to market the 'In'kumi Experience' as a Fitness-and Health regime. Walking all day, eating very little in the way of carbohydrate or protein and drinking only rainwater 'Works Wonders for the Waistline' as our potential tagline would say.

Our lifeline to the outside world, our satellite telephone, was used sparingly. Once a week calls of five minutes' duration, to save the dwindling battery power - me to my home to say all was well, whether that statement was true, or not - and Jane to Malabo base to say the same. On one of these nights, we were treated to an amazing display of fireflies. I had seen glow-worms in the UK, but they couldn't have made the spot as a warm-up act to what we experienced that evening. Brilliant flashes of fire, darting in impossible directions at high speed, lighting and filling up the inky-black night for an hour or more.

We asked Diosdado, replete with porters and some of our cash, to go to Nsork mid-way through our 'In'kumi Episode' to obtain some supplies. However, we explicitly forbade his driving the Pajero to achieve this simple objective as we had been warned that he had crashed the last vehicle he had driven and perhaps more importantly, he didn't actually possess a driving licence. He assured us he would only use a taxi.

Somewhat expectedly, word came back with the porters who returned with our supplies that the Pajero 'was broken' and that Diosdado was in hospital. We were not in the frame of mind to trek fifty kilometres to see either how our disobedient employee was faring or to deal with any police enquiries. We reckoned that if something serious was afoot, we would know soon enough.

However, the time eventually came to depart In'kumi for Nsork and with the last of the battery power in the satellite phone, we tried to raise Malabo base to begin organising transport for us, as we were now a Pajero-free zone. We met with a resounding lack of success. The ruling political party had decided to have its annual convention in Bata, so not only was everyone who was anyone in attendance, but all the resources of the town had been commandeered for the duration. We were stuck without transport back to Nsork, let alone to Bata or Malabo.

Jane and I were upset. We had been working non-stop in less-than-ideal conditions for weeks and now no-one could be bothered to consider us worthy of attention.

"Sod it," I said to Jane. "We'll walk back to Nsork - we'll get the porters to bring the sample concentrates and we'll see if we can hire a car to get us to Bata, at least."

Jane agreed and after fond farewells to In'kumi, and converting our treatment plant to a kids' playground with swings and a see-saw, off we set, including a one-night tented stop to collect the last two planned samples.

We finally reached the beginning of the Nsork road, tired, ratty of temperament, and very wet, the rainforest once again having lived up to its name. We noticed a small house a few hundred metres away and more importantly for us, an antique Toyota pick-up sitting outside. After a stilted conversation in Frespanglish, the owner agreed to take us, some porters and some luggage to Nsork, for some exorbitant sum equivalent to about ten dollars. If he'd haggled much, we would just have offered to buy his car. Or hi-jacked it, the mood we were in.

Nsork hadn't changed much in the weeks we had been away and nor had the Palace. However, being able to don fresh clothes after a cleansing tepid shower - it being one of the days when power was available - and to recharge our laptops and the satellite phone restored some good humour to the day. At least, until we tried to raise Malabo base again.

"No," we were told by our contact. "There are no vehicles available until next week, you will have to wait."

"Surely one car or truck is not impossible?" asked Jane. "Hanging around in Nsork is not doing much for the project, or for us!"

Back came the waspish reply, "You see what you can sort out then, because we can do nothing until next week!" With that, the connection was cut.

We visited our 'broken' Pajero which, bent as it was into a horizontal 'U' shape, looked and actually was beyond the skill of any repairer to resurrect. We also visited our broken employee who, well on the road to recovery, admitted he had done precisely what he had been instructed not to do. We left him as an ex-employee, lucky to be alive and lucky not to be prosecuted for theft and gross misconduct.

The amenable owner of the Palace of Broken Beds was able to find someone who would take us to Mongomo, on the Río Muni-Gabon border, where the tar road began for Bata to the west.

A very small and weary Datsun pick-up was loaded with our personal luggage and as many sample concentrates as we could fit aboard, the remainder being left with the owner at the Palace to be forwarded when possible. To his credit, and only a few days later, these samples arrived in Bata.

Meanwhile, after a very cramped journey, we arrived in Mongomo and were able to secure rooms at the imposing Mongomo Hotel. Lots of hot water, electricity and big rooms - this was luxury! Unfortunately, there wasn't any food to be had. Actually, genuinely, no food at all and not a beer in sight.

Jane and I had noticed on the way in that there were roadside stalls selling snacks and the like, so we quickly backtracked and bought what we could. The underemployed hotel chef was happy to turn the somewhat forlorn chicken we had found into something edible and the kitchen fridge was at our disposal to cool the beers and soft drinks we had foraged. Now we had a land-line telephone so once again we pestered Malabo. After some robust discussion, and some very much more than robust comment, it was agreed that a vehicle would be found in Bata and sent to Mongomo, post-haste.

The following morning, a comfortable Land Cruiser station wagon arrived and we set off for Bata. Owing to the conference, there was no accommodation available in the town, so a flight had been arranged back to Malabo. Not for us the ancient Soviet blunt weapon of an aircraft this time!

The make of aeroplane we flew on I never ascertained. It was a mid-size corporate-type jet with two engines seated high on the rear of the fuselage and a set of entrance steps which appeared by lowering the rear of the plane. The inside was decked out in mauve velvet, with large glass mirrors on the bulkheads and doors. The crew appeared to be citizens of somewhere east of Poland, and once again, apparently reliant on ethanol as a nerve-tonic and flying aid. I hoped they would dispense some of their beverage supply to their hapless passengers, but this was not to be.

Back in Malabo, the guesthouse once again awaited us and we spent a few days in organising export permits for the shipment of samples, finishing off the first part of a project report and sundry other administrative tasks. Then came the time to depart; this time without the HRO to clear away any administrative niggles. Fortunately, I had managed to acquire a stamped authorisation for my stay which, while not being exactly a visa, did, after some telephone conversation between the Immigration Officer and the HRO's boss, allow me access to the departure area. Almost.

I was aware that in our hurried entry to the country, there had been no checking or declaration of the foreign currency I had brought in, which was a couple of thousand United States Dollars. Any quantity above a couple of hundred dollars should have been declared, but I was actually leaving with a sizeable sum, because most of my expenses had been covered by the company. I had not stated this sum on the departure form, but had written a much lesser amount, given that there was no-one around to explain how he we had been 'helped' on arrival.

A rather seedy-looking and sinister individual standing behind the Immigration cubicle grabbed the stamped copy of my departure form from me as I exited. He gestured towards a dark area behind the Immigration desks.

"*Habla Espanol*?" he said.

"Sorry, I don't speak Spanish," I said. "Anyway, who are you and what is the problem?" I asked.

He grinned rather nastily and opened his jacket to show a holstered pistol. "I am Security Police. You must now show me all the foreign currency you are taking out of the country! Because I say you must, *entender*?"

"I have just filled out the declaration form," I said, gesturing towards the form he was clutching in his hand.

"Ah senor," he said. "It is well-known that many people seek to make us poor by taking out dollars they should not, so we must check."

Fortunately, I had been warned this sort of shakedown was not uncommon. I had taken a chance and hidden a good portion of my unused foreign currency in my suitcase, hoping that the good citizens who operated Swissair and Zurich airport would not somehow lose the luggage which, at this juncture, I could see being loaded onto the aircraft which I hoped to join in a few minutes.

I fiddled around and produced my wallet which had a few United States notes of various denominations, probably less than fifty dollars in total, and a few CFA francs. This didn't satisfy the man, who demanded to search my carry-on luggage. I protested, politely enough so as not to make him draw his gun, but enough so that he could see I was annoyed.

When he couldn't find any more currency, he demanded to know how I had paid for my stay as I had been in the country for six weeks and had not declared any currency on arrival, yet had some dollars. I opened my wallet.

Pointing to the credit cards, I said. "I have paid for flights and hotels with these - I did not need dollars."

He gave a disgusted "Go to your plane!" and went off to molest his next victim. At that point in Malabo's history, credit card transactions were all but impossible and certainly, with my preferred credit card, not possible at all. Of this fact, Mr. Nasty was unaware or had forgotten. I had been lucky.

Once aboard the safety of the Swissair jet, it seemed that the bulk of an incredibly arduous project was behind us and Jane and I looked forward to returning to the relative sanity of the United Kingdom, at least for a while. Fate still had a surprise in store.

After reaching Zurich at the end of the overnight flight, we switched planes and headed for Heathrow. About half an hour into the flight, I noticed a young man standing next to one of the plane's over-the-wing doors, close to one of the toilets. He was bopping about, seemingly in time to music from an undisclosed source, quite unconcerned with using the toilet and allowing other passengers to go ahead of him. I pointed him out to Jane.

"Don't know what's going on here, but he's a bit too close to that exit door for my liking!" I said jokingly. We both tightened our seatbelts.

Someone must have said something, because moments later, a cabin attendant asked the young man to return to his seat. He looked a bit vacant, but with a sloppy smile, he sauntered off down the aisle to his seat in a row somewhere behind us.

I dozed off, tired after the long haul, when suddenly, there was a commotion behind us and the same young man, now naked as could be, sprinted up the aisle. He was neatly caught in a pincer motion by two cabin attendants of the large variety and pinned to the floor. Handcuffs were found and applied and a blanket was draped over the form as it was picked up, yelling loudly, and taken to the back of the plane. Occasional yelps punctuated the rest of the flight. No announcements were made, but as we arrived at Heathrow's Terminal Two, we could see blue flashing lights on our stand and when the air-bridge was connected, four serious-looking officers of the law 'proceeded in an orderly fashion' to the back of the aircraft.

That should have been enough to end this trip, but on my return home, I caused an upset which lingers to this day. My young sons had been told that 'Dad will be home soon' and had counted off the sleeps until the last day. I walked through the door. Older son took a look at me and gasped, younger son hid behind his mother, yelling.

I had forgotten that not only had my hair and full beard grown since the boys had last seen me, but I had lost a couple of stones in weight and was very tanned. The boys eventually calmed down but I had to trim my beard back rather quickly before younger son was convinced that his dad had not been eaten by a hairy jungle monster. Perhaps one day I will tell him the truth.

CHAPTER 31

AUTHORITIES

Russia is an incredibly vast country about which, at least until 2001, I knew very little. The previous year, I had resigned from my employer of twenty-five years and had relocated to Scotland, from where I established my own geological consultancy. I had secured a few contracts since going-it-alone and owing to the positive feedback from one client, was now standing, in late November, in the immigration queue at Moscow's grey, oppressive and unwelcoming Sheremetyevo International Airport.

My passport had the correct type of visa, of that I had been assured, but I spoke no Russian, could read no Russian and was completely dependent upon there being an interpreter and guide waiting for me in the Arrivals Hall. The other problem was that I could not fill out the immigration forms properly, because the writing was all in Russian. Hastily consulting my travel guidebook, I took an age at the small desk provided for the completion of these documents and then scribbled what I thought were the correct responses, before handing the forms over to the severe-looking woman in the booth in front of me.

She looked at my passport and visa, checked what I had written on the main document and asked, "You beesneesman, da?" I couldn't have explained otherwise, so I just said "Yes" and then she asked, "How much dollars you bring?"

At that time, all imported foreign currency had to be declared. I replied, truthfully, "One thousand five hundred US dollars." A notation was then made in the appropriate box - which I had missed in my confusion - the form and my passport were both stamped and I was now allowed into Mother Russia.

A middle-aged, balding and shortish Igor Alexandrovich Petrov was waiting for me as I emerged from Customs, looking somewhat concerned. He had a card with my name on it, so I surmised (correctly) that he was the interpreter and after I had introduced myself he said, "You were a very long time coming through, I thought you had perhaps missed the flight."

I explained the language predicament which had caused the delay but he said cheerfully, "No matter now, here you are in wonderful Russia, let's go to your hotel."

He had arranged a car and driver so off we set for one of the Western chain hotels which are scattered through Moscow. Thankfully, as I would later discover, we were not travelling at one of Moscow's peak traffic times and the journey took less than an hour.

Igor was, in his day job, an eminent statistician at a prestigious Moscow institute, but, as he explained, 'prestige doesn't pay the dollars', so he moonlighted from time to time to buy the luxuries in life, like a warm winter coat or a new pair of boots. Bureaucrats' pay in post-perestroika Russia had not, in general, been adequately addressed and many of these well-qualified individuals, lacking the right contacts, struggled along on meagre salaries. The 'driver' from the airport was a colleague, he said, undertaking a little private enterprise with his own car, for which Igor would pay from his fee for escorting me around the country.

Igor had spent time in the USA on postgraduate work in the late Gorbachev era, before returning to Russia when his thesis was complete, so his command of English was good and he proved to be a witty and interesting travelling companion. He also had a keen interest in showing me, and having me test, the great variety of beers available. I thought this was a very reasonable way to pass an evening.

Our ultimate destination, reached the following morning, was the town of Apatity, some one hundred and ninety kilometres south of Murmansk - but still north of the Arctic Circle. There we would find the Tersky Exploration Company, a quasi-governmental organisation which had information on the geological potential of the Kola Peninsula and in particular, the possibility of diamonds.

I had secured a contract to review this tantalising possibility for a British company which had good Russian connections, an association with diamond projects in other parts of the world and the desire to expand its operations.

Apart from Moscow, which I hadn't really seen owing to a late arrival followed by an early morning departure, both in darkness, my first impression of Russian architecture took me back, immediately, to China.

Grey, rust-streaked concrete blocks of no commendable architectural virtue except, as I found out shortly, that they were always supplied with plenty of heat and light, courtesy of an otherwise under-utilised nuclear reactor nearby in the peninsula.

The hotel we had been booked into was very well kitted out and very Scandinavian in appearance - internally at least - with lots of blond wood furniture and functional, but aesthetically pleasing lamps, showers, beds and other fitments.

Tersky Exploration's offices followed an acceptably similar pattern and we were introduced to the Director, the Chief Geologist, the Chief Engineer, someone who was Mr. 'Fixit' and a variety of underlings with obscure, but long, titles. Eventually, we were left with a few, apparently key individuals, to start the information-gathering part of the proceedings.

Piotr Nabokov, a geologist with specialist knowledge in diamond prospecting, led the discussion, with Igor translating. It soon became obvious that the more esoteric terms were beyond Igor's capability, but by dint of graphs, photographs, diagrams and adding 'ski' to a lot of English terms, Piotr and I more-or-less understood what he was saying and I was asking.

This was to be the first of many visits I undertook to this part of the world, owing to my report, although not acted upon immediately, concluding that the general area was highly prospective for diamonds. After a day or two with Piotr, we returned to Moscow and the obligatory visit to Red Square, St Basil's Cathedral and the GUM store and then on to Sheremetyevo. Igor bid me farewell as he was not allowed past the Aeroflot check-in point.

I duly presented my stamped Immigration form to the male officer on duty who asked, "How many dollars you taking out of Russia?"

I looked in my travelling wallet and said, truthfully, "Eight hundred." I had paid Igor discreetly for his interpreting services, in the car on the way to the airport.

"No," said the Customs Officer. "Is not possible. You only bring in five hundred dollars and now you take out eight hundred - is illegal!"

I pointed to the form, "Look," I said. "I declared one thousand five hundred when I came in last week..."

"Nyet," came the stern reply. "This says in words, five hundred."

"But," I said. "I cannot write in your language so there is some mistake. I said to the officer on duty when I arrived that I had fifteen hundred dollars and she helped me fill out the form."

"Wait here," he said. "I consult my superior." With that he marched off with my money and my passport.

As a nation, we British are wedded to our passports and have great difficulty in surrendering them even to be stamped, let alone taken from our possession, never to be seen again. Despondency flooded over me because I couldn't even get a signal on my cellphone, so there was no way I could try to raise Igor, or anyone else, if things did not go well.

I waited for quite a time, then Mr. Customs returned, with a man who had an even bigger hat. "This form," he said as he waved my pidgin-Russian effort in front of me. "Is very bad filled out. This time, you keep money and go, but no more like this. Next time, we impose penalties!"

"Thank you, "I said, repeating in Russian. "Spassiba balshoy."

Next stop, Heathrow.

A few years later, without Igor, but with Sergei, an English-speaking geologist, together with one or two 'helpers' of unspecified purpose, I was getting ready to depart for the wilds of the Kola by helicopter from the largely-disused Kirov airport, near Apatity. My report had finally thawed some purses and generated an exploration programme, under the banner of a Joint Venture with Tersky Exploration.

On this occasion, I had not been billeted in the very comfortable hotel, but in a much more Soviet-era monstrosity with echoing concrete stairwells and rooms higher than they were wide. The smiling but rather fierce lady at reception had taken my passport overnight and secured a 'registration' permit for my visa from the appropriate authorities, which stated with which organisation I was working and how long I was permitted to stay. In those days, any visit of over two nights' duration required such a permit otherwise unspecified 'problems' could occur for both me and the host organisation, if anyone in authority checked on my documentation. This permit had to be surrendered when exiting Russia, and the details could be checked to ensure that I had not somehow slipped through the system.

I left the hotel, and was collected by Sergei in a typical Russian 4x4 jeep - no suspension to speak of and smelling strongly of petrol. I was armed with fishing waders, a fly-net, a tent, a sleeping bag and sundry other pieces of equipment.

We stopped en-route to the helicopter to pick up bread, salami, cheese, pickles, vodka, beer and the other necessities for a couple of weeks visiting the working areas, all of which were only accessible by helicopter, as there are no roads in the eastern part of the Kola peninsula. In summer, the whole area comprises boggy ground and lakes, interspersed with rivers and occasional 'islands' of slightly higher elevation which are covered in clumps of pine trees. The sampling crews are dropped off by helicopter near one of these islands, on which they build a camp and from which they work for a couple of weeks. They then strike camp, are picked up by helicopter and repeat the process, all through the field season from May until October. Fishing waders are the footwear of necessity.

At these latitudes, in mid-year there are several weeks of no darkness. The sun describes a flat arc trajectory above the horizon, so with twenty-four hours of daylight and with all the ice having thawed, the insect life has a ball. The mosquitoes, in particular, are of varieties which haven't subscribed to the notion of Mutually Assured Destruction and can probably cheerfully pierce 'Kevlar' body armour. They are certainly determined not to waste a moment in attacking any warm-blooded creature they can find. Hence the fly-net and industrial-strength insect repellent, the latter of which managed to corrode the plastic covering of my spectacles frame.

A monstrous MIL-17 helicopter hove into sight, its twin engines and huge rotors making an ear-splitting racket as it settled on to the concrete landing pad. This particular beast was owned by a charter company and was mainly occupied with ferrying very wealthy fishing enthusiasts into the eye-wateringly expensive lodges dotted throughout the Kola Peninsula.

The engineer descended from the fuselage steps and opened the rear clam-shell doors, inviting us to stow our gear inside, along with a variety of very costly fishing rods, owned by a couple of sportsmen who had turned up.

Loading and re-fuelling complete, we boarded the machine to find that seating hadn't changed from the days when the Russian Army had owned the helicopter, so we settled back into our canvas deckchairs, complete with seatbelts but with no ear protectors for the thundering exhausts at head height. Fortunately, I had some earplugs in my emergency kit, but even with these, I soon became proficient in Russian sign language (of sorts).

Two hours later, after earlier dropping off the fishermen at a fuel stop in the last permanent village in the southern part of the peninsula, the aerial behemoth descended into a controlled hover a few feet above some blueberry-covered swamp and we all bailed out, passing our luggage and accoutrements down a human chain. The last link to the outside world departed and there we were, just on the edge of a field camp.

A familiar figure appeared – Piotr. Not the Piotr of the office, but Piotr, Wild Man of the Kola. It transpired that Piotr's beard had a once-yearly trim back to basics, at the end of the field season in October, when he returned to civilisation. At that time, he had to don apparel other than his canvas smock, triple-weight trousers and chest-high waders, or his wife wouldn't allow him in their apartment. The beard, however, which led its own independent lifestyle, submitted to an annual topiary adjustment, but nothing more frequent.

Sergei explained to me, "Piotr, he like the field. Comes out in May and goes back in October."

"What," I spluttered. "He doesn't have a break for five months?"

"Is correct," said Sergei. "Secret of happy home life. Field work is paid double town work, so his wife is able to buy many things. Piotr not have to worry about all things womens wants mens to do and he can work, fish and hunt with no - not sure of English word - domestic problems."

He continued, "Piotr not know other life, his work his life."

Piotr and his crew lived hard existences in the field, as did all the Russian geologists who worked on the projects my company financed. Their tents were simple canvas covers stretched over pine poles, with no groundsheets or flysheets. Each bed, *cum* desk, *cum* table was an old door, nailed to six pine stakes hammered into the moss or swamp floor of the tent. Each tent was equipped with a simple wood-burning stove and food came from a helicopter drop every two weeks or so, coupled with what could be caught or trapped. Communications were limited to the odd radio call to the nearest fishing lodge with a telephone, where messages were re-transmitted to the exploration base at Apatity or to the helicopter charter company.

The field notes these geologists compiled are probably the most complete I have ever seen in any culture with which I have been associated. I could, with one hundred per cent confidence, return to the site of every sample ever taken and be sure that the notes would be absolutely accurate. Russian geologists, in my estimation, have no equal when it comes to being professional. They are also among the least pampered and the least likely to complain.

Piotr was an avid consumer of 'papirosi' cigarettes. These comprise a hollow cardboard tube, attached to a thin cigarette paper cylinder filled with cheap tobacco. The cardboard tube plays the role of a disposable cigarette holder. The smell of one of these smouldering was akin to burning wool or something equally noxious. However, he explained, through Sergei, that smoking cigarettes could be good for you.

"Two years ago," he said. "When starting work in Varzugskaya area in spring, I alone, coming back to camp, when I come across brown bear mother with cubs. She not happy with me and make big grumbling noises. I have no gun but I have papirosi, so I think I will make smoke like forest fire. I strike match to light papirosi and mother bear get very afraid and run away with cubs."

"So," he finished with a smile. "Only conclusion is cigarettes not so bad for Piotr health!"

The camp was situated high on a bluff overlooking a wide river, which, as I discovered, was teeming with fish, the likes of which the wealthy fishermen paid small fortunes to catch in the areas of the peninsula set aside for their sport. This was not one of those areas, so the crew caught salmon, perch and pike for their needs. It was quite novel to sit in a smoky, poorly equipped tent, at two o'clock in the morning in full sunlight, eating salmon caviar on freshly baked brown bread. Admittedly, there was a lack of champagne but the odd shot of vodka from a tin mug helped matters along.

After two weeks of visiting not only Piotr's operation but also using the helicopter to reach three other geologists, including assisting with a camp move and re-build, the time came to return to Apatity. Back at the same hotel, the guardian of the room keys accepted my passport, showed me to a different room and left me to my own devices. Two weeks of living in waders, sleeping in ill-ventilated tents and generally being attacked by insect life at every opportunity, thus limiting ablution time, meant that a shower - a very long shower - was required.

Duly scraped clean, dressed in fresh clothes and with a bottle of cold beer to hand, I was transcribing my field notes into a report when a knock came to the door.

"Come in," I said.

Clutching my passport, the guardian lady appeared, with three other people. One bearded fellow introduced himself. "Good afternoon," he said. "I am here because I speak English and I work next door. There is problem with your passport. The young lady here is from Immigration, the gentleman is from Militsiya - Police - and you know the lady from hotel."

I was taken aback. "I am sorry, I do not understand," I said. "I've just returned from visiting some work in eastern Kola and there was no problem with my passport before I left. Why is there a problem now?"

The interpreter translated all of this and the Immigration lady replied. "The problem not passport. The problem you have no registration stamps. You cannot live in Russia illegally; you must have stamps to say where you stay. Is law."

I turned to the interpreter. "Where I've been for the last two weeks, there are no villages, no roads, no people, nothing. The only places I've stayed in were tents for geologists. There was no-one to give me a registration stamp and no place to get one. Please contact the Tersky office and they'll confirm what I have said is true."

Some fierce-sounding translation of my statement went on.

"You have been in, I think word is, boondocks?" asked the interpreter.

"Yes," I replied. "That is a very good word." I fished around in my rucksack for Sergei's business card. "Here," I said. "Please telephone this man for confirmation."

The policeman went off downstairs with the card, presumably to find a telephone and the others talked amongst themselves.

"OK," said the interpreter. "I think everything going to be good, but lady from hotel is causing big noise because you have no registration form and she will get in big trouble if not report this."

The policeman returned, conferred with his colleagues, then the Immigration lady spoke again. "Is big problem that you not have registration stamps, but Tersky man say his fault, not yours. This time, no penalty but not to do again. Do again, will be jail and then deport!"

With that, they all left, the guardian lady keeping my passport, now that she would not get into trouble for overlooking the issue.

Sergei appeared about ten minutes later, looking very concerned. "You all right Tom?" he asked.

I said I was fine, then he went on. "This problem, I am very sorry, not think about registration. These *people*, they have all regulations, rules and permits but all nonsense."

I calmed him down with a beer, assured him that I was fine and that I understood that people in authority liked to show off their importance from time to time, and that this was not a uniquely Russian problem. When he'd settled down a bit, I told him of a recent incident in Africa, just to show him that there are – a good French expression taught to me by Geoffrey, my boss in China – *petit fonctionnaires* in all cultures.

The last Friday of the month is, in Zimbabwe, very much like most of the rest of the world. It is payday. However, in the hyper-inflationary Zimbabwe of the twenty-first century noughties, where a wheelbarrow-full of Zimbabwe dollars would just about buy a loaf of bread, if there was any bread to be had, payday was largely irrelevant. Barter or bribes were the order of the day, with bribes being in the hard currencies of the United States Dollar or the South African Rand. Life in Mr. Mugabe's paradise had one or two drawbacks - not for Mr. Mugabe or his close minions - but for most of the citizenry. It was early morning in Bulawayo and I, in my capacity of independent reviewer, was off to inspect some mines and a laboratory owned by a British company, with the objective of writing a report suitable for a sales prospectus. My guide for the visit was Phil Williams, a company geologist of English extraction.

As we headed out into a sunny African morning, the bush looked fairly green, owing to a good wet season, but the landscape to the north of Bulawayo was fairly flat and boring for the first few miles. Phil and I chatted of mutual acquaintances, life in Zimbabwe and similar matters, until we came upon a police roadblock.

"Whoops," said Phil. "They'll be checking everything today, 'cause they won't have been paid. There'll be 'fines' for everything wrong they can think of. I know we haven't got an up-to-date licence for the truck's radio (the normal, installed-in-the-factory, commercial radio and tape-player unit) but that's because the Radio Office hasn't got any licences printed, because they have no funds. What the guards will want is a few dollars or Rands to change hands and the fines won't be written up."

"Good morning gentlemen," said an unarmed police constable, as Phil wound down the driver's window. "We are checking for vehicle licences, general roadworthiness, guns and drugs."

"Good morning to you, Officer," said Phil. "Please carry on." He continued, "Just for your information, this is a company vehicle, not owned by me or my colleague here."

"Very good sir," the constable replied. "Now please sound your hooter. Good. Now the indicators please." He walked around the Toyota double-cab pick-up, inspected the lights, the brake-lights, the tyres, the vehicle licence and his gaze then focused upon the radio licence disc in the windscreen.

"Aha, sir," he said. "I'm afraid your radio licence is out of date. I must issue a fine."

Phil said, "Officer, we both know that the office in Bulawayo has no new licences to issue. How can you issue a fine when I can't, or rather the company can't, possibly obtain a new licence?"

The constable looked at Phil. "That, sir, is not my concern. You do not have a valid licence on this vehicle and that is in breach of the law."

There was no point in arguing further, so Phil gave the company details, a form noting that a penalty had been issued was duly handed over and we made to head off north.

Phil started the vehicle, but the constable said, "I need to inspect the interior of this vehicle sir, in case you are carrying contraband. Please switch off the engine and both of you step outside."

Phil muttered to me, "Shakedown time, watch out."

The constable inspected the driver and passenger area, behind and under the seats, then asked Phil to open up the rear canopy. There, in the back, were six bags of rock samples which were on their way to the laboratory for analysis.

"What are these?" asked the officer, pointing to the bags.

"Rock samples, for the company laboratory," said Phil.

"What is in these samples?" asked the policeman.

"I don't know," muttered Phil. "That is why they are going to the laboratory. The chemists there will analyse the rocks and tell us if there is anything worthwhile in them."

The constable then asked, "Where do they come from?"

"They are from our company's mine south of Bulawayo," said Phil.

"What mine is that?"

"The Wonderboom Gold Mine," replied Phil.

The policeman frowned. "So, you are carrying gold? That is illegal without the proper documents. Where are your documents?"

Phil sighed in frustration. "We are carrying rock samples which may have, but probably do not have, very small amounts of gold. There is no gold to be seen, because if it is there, it would be mixed up with other minerals. Only by crushing the rocks at the laboratory can any gold be detected. These are samples and I have the paperwork which allows us to transport samples."

Back came a peremptory demand. "Show me this paperwork you say you have!"

Phil rummaged around in his briefcase and produced a rather large bundle of paperwork, all stamped with company seals, signed on every page and generally looking very official. Most of it was simply a set of chain of custody documents which would authenticate the eventual results as having come from this or that location.

After about twenty minutes of opening and closing bags, ticking off items on the documents, the policeman proudly announced that one bag had no documents, so we were, in fact, illegally transporting gold.

Phil looked at me. "Sorry, the blasted idiots at the mine are always getting the paperwork wrong, but it doesn't ever end up like this. This guy just wants a few US Dollars and everything will be OK and the problem will mysteriously go away. Only thing is, I won't, and the company doesn't, pay bribes. Do it once and you're marked forever. I'll go and see his sergeant and explain things."

Around thirty minutes later, we were forcibly escorted into the truck, with the sergeant sitting behind me and an armed constable behind Phil.

"Drive," said the sergeant. "We must go to Bulawayo Central Police Station, where you will be held until this matter of the illegal transport of gold is sorted."

Phil said, angrily. "You are making a serious error, Sergeant." Pointing to me, he continued. "This gentleman arrived last night with the intention of writing a report which could bring much-needed foreign investment into your country; now you are treating him as a criminal when there is no offence committed. We will divert to the company office and drop him off there and then the three of us can go to the Police Station."

The sergeant bellowed back. "You will drive straight to the Police Station or I will telephone for reinforcements and have you handcuffed because you are kidnapping us!"

Phil pulled over to the side of the road.

"What are you doing now?" screamed the sergeant.

"I am telephoning the office to tell them what is happening and I cannot do that while driving because that is an offence, for which you will charge me."

The sergeant was nearly apoplectic at this point so Phil asked me what I thought we should do. I said, "Make the phone call and then we go to the Police Station."

Turning to the sergeant, I said, "Officer, I would like your badge number and your name please, for my report to the British Embassy in Harare on this deplorable introduction to your country."

The sergeant calmed down a bit and tried to soft-soap me with pointless references to rules and regulations, by which time Phil had reached the 'Mr. Fixit' at the company office and explained our situation. We continued on to Bulawayo Central Nick, where the sergeant refused to allow us to park outside but demanded we drive in through large, heavy wooden doors which opened on to the central courtyard of the square building. Two police officers were letting the packed inmates from some foetid-looking cells out into a fenced compound, from where they were carted off to an adjacent magistrate's court.

Our two escorts jumped out. The sergeant instructed our armed constable to see we did not run away. "To where, exactly?" I thought. Or try to dispose of the evidence. "Evidence?"

The sergeant then went off to find some or other superior being. Phil called the office again and was told Mr. Fixit was on his way and that we should just do as little as possible to annoy anyone.

The sergeant returned half an hour later, in the wake of someone with metres of gold braid on his uniform and scrambled egg upon his hat. The Personage spoke. "You are very impudent fellows. Not only are you transporting gold illegally, but you are trying to kidnap my officers at the same time. These are very serious offences, you understand."

Phil went bright red and said, "How exactly are we supposed to be trying to kidnap an armed police constable and his sergeant, when we are unarmed and sitting in front of them? This is ridiculous nonsense!"

The Personage seemed unruffled. "Well, you can wait out here, or you can wait in the cells until the Senior Assistant Commissioner has time to see you. What would you prefer? Any more outbursts and the choice will be taken away from you."

I intervened. "We will stay with our vehicle, thank you." The Personage and the sergeant disappeared into the offices.

Phil and I slouched around, keeping in the shade. I took the opportunity to text Sue back in the UK to warn her of my impending gaolbird status. Then Mr. Fixit arrived. Philemon Chibatse, owner of a dazzling smile, politically savvy, politically connected and quite ruthless in getting things done.

I was introduced to him by Phil, then the two of them had a discussion about what had transpired. Philemon consulted his cellphone and called someone. "It's his brother he's calling," said Phil. "He's a big wheel in CID here."

A very few minutes later, a youngish chap in a floral shirt and jeans strolled into the yard from the direction of the front offices. Philemon introduced us to his brother Solomon, a Detective Chief Inspector. "Right," said Solomon. "What's all this about?"

Phil duly related the sorry tale, at the end of which Solomon guffawed loudly. "So, you go around kidnapping poor little armed policemen, do you? How do you find the time in between ferrying gold around the country? No wonder that lot are still in uniform, they haven't got the sense of a dung-beetle!"

"Wait here," said Solomon. "We'll have this sorted pretty damn quick."

He must have lit a fire under the uniformed branch because in no time at all, Philemon was escorting me out of the police station back to the office. Phil had to stay around while his credentials and residence permit were checked - uniform had to salvage some pride - but after a while, he joined me back at the office.

"So," he said, "welcome to Zimbabwe. It's a lovely country, speaking geographically and for a lot of the people, but is it being stuffed out of existence by the politicians! The teachers don't get paid, the police don't get paid, yet the Minister of Mines, who is technically on a salary of US$ 20,000 a year, has three farms, six personal Mercedes limos and God knows how much dosh in Switzerland. Five years ago, he had two suits and that was about it!"

Back in Apatity, Sergei had listened to this tale of woe with astonishment. "I thought only in Russia is such incompetence and corruption." He went on. "Is all Africa like this?"

"No," I said. "Many countries in Africa are very much worse, I'm afraid".

It's a sad reflection on the human race that so many people on Earth live in squalor, misery and fear simply because of the ego of an individual, and the systems that allow them and their acolytes and sycophants to prosper and to subjugate others with impunity. Many politicians and world leaders 'talk the talk'; very few, if any, 'walk the walk'.

I've been lucky, not only through having a decent education and family background, but also in possessing a passport that's still regarded as having some weight behind it, so my brushes with the authorities have been relatively minor. Thus far.

CHAPTER 32

LANDSCAPES

Geologists tend to go to strange - meaning isolated, difficult and dangerous - parts of the world, both on the surface of the Earth and within its crust. Most of the easy-to-locate mineral deposits have been found and it is now, with the huge advances in technology not available only twenty or thirty years ago, that projects in the previously 'too difficult' basket are being addressed. More often than not, these types of projects are in areas of the world where the average tourist does not venture, with good reason. Too many flies, or creepy-crawlies, or people waving AK-47's about, or perhaps there isn't a cold beer or a decent bed to be had in several days' travel in any direction. All too frequently, these intrepid geologists simply get to site, work until the project is finished and pay little attention to anything cultural or scenic, before leaving for Rest and Recreation and then the next project.

I have been fortunate in not only working but also living for extended periods in several countries, and doubly fortunate because through work, I have had experiences many tourists pay extravagant quantities of money to acquire.

Take Mount Taishan in Shandong Province in China, for example. The first thing for an Emperor to do on ascending to the throne was to climb Mount Taishan, there to pray to heaven and earth or their ancestors. It is reported that seventy-two emperors of different dynasties made pilgrimages here and the mountain played an important role in the development of Buddhism and Taoism. The highest point is just over one thousand five hundred metres above sea level and can be reached by either driving to mid-way, then taking a cable car, or by climbing the six thousand-odd steps from the bottom.

Simon Webster and I, being supposedly young(ish) and fit(ish), decided on the steps. Geoffrey Waters, being in his very early fifties and the recipient of two replacement hip joints, took the easy option, and our luggage. We had planned to spend the night in a hotel on the summit, to view the sunrise, which had been sold to us a 'magical' experience. The first half of the climb took us through a wooded valley, complete with a clear stream burbling away. The gradient was manageable and although it was a hot day, the exercise wasn't unduly strenuous. However, as we reached the bottom cable-car station, the shade disappeared and so did the gentle gradient.

We also encountered an exponential increase in the numbers of would-be ascendants who had arrived at the mid-point by bus, but who were determined enough, or perhaps impecunious enough, to want to expend some effort in reaching the top of this sacred spot. Venerable grandmothers, young couples on a date, British idiots - the mixture was many and varied.

After a brief stop to obtain a drink from one of the many available kiosks, Simon looked at me and said, "Last one to the top buys the first round... ready?"

He took off at rather a fast pace, leaving me in his wake. Three thousand steps don't, perhaps, sound too many, but the dimensions of the stairway were calculated for a race of quite small people, so each pace upwards wasn't a full step for me, but somewhere between a half and a third less than my legs had been accustomed to for the previous thirty years or so. The adjustment took some time.

Meanwhile, although I wasn't being passed by the grandmothers, I was being overtaken by porters, carrying amazing quantities of goods on poles across their shoulders. Some had up to twenty-four one-litre bottles of beer balanced in two bundles, one on each end of the pole. Others carried soft drinks, cooked ducks, water, boxes of cigarettes... the list was endless. Whatever would sell either part-way up the mountain or at the top came by porter. These men had leg and calf-muscles on display which even an Olympic athlete might envy and, so we were told later, some made the return journey three times each day.

Simon reached the top and I wheezed in ten minutes or so later, to be met by a cheery Geoffrey with a "What kept you then?"

"Come on," he said. "We've got the rooms organised at the hotel. Only thing is there's no running water or flush toilets, so it might be a bit whiffy. Still, we'll see the sunrise!"

After lying down for a half-hour or so, my legs had recovered enough to transport me in search of beer - the same beer which had overtaken me a couple of hours or so previously. Simon had managed to obtain some peanuts, so the three of us and Mr. Yang the interpreter sat outside our rooms and admired the view. It seemed as if only a few hardy souls braved the hotel, as there were few other guests. Apparently, most of those keen to see the sunrise ventured up in the pre-dawn darkness, well before the cable car started operations for the day, which can only be classed as an intrepid undertaking.

The evening meal wasn't in any way memorable, but sunrise the following morning was. Scores of visitors, most huddled into duck-down coats against the cold, watched the grey eastern sky give way to red-streaked white clouds being blown in from the Bohai Gulf and then to the sunrise itself. The winds pushing the clouds also managed to clear the ever-present pollution from the low ground around the base of the mountain, so we were treated to the fairly rare sight of a China uncloaked by smog, dust or smoke.

Environmental pollution of every description was ever-present in the China of the 1980's, from rivers running black with slag from coal mines or cement factories to backyard blast furnaces pumping out sulphurous clouds of grey and yellow evil-smelling smoke in the pointless pursuit of very low quality, mostly unusable, iron and steel. Countless factories released untold quantities of unspecified toxic metals into the air and the surrounding lands and watercourses, manufacturing white goods which were despatched to stores, there to remain unbought, but whose production kept the factories' books balanced when the productivity inspectors came around. 1980's industrial and social China was very definitely foreseen by Tolkien and Orwell, but on this one day, it was possible to see how China might have looked less than a hundred years earlier. Strips of varied green cultivated land filled the view, interspersed with straight rows of poplar trees alongside waterways and roads. Little clusters of villages were dotted about, in no particular pattern. It all looked very rural and peaceful without the usual greyish background.

Thoughts of pollution were very far from my mind when I first visited South West Africa's Skeleton Coast and Damaraland back in the late 1970's. Much of the area was off limits to the casual visitor, but to those whose companies had prospecting licences, hidden vistas awaited. The area north of Cape Cross had experienced both exploration for oil and mining for diamonds and being diamond explorers, the participants on the trip were keen to look at the sediments reported to have contained these gems, which were believed, by some, to be related to the beach deposits over a thousand kilometres to the south at Luderitz and Oranjemund. Our Man in Windhoek, Frik van der Staal, didn't hold with this theory.

"Ag, there is just too much distance from the Orange River for these diamonds to be the same population, especially if that big stone at Toscanini is real."

What he was referring to was the alleged discovery of a 2.5 carat diamond by a land surveyor of the German Schutztruppe near Cape Cross in 1910. On the basis of this information, a couple of entrepreneurs, Ben du Preez and Jack Scott, built a large scale diamond processing plant at Toscanini in the 1960's and later took over the prospecting licence from De Beers' Consolidated Diamond Mining Company (CDM) for Terrace Bay. Both operations closed in 1972, with the camp at Terrace Bay being taken over by the Department of Nature Conservation and turned into visitor accommodation.

Frik's theory was that the diamonds in this part of the world came from the erosion of Dwyka-age (around 300 million years ago) diamond-bearing glacial sediments inland from, and therefore much closer to, the Skeleton Coast than the known deposits well to the south. On this premise, he obtained prospecting licences for large parts of Damaraland, which allowed us to visit these otherwise forbidden areas. It was a bit of a leap of faith on Frik's part, as not only was he pre-supposing that diamondiferous kimberlites existed in central Namibia but also that they were old enough to have been eroded by the Dwyka glaciers. The evidence for the existence of the basal Dwyka tillite (a sequence of sediments formed in basins left by retreating glaciers) also required some verification. Nevertheless, it was a hypothesis worthy of investigation and this particular reconnaissance trip began inland, working our way to the coast.

Parts of Damaraland resemble the scenery of the typical 1950's Western movies shot in Monument Valley - mesas and buttes rising out of a sandy landscape, dotted with various low bushes. Other parts are more rugged and this area is home to the Brandberg - a large, brooding mountain, in fact Namibia's highest peak at over two thousand five hundred metres high - so named because it appears to 'burn' in the light of a setting sun.

Throughout Damaraland are ancient watercourses which only flow in the rainy seasons but which otherwise retain moisture deep in their sands and gravels. Along these rivers, many of which have carved magnificent canyons into the stony Namibian plains, trees and rough grasses grow and waterholes have developed. Black rhino, elephant, gemsbok, springbok and lion, amongst other species, are to be found in this starkly desolate land.

A curious two-leaved plant, the *welwitschia mirabilis*, distantly related to pines and cycads, is found nearer the coast, where moisture is obtained both from the ephemeral water courses and from the precipitation of fog. This succulent plant can live for up to fifteen hundred years and is only found in a strip of land running from southern Angola to Damaraland. It is believed to be a relic from the Jurassic Period (about 200 million years ago) and appears to have changed very little since then.

Yet nearer the coast, there are belts of sand dunes, neither the height nor the red colour of those at Tsossusvlei, further south, but in which can be found the occasional oasis, complete with palm trees. These dunes lead on the Skeleton Coast proper, a place of eerie fogs and the plaintive screeches of seabirds fishing the waters of the cold, nutrient-rich Benguela current, flowing northwards from Antarctica and teeming with aquatic life.

Wrecks of ships of all types are found along this forbidding place, as are the remains of whales and sea lions, whose bones gave the area its English name but which was referred to by the aboriginal Bushmen as 'The land God made in anger'. Portuguese seafarers called this desolate part of the world 'The Gates of Hell'.

It is reported that as the sun sets over the Atlantic that sometimes, a green 'flash' can be seen - if there's no fog about - but none of us on that trip experienced this rare sight. What we did see, close to the beach strand lines, were small herds of springbok antelope, feeding on grass and reeds growing alongside several of the small freshwater streams, fed by the ever-present fog. Jackals and brown hyena could also be found near the coast, seemingly enjoying a diet from both land and sea sources.

The Skeleton Coast is a mesmerising place and even hard-boiled geologists could feel something of the supernatural here, although, as Trev Callaghan remarked, "It's probably just the effects of too much biltong and beer too late at night." He was, and is, a sensitive soul, with all the sophistication and empathy of a brick.

The loneliness of this area is very reminiscent of outback Australia and parts of Namaqualand, to the south and east of the Skeleton Coast, share a floral peculiarity with inland Western Australia. The Richtersveld daisies - principally yellow and orange in colour - carpet the ground in spring and bring tourists by the busload.

Outback Western Australia has over twelve thousand species of wildflowers, of which sixty per cent can't be seen anywhere else on Earth. The flowering season begins in the north of this vast state in late June, then, as the weather moves south, the flowers follow until fading in November in the southern Albany-Esperance area. It is almost impossible to describe how the normally bare earth, scattered with occasional bushes, becomes a vista of pink, white, yellow and purple flowers flowing to as far as one's eye can see in every direction. These are not solely 'everlasting' daisies such as those in the Richtersveld, but their scientific variety is immaterial to the annual colour transformation of such an otherwise majestic, but desolate, and unremittingly red landscape.

Wildflower tours are common here, too, and a whole industry has been built on the back of this natural phenomenon. It has, however, been my immense privilege to go far beyond the tourist routes and to truly appreciate the sheer geographical immensity of this biome and to share this special annual event with a number of family members. That's something money just can't buy.

CHAPTER 33

THE MYSTERIOUS CASE OF THE POISONED PRAWN
(In memory of a departed colleague)

Another velvet early summer dusk settled on that mid-1980's home of rest and bewilderment, the Jinqueshan (Golden Oriole Hill) Guesthouse, in the City of Linyi, somewhere well to the south of Beijing in the People's Republic of China.

Two of the city's foreign contingent of three - the remaining 249,997 inhabitants being of wholly Chinese extraction - sat down to their evening meal. The third member of the British geologists' team was on leave in some or other exotic location.

Thankfully, after a considerable period had been spent in educating various cooks that dishes such as Scorpion Surprise or Duck's Bill Delight were far too exotic to be truly appreciated by us *'dà bízi'* (lit. big noses), the food served up was ordinary, if slightly modified from the original, fare.

Some steamed fish, possibly a soup dish, certainly some form of green vegetable - no meal for Geoffrey was ever complete without vegetation - and the main event, whole prawns in a bean sauce. The prawns were truly magnificent; large, succulent, beautifully cooked and plentiful. But they were served up as an odd number. After much persuasion, Geoffrey demolished the last one and off we went to spend the rest of the evening on whatever pursuits we wished.

In those far-off days, breakfast tended to be fairly rudimentary and quite often eaten in a rush if we were off to the field, rarely together as foreigners, but each in the company of a host of young, English-speaking geologists and each group heading somewhere different.

I had not seen Geoffrey at breakfast the following morning but when I was all kitted up to go off and be a geophysicist for the day, I knocked on the door of his bedroom to let him know I was on my way to the assigned work area.

A slightly hesitant voice bade me "Come in" and I encountered a rather grey-faced, somewhat shrunken, shivering individual, clad in not much but a t-shirt and a pair of elderly shorts. More truthfully, holes held together by bits of short. His eyes were not merely pinpoints; they were reflections at the bottom of a pair of deep wells. Dug by trolls.

"What's up?" I asked.

"Just a slight touch of GreenApple Quickstep," replied Geoffrey. "But have you anything for cramp?"

After some questioning, it transpired that he had been up for much of the night and had lost a serious amount of fluid, and was obviously majorly dehydrated. He didn't want a fuss made, but asked me to get him some sugared water and to let our interpreter, Mr. Yang Siji, know that he would be late into the office.

Instructions were given.

"I do not need any quack, and I am not, repeat not, going into hospital," stated Our Fearless Leader.

At this point, both his legs went into cramp. That didn't do much for his ability to stand.

I called Mr. Yang, advised him that Mr. Waters was seriously ill, that a doctor was required immediately and that Mr. Waters would need treatment for dehydration. Cue, one ambulance, several doctors and a trip to hospital. Followed by an overnight stay. Allowing a 'foreign expert' to remain sick, or for such a condition to worsen, would have had consequences for our Chinese colleagues that I did not dare imagine.

As I recall, over twelve litres of fluid went into Geoffrey over the next 24 hours. He was watched over every minute of that period by a relay of our young English-speaking geologists, so that he would never be in a situation where he needed something but could not be understood.

My visit to hospital to see him wasn't, perhaps, accompanied by the easiest of conversations that we ever had, given I had disobeyed a direct instruction, but Geoffrey did acknowledge that perhaps he hadn't been at his most rational at that point. He was puzzled though.

Given that we had both eaten the same things - why was I perfectly well and he was not? It had to be that last prawn, did it not? But how did I know which was the Poisoned Prawn? Had I discovered a fiendish way to accelerate promotion?

I just nodded and said nothing, neither then nor later. As I've often told my family “best say nothing and be thought a fool, than open your mouth and prove it.”

The mystery remains unsolved, but it did have one legacy. Never, to my knowledge, did Geoffrey eat the last of anything at a banquet - just in case!

THE END

Lightning Source UK Ltd.
Milton Keynes UK
UKOW01f2338181016

285623UK00001B/124/P